Futur

Futures of the Past

An Anthology of Science Fiction Stories from the 19th and Early 20th Centuries, with Critical Essays

Edited by IVY ROBERTS

McFarland & Company, Inc., Publishers
Jefferson, North Carolina

This book has undergone peer review

Library of Congress Cataloguing-in-Publication Data

Names: Roberts, Ivy, 1982– editor.
Title: Futures of the past : an anthology of science fiction stories from the 19th and early 20th centuries, with critical essays / edited by Ivy Roberts.
Description: Jefferson, North Carolina : McFarland & Company, Inc., Publishers, 2020 | Includes bibliographical references and index.
Identifiers: LCCN 2020021783 | ISBN 9781476675046 (paperback : acid free paper ∞) ISBN 9781476638928 (ebook)
Subjects: LCSH: Science fiction—19th century. | Science fiction—20th century. | Science fiction—History and criticism.
Classification: LCC PN6071.S33 F86 2020 | DDC 808.83/8762—dc23
LC record available at https://lccn.loc.gov/2020021783

British Library cataloguing data are available

ISBN (print) 978-1-4766-7810-8
ISBN (ebook) 978-1-4766-3955-0

Front cover illustration by Harry Grant Dart for the October 1908 issue of *The All-Story* magazine (Library of Congress)

Printed in the United States of America

McFarland & Company, Inc., Publishers
  Box 611, Jefferson, North Carolina 28640
  www.mcfarlandpub.com

Table of Contents

Introduction

Ivy Roberts

If you ask five science fiction scholars to date the emergence of the genre, you will inevitably receive five different answers. While it is generally accepted that science fiction emerged as a recognizable genre in the early to mid–20th century, its historical lineage is contested. The so-called "Golden Age" of science fiction began in the 1940s, with authors such as Heinlein, Asimov, and Clark writing about space exploration, inventing alien races, and speculating about future technology.[1] Many scholars also agree that the science fiction genre developed from a 19th-century climate reeling from the advances of the second technological revolution, a literature known as scientific romance (*roman scientifique*) (Suvin 1983; Stableford 1985; Westfahl 1998, 6). According to Adam Roberts (2016), "most scholars in the history of SF [science fiction], and most fans too, 'believe in' a shorter-scale history of the genre, dating the beginning of science fiction to the early 19th century..." (vi). Alternatively, as Roberts forwards in his *History of Science Fiction*, the genre has roots in mythology, classical literature, and Renaissance Era Utopian fiction. This anthology sides with Brian Aldiss' (1986) position that science fiction emerged at the beginning of the 19th century with Shelley's *Frankenstein* as its first major work (see also Roberts, xviii; Westfahl, 3).

While it must be acknowledged that science fiction scholars take a variety of approaches in identifying the concept of science fiction, such as Suvin's theoretical approach (1979), Istvan Csicsery-Ronay's "beauties" (2008), Freeman's philosophy (2013), or Jameson's political one (2005), this anthology adopts a historical-contextual perspective like that of Roger Luckhurst (2005): "representative SF [science fiction] works ... are rich and overdetermined objects [that] speak to the concerns of their specific moment in history" (3). The problem of periodization also dovetails with the question of the identity of the genre itself. As it turns out, the identity of science fiction is deeply and innately reflexive. Or, as Aldiss pithily remarks: "the model is flexible, changing with the times" (14).

1

Additionally, such scholars as Teresa De Laurentis (1980) and Donna Haraway have explained SF as a multiple acronym referring at once to science fiction, speculative fiction, and science fact. Indeed, the territories overlap and intermingle in the technological imagination. In the words of Istvan Csicsery-Ronay (1991):

> SF names not a generic effects engine of literature and simulation arts (the usual sense of the phrase "science fiction"), so much as a mode of awareness, characterized by two linked forms of hesitation, a pair of gaps. One gap extends between, on the one hand, belief that certain ideas and images of scientific-technological transformations of the world can be entertained, and, on the other, the rational recognition that they may be realized (along with their ramifications for worldly life) [387].

The literature reprinted in this volume engages readers in modes of questioning historical fact and future knowledge. This anthology assumes the plural, "histories," to demonstrate the peculiar ways in which science fiction merges historical-cultural contexts, speculations on the future, and facts from science.

As Luckhurst observes, "Naming is not the same as origin, however, and there are divergent critical accounts of the beginnings of the genre, depending on how SF is conceptualized" (15). Given the differing accounts of *scientific romance* and *scientifiction* in the Victorian Era and Radium Age, some definitions require explanation. Victorian Era science fiction generally encompasses literature written during the reign of Queen Victoria (1837–1901). Science fiction from this era incorporates Gothic themes that overlap with horror while also reflecting on the dramatic changes taking place in technology, industry, science, and culture. Victorian Era science fiction also addresses ramifications of the industrial revolution and second technological revolution of the 19th century.

When the 20th century rolled around, genre literature found new venues in pulp and popular science periodicals. Notorious author and editor Hugo Gernsback introduced the portmanteau *scientifiction*, a precursor to the term that would eventually be used to identify the genre.[2] In "The Evolution of Modern Science Fiction" (1952), Gernsback presents a short history:

> Usually authors not quite familiar with the writer's [Gernsback's] early work set the date of the start of modern science fiction in the year 1926, which date coincides with the first science fiction magazine, *Amazing Stories*, the first issue of which was launched by the writer in April, 1926. We would like to correct this view for historical purposes. Modern science fiction, like so many other endeavors, had an orderly evolution…. The date which the writer [Gernsback] would like to fix is the year 1911, not 1926. 1911 was the year in which the writer's [Gernsback's] novel, RALPH 124C41+, ran serially in *Modern Electrics*… [1].

Gernsback goes on to list a dozen or so authors whose work was published in his magazines (*Modern Electrics, The Electrical Experimenter, Science and*

Invention, Radio News, Practical Electrics, and more). The variety of stories Gernsback includes serves to elucidate his conception of *scientifiction* as a melting pot of mystery, thriller, humor, adventure whose generic relevance comes down to their commonality in themes of science and engineering.

Gernsback includes some works because they feature electrical inventions and technical innovations as pivotal plot devices. For instance, in "The Feline Light and Power Company Is Organized," Jacque Morgan inaugurates his humorous series "The Scientific Adventures of Mr. Fosdick" (*Modern Electrics,* October 1912). Fosdick is an inventor, and his adventures aim to popularize facts about electrical engineering and science. In the case of "Feline Light and Power," it is static electricity. In Herbert L. Mouton's "Mystery of the Dampt-Undampt," an amateur radio enthusiast investigates a mysterious broadcast using his expertise in cryptography and sound engineering (*Radio News,* January 1921). The story creatively integrates specialized scientific knowledge with the goal of introducing readers to the exciting world of radio. Gernsback's Radium Age magazines also included lectures in hard science, how-to articles by radio and electrical engineers, and industry news. The integration of short fiction served much the same purpose as the popular science articles: to make science and technology accessible to amateur enthusiasts and tinkerers.

Gernsback's coinage of *scientifiction* overlaps with the new periodization of the "Radium Age," introduced by author and editor Josh Glenn. Glenn describes it as a discrete period in the history of science fiction in an article published in *Nature* (2012a): "More cynical than its Victorian precursor yet less hard-boiled than the generation that followed, this is sci-fi offering a dizzying, visionary blend of acerbic social commentary and shock tactics. It yields telling insights into its context, the early 20th century." Nestled between the scientific romances of Wells and Verne and the Golden Age yet to come, Radium Age stories have been too long overlooked as low or pulp fiction. Glenn (2012b) further explains:

> I've dubbed this unfairly overlooked era science fiction's "Radium Age" because the phenomenon of radioactivity—the 1903 discovery that matter is neither solid nor still and is, at least in part, a state of energy, constantly in movement—is a fitting metaphor for the first decades of the 20th century, during which old scientific, religious, political, and social certainties were shattered.

In retrospect, Glenn offers a vision of the era's science fiction infused with socially-relevant themes.

In presenting Victorian Era stories alongside those from the Radium Age, this anthology reflects upon the ways that literature and culture adapt to and correspond with sociotechnical conditions. The first six contributions consist of Victorian Era science fiction. Stories from the early 19th century are marked by Gothic overtones and deal with themes relevant to the time. Several of the stories anthologized here also include themes that would become recognizable hallmarks of the science fiction genre during the Golden Age, for instance cryogenics (Shelley) and artificial intelligence (Bierce).

Joanna Harker Shaw opens up our discussion of Victorian Era science fiction with a consideration of Mary Shelley's role in the formation of the genre. Shelley's story combines the concept of the long-time sleeper, borrowed from "Rip Van Winkle," with the early 19th century trend of the literary hoax. "Roger Dodsworth: The Reanimated Englishman" also touches upon themes relevant to science fiction such as time travel and cryogenesis. Written in 1826 and published posthumously in 1863, "Dodsworth" raises questions about the contexts of audience reception and the influence of scientific progress on society. Harker Shaw introduces the story in regard to the importance of Shelley's reputation, during and after her death.

Beth Atkins follows up with an essay on Edgar Allan Poe's "The Thousand-and-Second Tale of Scheherazade" (1845). Poe's sequel to *Arabian Nights* draws on a historical literary tradition while integrating relevant details about 19th century technology. Atkins situates the story in the context of the 19th century history of science. Instead of approaching Poe's tale as a fantasy, which its relation to *Arabian Nights* suggests, Atkins pictures it as "an allegorical journey exploring the 19th century scientific imagination, centering around mesmerism."

The science fiction of the late 19th century addresses the evolution of social and technological progress, as demonstrated in the works of Mitchell, Bose, Lathrop, and Bierce. Rob Welch introduces work from this period with his first contribution, which examines Edward Page Mitchell's futuristic "The Senator's Daughter" (1879). Welch explores "The Senator's Daughter" as an analogy for Reconstruction and postbellum American life. His essay also explores themes of race and politics in Mitchell's story of star-crossed love.

Christin Hoene travels to the other side of the globe for a consideration of "Runaway Cyclone" (1896) by Bengali author Jagadish Chandra Bose, a story only recently available in English translation. Hoene explains Bose's rationale for including a popular Indian hair product in his story, and reflects on the story's mixture of science fiction and disaster genres. Her essay also looks at what makes Bose's work important for its non–Western perspective on science and technology in speculative literature.

My first contribution is entitled "Thomas Edison's Hypnotizing Machine: Technology, Science Fiction and 'Progress.'" The essay introduces George Parsons Lathrop's short story "In the Deep of Time," which was serialized in a syndicated column published in select American newspapers in 1896 and 1897. After explaining the origins of Lathrop's collaboration with Thomas

Edison, I focus on the portrayal of a "hypnotizing machine" within the context of early cinema culture.

In "The Emotional Birth of AI in 'Moxon's Master,'" Rob Welch looks at Ambrose Bierce's literary contribution to the genre of science fiction. Welch explains the appearance of the mechanical Turk in Bierce's story and connects it to the early history of artificial intelligence and humanoid robots. Welch argues that "Moxon's Master" (1899) indicates a shift in thinking about AI from mechanical to emotionally intelligent machines.

In contrast to the themes and contexts in which Shelley and Poe wrote, stories from the early 20th century reflect upon revolutionary scientific theories of the time against dramatic backdrops. Jessie F. Terrell, Jr., explores the worlds of Edgar Rice Burroughs. His essay also works to contextualize Burroughs' 1914 novel *At the Earth's Core* in the history of science fiction, in particular in relation to Jules Verne's *Journey to the Center of the Earth* (1864). He focuses on the characteristic traits that distinguish Burroughs from Verne and his contemporaries.

Riccardo Gramantieri's first contribution situates the work of H. Rider Haggard in science fiction's Radium Age. Gramantieri discusses the role of radium in early 20th century American culture. He also explains the unusual representation of radium and radioactivity in Haggard's pulp adventure novel *When the World Shook* (1919).

The discussion of Radium Age science fiction continues in my second contribution, an introduction to the speculative future "In 1999." Burrell Franklin Ruth's short story, written in 1921, takes the form of an address to a scientific society at the dawn of the 21st century. Ruth explores a future history in which atomic energy has brought about world peace. In this essay, I focus on the representation of atomic energy and the resemblance of Ruth's story to H.G. Wells' novel *The World Set Free* (1914).

Our anthology concludes in the year 1923. Riccardo Gramantieri's second contribution considers G. Peyton Wertenbaker's "The Man from the Atom" as a work of scientifiction in the context of Hugo Gernsback's pulp magazines. After a brief explanation of Einstein's theory of relativity and the development of atomic theory in the early 20th century, Gramantieri discusses the significance of Wertenbaker's description of the multiverse among other works of Radium Age science fiction.

By pairing critical introductions with primary sources, it is our hope that this anthology will reframe these works of science fiction in their cultural and historical contexts. The stories are arranged chronologically by date of publication. In some cases where the stories were published at a later date, as in the cases of Shelley and Bose, they are arranged by date of authorship with both dates also listed. This anthology is not intended to be read cover to cover. Readers are encouraged to explore science fiction from eras that most appeal to their curiosity, and use introductory essays as guidance for further research and engagement.

NOTES

   1. The "Golden Age" is also sometimes referred to as the Campbellian era, after author John W. Campbell, who "played a larger role than anybody else in disseminating prescriptive ideas of what SF ought to be" (Roberts, 287; See also Luckhurst, chapter 4).
   2. Gernsback is also credited with coining the term "science fiction."

BIBLIOGRAPHY

Aldiss, Brian. 1986. *Trillion Year Spree: The History of Science Fiction*. Gollancz.
Csicsery-Ronay, Istvan. 1991. "The SF of Theory: Baudrillard and Haraway." *Science Fiction Studies* 18, no. 3: 387–404.
Csicsery-Ronay, Istvan. 2008. *The Seven Beauties of Science Fiction*. Wesleyan UP.
De Laurentis, Teresa, Andreas Huyssen, and Kathleen M. Woodward, eds. 1980. *The Technological Imagination: Theories and Fictions*. Coda Press.
Freedman, Carl. 2013. *Critical Theory and Science Fiction*. Wesleyan UP.
Gernsback, Hugo. 1952. "The Evolution of Modern Science Fiction."
Glenn, Josh. 2012a. "The Radium Age Science Fiction Library." Boing Boing (Feb 14). Retrieved from https://boingboing.net/2012/02/14/the-radium-age-science-fiction.html
Glenn, Josh. 2012b. "Science Fiction: The Radium Age." *Nature* 489 (13 September): 204–205.
Jameson, Fredric. 2005. *Archaeologies of the Future: The Desire Called Utopia and Other Science Fictions*. Verso.
Luckhurst, Roger. 2005. *Science Fiction*. Polity.
Roberts, Adam. 2016 [2007]. *The History of Science Fiction*. Palgrave Macmillan.
Stableford, Brian. 1985. *Scientific Romance in Britain 1890–1950*. Fourth Estate.
Suvin, Darko. 1979. *Metamorphoses of Science Fiction: On the Poetics and History of a Literary Genre*. Yale UP.
Suvin, Darko. 1983. *Victorian Science Fiction in the UK: The Discourses of Knowledge and Power*. GK Hall.
Westfahl, Gary. 1998. *The Mechanics of Wonder: The Creation of the Idea of Science Fiction*. Liverpool UP.

The Future from the Past

Mary Shelley's "Reanimated Englishman"

Joanna Harker Shaw

It is appropriate that a collection such as this should begin with Mary Shelley, the long-acknowledged mother of modern science fiction. The infamous animation of dead clay executed by the young promethean scientist in Mary Shelley's *Frankenstein* has been adapted and referenced more times than it is easy to count, and one of the most common amendments adaptors make to Shelley's text is to give character to what the nameless creature was before he was "animated." For example, Kenneth Branagh's 1994 film, *Mary Shelley's Frankenstein*, saw the creature made with the body of a criminal and the brain of Dr. Frankenstein's university professor, drawing upon a famous scientific experiment of Shelley's day in which electric current was passed through the corpse of a recently deceased convict. But literary scholars remain faithful to Mary Shelley's original decision to disclose nothing about the parts from which the creature was assembled, truly allowing him to be a tabula rasa.

There are, however, two stories in Shelley's repertoire of not merely *animation* but *reanimation*. The first was "Valerius: The Reanimated Roman," first published in 1976 though it was written in 1819. The second, the work anthologized here, is "Rodger Dodsworth: The Reanimated Englishman," first published in 1863 and written 1826.[1] The former provides neither cause of nor detail about the reanimation. It is only a fragment, and Shelley never submitted it for publication. The reanimation is really only a *deus ex machina* to allow Shelley an opportunity to lament the decay of Italy. "Roger Dodsworth," however, is a very different and much more interesting case. "Roger Dodsworth: The Reanimated Englishman" is a short story masquerading as a newspaper article commenting upon the discovery of a body frozen in an avalanche in the Alps. The body was, miraculously, preserved, and subsequently brought back to life, making "Roger Dodsworth" one of the very first "suspended animation" stories.

Suspended animation, in which life is temporarily halted, usually by means of cryogenic freezing, has become a staple of science fiction. From *Star Trek* to Edgar Allan Poe's short stories, to Marvel's *Captain America*, it seems everyone is doing it. Prior to Shelley's story there were plenty of fantasy takes on the theme in tales, folklore and mythologies across the world (think of Sleeping Beauty, or one of the many King under the mountain myths). However, Shelley is certainly one of the first (if not *the* first) to write on this theme with a clear eye to the scientific likelihood, as she said of the events depicted in *Frankenstein*, that such things are "not of impossible occurrence" (Shelley 1996, 5). Shelley is adamant that this is not an enchanted sleep, clearly stating that "Mr. Dodsworth did not sleep; his breast never heaved, his pulse never stopped" (153). She acknowledges the likelihood of such an event by citing scientific consensus: "animation (I believe physiologists agree) can as easily be suspended of an hundred or more years, as for as many seconds" (152). However, few have identified Shelley as being the first science fiction writer to approach the topic, with most critics pointing to William Clark Russell's *The Frozen Pirate* (1887) as the progenitor of the trope.

Despite the hundreds of people currently frozen in cryogenic facilities across the world, cryonic freezing, as Grant Shoffstall (2010) points out in his history of cryonic suspension, is, even today, a form of science fiction (285–286). While frogs, fish and some small mammals can withstand freeze during hibernation, no human has yet been successfully reanimated after deliberate freezing. Indeed, the contemporary practice of freezing yourself in the hope of someone one day discovering a means of reanimating you came from Robert C.W. Ettinger, who openly says he found his inspiration in the pages of 1930s science fiction, most notably Neil R. Jones' *The Jamieson Satellite* (Shoffstall, 288). Though life has repeatedly tried to copy art, in this case life has not been successful. It is what Shoffstall calls the "realm of possibility: the what if or the what could be of a given future, as opposed to attending the actual, the what is of the here and now" (267).

It is easy to see the train of thought that leads to this hope, though. The benefits of freezing have long been studied. In 1626, Francis Bacon experimented with preserving meat in the snow. In 1766, not so very long before Shelley was writing, John Hunter undertook an experiment attempting to reanimate a fish that had been frozen. By Shelley's time there was lively scientific inquiry for a means of suspending animation, even for just a short time to allow for painful or difficult surgeries (remember, these are the days pre-anesthetic).

So when, in June 1826, what has become known as the "Roger Dodsworth Hoax" began to circulate newspapers, there were grounds for believing the story possible, even if it were not actually true. The London magazine *The New Times* republished a translation of an article from the *Journal Du Commerce De Lyon* which claimed that a frozen body had been found in the Alps and was subsequently restored to life. The story ran that the reanimated Englishman was one Roger Dodsworth, born in 1629. The story prompted discussion and debate (of varying levels of credulity). Notable commentators included radical MP and journalist William Cobbett, as well as Thomas Moore, once friend of Shelley's family and soon to remake her acquaintance, who wrote a witty piece suggesting that Dodsworth, with his seventeenth-century values, could easily step into the shoes of noted politician the Lord Chancellor John Scott, Earl of Eldon.

It seems that Mary Shelley had already begun her first reanimation story in 1819, not long after the publication of *Frankenstein,* "Valerius: The Reanimated Roman." All we have of this story are a few fragments which do not engage with the means of Valerius' reanimation, but only speak upon the Roman's feelings on being returned to his world.

This theme is lightly mentioned in Dodsworth when the narrator says, "we have ... often made conjectures how such and such heroes of antiquity would act, if they were reborn in these times" (162). Valerius is exactly one such individual. In this fragment, Shelley shows modern Italy through an ancient Roman's eyes, and takes his wisdom to pass judgment upon the folly of the day.[2] Valerius looks upon modern Italy with bitterness, just as Dodsworth initially sees that "the later generation of man is much deteriorated from his contemporaries." However, "Valerius" does not seem to be complete. It was never submitted for publication and, as Anastasaki (2006/7) notes, is often fragmentary (29). "Roger Dodsworth," on the contrary, is complete. With time, Dodsworth grows "to doubt this first impression," which perhaps suggests where "Valerius" may have been heading. It may well be that work on this narrative predisposed her to pick up the Roger Dodsworth story herself.

Shelley no doubt found the Dodsworth controversy highly amusing. She wrote her own piece to contribute to the ring, fuelled with the political satire and humor that is rarely credited to her. She sent it to the *New Monthly Magazine* for publication, but they did not choose to print it at that time.

After her novels *Frankenstein* (1818) and *The Last Man* (1826), this was an obvious topic for Shelley. Indeed, recent tepid reviews of *The Last Man* had criticized her depiction of a future (2092) with post-chaises and hackney cabs, perhaps prompting her to turn to the more familiar past (see Seymour 2000, 361). Dodsworth's era was one she had studied previously, including while her husband, Percy Shelley, endeavored to write a play on Charles I. The idea may have further suggested itself to her as she had recently been reading the works of Washington Irving, which most likely included the tale of "Rip Van Winkle" who slept for twenty years.

When shaping her own Dodsworth story, Shelley diverged significantly from her fellow commentators in setting the reanimation "a score or two of years ago." A journalistic narrator elaborates first upon the particulars of the case with endearing sincerity, includes a brief history of Dodsworth before his accident in 1654, and outlines the present day response to the news of his reanimation, before coming to their principal point: that they are frustrated at the lack of information forthcoming and believe Dodsworth should come forward to give an account of himself ("it is hard, very hard, that Mr. Dodsworth refuses to appear") (152). As there is no sign of Dodsworth doing so, the journalist takes it upon themselves to hypothesize the feelings of Dodsworth at this extraordinary event and soon descends into a speculation of the first conversation between Dodsworth and his discoverer, Dr. Hotham.

This conversation forms Shelley's set piece, which spirals into a satire on political opinions of the day, as Dodsworth and Hotham try to understand each other's political position and maintain a political correctness. Dodsworth, it must be remembered, last saw England in 1660, a time in which the monarchy had been terminated and the Commonwealth installed; Shelley hypothesizes that his absence from his homeland points to a royalist who chose exile under the rule of Oliver Cromwell, but who was able to keep his opinions sufficiently quiet to allow him to return to England unimpeded. Hotham, meanwhile, is a high tory who suspects his companion of a pre–French-revolutionary radicalism. The two amusingly misunderstand and bewilder each other. As Dr. Hotham listens critically to Dodsworth's questions and "suspects a radical," Dodsworth in his turn "suspects the Republican" (156). Dodsworth is pained to conceal his political opinions and endeavors to put forward the most palatable front as he asks for news from England, until he hears Hotham's casual reference to the King, at which point "his loyalty late a tiny bud suddenly expands into full flower" (157). Poor Dodsworth is raised to the highest joys on hearing what he believes to be the crowning of Charles II, only to be shot down by Hotham's reply:

> Surely, sir, you forget ... that of course is impossible. No descendant of his fills the English throne, now worthily occupied by the house of Hanover. The despicable race of the Stuarts, long outcast and wandering, is now extinct, and the last days of the last Pretender to the crown of that family justified in the eyes of the world the sentence which ejected it from the kingdom for ever [158].

"Such," Shelley regretfully comments, "must have been Mr. Dodsworth's first lesson in politics." Poor Roger Dodsworth is disillusioned and the full force of his situation hits him. For Dodsworth, the suspension of his life forms a kind of time travel, as he wakes to find that "now every human being he had ever seen is 'lapped in lead,' is dust, each voice he ever heard is mute. The very sound of the English tongue is changed" (158). He is a stranger in his own country. There are parallels between Shelley's sympathy for Dodsworth and the emotional journey of Lionel Verney, the eponymous protagonist of *The Last Man* who witnesses the deaths of all his peers in a savage plague. Numerous critics have looked at the biographical analogies between this loneliness and the suffering Mary Shelley underwent as, at the age of 29 in 1826 she had lost her mother, three of her four children, her husband, her sister and several dear friends.

As well as this engagement with Dodsworth's emotional journey and an acknowledgment of all he must undergo to fit into 19th century society, Shelley also meditates upon the philosophical considerations of this technological development. What Mary Shelley saw in the story, as she saw in the discussion of galvanism and applied so brilliantly to *Frankenstein*, is a consideration of implications, and it is here the story's real poignancy lies.

If a person could come from the past, would we not learn to transcend our petty differences? What the misunderstanding shows is the irrelevance of daily politics, even though Mary was acutely interested in political matters and once wrote to a friend "you see what a John or rather Joan Bull I am so full of politics" (Shelley 1995, 59). Nonetheless, she valued the ability to see beyond the squabbles of the day.

Shelley was a formidable historian, writing considerable amounts of both historical non-fiction and historical novels across her life, and in "Dodsworth" she explicitly expresses the importance of knowing our history. As Dodsworth himself adjusts to modern life, a great deal of what was formerly important to him fades away. From this, Shelley goes on to consider the theories of past lives and the great insight it would be if we all had some intimate knowledge of the past. She makes a particular example of how a "judge as he passed sentence would suddenly become aware, that formerly he had condemned the saints of the early church to the torture, for not renouncing the religion he now upheld—nothing but benevolent actions and real goodness would come pure out of the ordeal," highlighting how a person of one spirit could claim extraordinarily different values at a different time in history (163–4). She may here have considered the widespread condemnation of her late husband for his atheist beliefs, that would, in another day in time, be easily accepted. She cites eminent politicians and writers of the day and aligns them with historical counterparts, expanding upon what knowledge of such a past might have given to them. While the "Honorable" Charles Fox might have been "soothed" to know his past, she councils that Richard Sheridan may have learned from former mistakes and chosen instead a different path. Such knowledge, she argues, would eradicate our narrow-minded beliefs.

Publication

Had this work been published in 1826, when it was written, it would have joined a dialogue of several articles (with varying degrees of satire and sincerity) discussing the discovery of the frozen man and his subsequent reanimation. Robinson (1975) notes how the story was reprinted in the *Morning Chronicle,* the London *Sun,* the *Manchester Guardian,* the Edinburgh *Scotsman,* and the tory *John Bull* (22).

However, Mary Shelley's piece did not join the debate at the time. She sent it to the *New Monthly Magazine* in 1826 while the issue was hot, but one of the magazine's editors, Cyrus Redding, only chose to publish the work a full 37 years later, in 1863.

The world "Roger Dodsworth: The Reanimated Englishman" was published into was very different from the one in which it was written. Long gone were the anxieties of revolution and reform that haunted the start of the century; Queen Victoria was long-established on the throne, and the British Empire was expanding as industry and science made game-changing inroads. Scientific discussions moved from the theories of Erasmus Darwin, who had no small influence upon *Frankenstein,* to those of his grandson, Charles Darwin. With such great developments in scientific inquiry came, almost inevitably, a development in the genre we today know as science fiction (though the genre had not yet acquired its name). Everett F. Bleiler's impressive encyclopedia, *Science Fiction: The Early Years,* lists only three science fiction texts published in the five years preceding the composition of "Roger Dodsworth," one of which was Shelley's own *The Last Man.* Ten science fiction texts appeared in the five years prior to the story's publication.

The day of science fiction was dawning. The year that saw the publication of "Roger Dodsworth" would also see the publication of Jules Verne's first novel, *Cinq Semaines en Ballon* (*Five Weeks in a Balloon*). Between the composition and publication of "Roger Dodsworth" exists Edgar Allan Poe's entire publishing life.

It is apt that the works of Poe, who is in so many ways Shelley's successor with his perfect mix of gothic and science fiction, should pave the way for the publication of "Roger Dodsworth" with his own hoaxes. Today media is abuzz with the Trumpian term "fake news," but fake news is nothing new, and the 19th century, with its curiosity, its enthusiasm and its constant scientific development, was a peak time for journalistic hoaxes.

One of Poe's famous hoaxes is "The Unparalleled Adventure of One Hans Pfall" (1835). Published in the *Southern Literary Magazine,* this tale is an openly satirical piece that tells of a balloon flight to the moon. Mario Castagnaro (2012) identifies this story as "clearly a satirical hoax in the vein of Jonathan Swift or Benjamin Franklin" (253). In saying this, Castagnaro makes a key distinction between this and later hoaxes; this earlier style, characterized by its far-fetched content, its comic tone and exaggerated names such as Mynheer Superbus Von Underduk and Professor Rub-a-dub, is not intended to be believed, just as no one is *meant* to take Jonathan Swift's *Modest Proposal* (1729) seriously. It is meant as a commentary.

However, Poe's later and far more successful publishing hoax was the Balloon Hoax (1844) which, as with the Roger Dodsworth hoax, wears the mask of earnestness. Published in the New York *Sun* newspaper, it claimed that a balloon had crossed the Atlantic in only seventy-five hours. Here there is no exaggerated caricature, but instead exactly the kind of meticulous journalistic reportage and reflection as the presses of the day were using. The article relates the events as follows:

> By the energy of an agent at Charleston, S.C., we are enabled to be the first to furnish the public with a detailed account of this most extraordinary voyage, which was performed between Saturday, the 6th instant, at 11, A.M., and 2, P.M., on Tuesday the 9th inst.: by Sir Everard Bringhurst; Mr. Osborne, a nephew of Lord Bentinck's; Mr. Monck Mason and Mr. Robert Holland, the well-known aeronauts [Poe 1844].

Throughout, it never lets the mask of sincerity slip. Indeed, it is so successful as a piece of reportage that it fails as a piece of literature, where Shelley's story does not. Without the wonder that such events might be real, the piece holds little more than historical curiosity to fascinate today's reader.

It is this tone of seriousness that we see the many great hoaxes of the 19th century using: an earnest enquiry that gets most of its kudos from the false appearance of fact. Castagnaro notes that "the amount of technical and scientific detail contained within the piece [the Balloon Hoax] indicates a shift in hoaxing away from literary satire toward a more contemporary understanding of the term that invokes the idea of intentional deception" (253). Poe drew heavily on scientific writings of the day to create a verisimilitude (Wilkinson 1960, 1960). Similarly, Richard Adams Yorke, orchestrator of one of the greatest hoaxes of the day, "The Great Moon Hoax" (1835), lured many to credulity by including William Herschel as one of his major players. It is exactly this movement that Shelley anticipated in "Roger Dodsworth" by acknowledging popular scientific consensus ("physiologists agree"), and elaborating upon the premise of suspended animation by freezing with an authoritative air, commenting that "a body hermetically sealed up by the frost, is of necessity persevered in its pristine entireness" (152). Readers in 1863 would have the increased awareness of this hoax language, which may have encouraged Redding to publish it when he did.

Adam Roberts' *The History of Science Fiction* charts the development of science-fiction texts alongside contemporary scientific developments, and demonstrates a movement from the enthusiasm of European Enlightenment science fiction (such as that of Swift and Voltaire) to a 19th century ambivalence that strays between optimism and pessimism in the later part of the century (106–108). Much of early science fiction formed a philosophical political critique. Just as Jonathan Swift, in the previous century, had used his *Travels into Several Remote Nations of the World* (best known as *Gulliver's Travels*) (1726) as a means of hypothesizing different cultural situations, Shelley brought a fantastical element in to address a real-world consideration (see Roberts 2016, 68–72). Into this frequently oppressive miasma of cultural anxiety, Shelley's optimism of the lessons to be learnt from a visitor of the past may have provided some comfort.

Mary Shelley's Reputation

Amidst the 19th century rise of science fiction, one might expect one of its greatest contributors to obtain notoriety, but such was not the case with Mary Shelley. Although *Frankenstein* continued to dominate popular culture, appearing in play adaptations and referenced in newspaper cartoons, its creator was carefully avoiding personal celebrity.

Here it is pertinent to point out that there are (at least) two reputations to Mary Shelley. The one we know best today is the wild sixteen-year-old who ran away with the already-married poet Percy Shelley and spent a glorious summer of 1816 with Lord Byron in Geneva, during which she famously wrote her novel *Frankenstein* that would become a peak of gothic culture. This is the image that is most widely propagated in biographies and films today: a prodigiously talented young woman living outside the rules. However, this was not the image her contemporaries held of her.

For the most part, Shelley published anonymously. Even her most famous work, *Frankenstein,* was initially published anonymously. She had good reason to avoid the public eye; she knew what devastation scandal could cause from public response to her parents and husband. Her younger days courted a little of it as she spent the summer with her married lover, Percy Shelley, and Lord Byron in what contemporary reporters suggested might be a "league of incest" (see Seymour, cii). But after Percy Shelley's death there was a more pressing need for silence; her disapproving father-in-law, Sir Timothy Shelley, stipulated that he would only continue to support her and her infant son so long as the Shelley name was kept out of publication. The allowance he did allow was pitiful and unreliable, and Mary Shelley turned to writing to support herself.

She got around Sir Timothy's edict by publishing her first few short stories anonymously, but in 1828 she began to publish short stories under the rather coy pseudonym "The Author of *Frankenstein.*" By 1833, however, having acquired a greater level of autonomy, she adopted a version of her own name—not the way she signed it in her correspondence, "Mary Wollstonecraft Shelley," but the socially acceptable name of a proper lady writer: Mrs. Shelley.[3]

Shelley is a fascinating example of woman writer in a difficult age. She was born into radical stock, the daughter of one of the earliest proto-feminists. She knew all too well the pains of being a social outcast, and was prepared to sacrifice for social acceptance. A great deal of rewriting history and careful concealing of past and present irregularities went into maintaining this image, much of it done by Mary and her daughter-in-law Lady Jane Shelley. Much of this is related to the careful curation of Percy Shelley's literary legacy that Lady Jane Shelley was manipulating to a considerable degree. When Mary Shelley died in 1851 she had managed to maintain a serious and sober reputation; she was the "Mrs. Shelley" who may have committed some indiscretions in her youth, and certainly came from unsuitable stock, but was essentially a respectable person on the surface. Thus, when Cyrus Redding (the editor she sent "Roger Dodsworth" to all those years ago) was compiling his memoirs of the great, the powerful, and the interesting, he came across the story and was more than happy to claim acquaintance with its owner.

Redding was clearly attempting to bolster his own reputation with his records of the past, as recent publications included *Fifty Years' Recollections, Literary and Personal, with Observations on Men and Things* (1858), and would in the next few years include the multi-volume *Personal Reminiscences of Eminent Men* (1867). He had also written a memoir of William Beckford, author of *Vathek*. He found a place for Shelley's story in the three-volumed *Yesterday and Today* (1863). By that time, Shelley had been dead for twelve years.

Yesterday and Today was Redding's self-proclaimed follow up to his *Fifty Years' Recollections, Literary and Personal* that included recollections of such eminent persons as William Wilberforce, Richard Sheridan, Lord Erskine, and Lord Cochrane. Redding is clearly making a name for himself, remarking it as unusual when there is a celebrity of the day that he does not know: "It is singular that while I knew by person almost all the literary men of that time, and was acquainted with most of them, I never even saw Byron" (Redding 1863, 106).[4] This claim seems frankly laughable once one examines some of the tenuous connections of his "remembrances."

Redding had some further correspondence with Mary Shelley after the writing of "Roger Dodsworth" when he compiled a collection of poetry of her husband, Percy Shelley, John Keats and Samuel Taylor Coleridge. Despite Shelley's offer to write the memoir of her husband, Redding ended up interviewing her and writing it himself, only acknowledging the debt in *Yesterday and Today*.

It is clear Redding does not have a conception of what he has on his hands. He opens the chapter in which "Roger Dodsworth" is contained with an anecdote on Shelley's father, William Godwin, implying he is more worthy of note. This leads him to a brief introduction of Mary herself. His introduction is a condescending stoop to propriety and gender mores of the day. "I had a great respect for this lady," he says, "as one of those of her sex who did it honour by her talents and agreeable manners" (Redding 150). This polite but underwhelming introduction leads to a brief discourse on the receiving, subsequent shelving, and eventual rediscovery of the manuscript. Redding's collection attained a certain ephemeral popularity in its day, but there is little mention of Shelley's short story until the surge in studies of her work commencing in the 1980s.

Redding's role in the history of "Roger Dodsworth: The Reanimated Englishman" is little like that of the story's Dr. Hotham. He stumbles upon something in the course of his daily life, and resurrects it with little real idea of the significance it has. Whatever the reason for Redding's original decision not to publish in 1826, the effect of delayed publication meant that Shelley's story was frozen in Redding's office, and emerged at last thirty seven years later with a new poignancy. Its author, like the rest of her generation, was dead, but here was a last piece of her voice. At the end of the story the narrator wonders if perhaps Dodsworth is already dead: "perhaps he is again once more. Perhaps he opened his eyes only to shut them more obstinately" (165). Hearing the voices of the dead in our present day is ever a stirring experience, and one that, as Shelley advised, we can learn from. Let us hope there still remain more as yet unidentified Mary Shelley stories out there frozen in ice, simply awaiting reanimation.

NOTES

1. Both of these titles were applied, as far as I can tell, for the first time by Charles E. Robinson in *Collected Stories and Tales,* rather than by Shelley herself.
2. Some critics speculate the fragment to have been written in 1819, thus predating Dodsworth by some years. See Nitchie 1953, 103.
3. The following full list of Shelley's published short stories is compiled from the notes to Robinson's edition (1990):
Anonymous, "A Tale of the Passions," *The Liberal,* 1823.
Anonymous, "The Bride of Italy," *The London Magazine,* 1823.
Anonymous, "Recollections of Italy," *The London Magazine,* 1824.
The Author of *Frankenstein,* "The Sisters of Albano," *The Keepsake,* 1828.
The Author of *Frankenstein,* "Ferdinando Eboli: A Tale," *The Keepsake,* 1828.
The Author of *Frankenstein,* "The Mourner," *The Keepsake,* 1829.
The Author of *Frankenstein,* "The Evil Eye," *The Keepsake,* 1829.
The Author of *Frankenstein,* "The False Rhyme," *The Keepsake,* 1829.
The Author of *Frankenstein,* "Transformation," *The Keepsake,*1830.
The Author of *Frankenstein,* "The Swiss Peasant," *The Keepsake,* 1830.
The Author of *Frankenstein,* "The Dream," *The Keepsake,* 1831.

The Author of *Frankenstein*, "The Brother and Sister: An Italian Story," *The Keepsake*, 1832.
The Author of *Frankenstein*, "The Invisible Girl," *The Keepsake*, 1832.
Mrs. Shelley, "The Smuggler and His Family," *Original Compositions*, 1833.
The Author of *Frankenstein*, "The Mortal Immortal: A Tale," *The Keepsake*, 1833.
The Author of *Frankenstein*, "The Trial of Love," *The Keepsake*, 1834.
Mrs. Shelley, "The Elder Son," *Heath's Book of Beauty*, 1835.
Mrs. Shelley, "The Parvenue," *The Keepsake*, 1836.
Mrs. Shelley, "The Pilgrims," *The Keepsake*, 1837.
Mrs. Shelley, "Euphrasia: A Tale of Greece." *The Keepsake*, 1838.
    4. As a note of how unreliable a source Redding is, consider the following anecdote on how he met Mary's husband: "I imagine I once met [Percy Bysshe] Shelley at his [Leigh Hunt's] house with others, but I forget most of their names" (Redding 1863, 104).

BIBLIOGRAPHY

Anastasaki, Elena. 2006/2007. "The Trials and Tribulations of the *Revenants*: Narrative Techniques and the Fragmented Hero in Mary Shelley and Theophile Gautier." *Connotations* 16, no. 1–3: 26–46.
Bjork, Ulf Jonas. 2001. "Sweet Is the Tale." *American Journalism* 18, no. 4: 13–27.
Castagnaro, Mario. 2012. "Lunar Fancies and Earthly Truths: The Moon Hoax of 1835 and the Penny Press." *Nineteenth-Century Contexts* 34, no. 3: 253–268.
Grossman, Marshall. 2011. *The Seventeenth-Century Literature Handbook*. Wiley-Blackwell.
Markley, A.A. 1997. "'Laughing That I May Not Weep': Mary Shelley's Short Fiction and Her Novels." *Keats-Shelley Journal* 46: 97–124.
Nitchie, Elizabeth. 1953. *Mary Shelley: Author of "Frankenstein."* Rutgers UP.
Poe, Edgar Allan. 1844. "Astounding News!" (The Balloon Hoax). New York *Sun*, 13 April.
Poe, Edgar Allan. 2004. *Collected Tales and Poems of Edgar Allan Poe*. Wordsworth Editions.
Redding, Cyrus. 1863. *Yesterday and To-day*. T.C. Newby.
Roberts, Adam. 2016. *The History of Science Fiction*. Palgrave Macmillan.
Robinson, Charles E. 1975. "Mary Shelley and the Roger Dodsworth Hoax." *Keats Shelley Journal* 24: 20–28.
Seymour, Miranda. 2000. *Mary Shelley*, Picador.
Shelley, Mary Wollstonecraft. 1863. "Roger Dodsworth: The Reanimated Englishman" in *Yesterday and To-day*, edited by Cyrus Redding, 150–165. T.C. Newby.
Shelley, Mary Wollstonecraft. 1990. *Mary Shelley: Collected Tales and Stories*. Edited by Charles E. Robinson. Johns Hopkins UP.
Shelley, Mary Wollstonecraft. 1995. *Selected Letters of Mary Wollstonecraft Shelley*. Edited by and Betty Bennet. Johns Hopkins UP.
Shelley, Mary Wollstonecraft. 1996. *Frankenstein*. Edited by J. Paul Hunter. W.W. Norton.
Shelley, Mary Wollstonecraft. 2008. *The Last Man*. Oxford.
Shoffstall, Grant. 2010. "Freeze, Wait, Reanimate: Cryonic Suspension and Science Fiction." *Bulletin of Science, Technology & Society* 30, no. 4: 285–297.
Wilkinson, Ronald Sterne. 1960. "Poe's 'Balloon-Hoax' Once More." *American Literature* 32, no. 3: 313–317.

"Roger Dodsworth:
The Reanimated Englishman"
(1826/1863)

MARY WOLLSTONECRAFT SHELLEY

It may be remembered, that on the fourth of July last, a paragraph appeared in the papers importing that Dr. Hotham, of Northumberland, returning from Italy, over Mount St. Gothard, a score or two of years ago, had dug out from under an avalanche, in the neighborhood of the mountain, a human being whose animation had been suspended by the action of the frost. Upon the application of the usual remedies, the patient was resuscitated, and discovered himself to be Mr. Dodsworth, the son of the antiquary Dodsworth, who perished in the reign of Charles I.[1] He was thirty-seven years of age at the time of his inhumation, which had taken place as he was returning from Italy, in 1654. It was added that as soon as he was sufficiently recovered he would return to England, under the protection of his preserver. We have since heard no more of him, and various plans for public benefit, which have started in philanthropic minds on reading the statement, have already returned to their pristine nothingness. The antiquarian society had eaten their way to several votes for medals, and had already begun, in idea, to consider what prices it could afford to offer for Mr. Dodsworth's old clothes, and to conjecture what treasures in the way of pamphlet, old song, or autographic letter his pockets might contain. Poems from all quarters, of all kinds, elegiac, congratulatory, burlesque and allegoric, were half written. Mr. Godwin had suspended for the sake of such authentic information the history of the Commonwealth he had just begun. It is hard not only that the world should be baulked of these destined gifts from the talents of the country, but also that it should be promised and then deprived of a new subject of romantic wonder and scientific interest. A novel idea is worth much in the commonplace rou-

18

tine of life, but a new fact, an astonishment, a miracle, a palpable wandering from the course of things into apparent impossibilities, is a circumstance to which the imagination must cling with delight, and we say again that it is hard, very hard, that Mr. Dodsworth refuses to appear, and that the believers in his resuscitation are forced to undergo the sarcasms and triumphant arguments of those skeptics who always keep on the safe side of the hedge.

Now we do not believe that any contradiction or impossibility is attached to the adventures of this youthful antique. Animation (I believe physiologists agree) can as easily be suspended for an hundred or two years, as for as many seconds. A body hermetically sealed up by the frost, is of necessity preserved in its pristine entireness. That which is totally secluded from the action of external agency, can neither have any thing added to nor taken away from it: no decay can take place, for something can never become nothing; under the influence of that state of being which we call death, change but not annihilation removes from our sight the corporeal atoma; the earth receives sustenance from them, the air is fed by them, each clement takes its own, thus seizing forcible repayment of what it had lent. But the elements that hovered round Mr. Dodsworth's icy shroud had no power to overcome the obstacle it presented. No zephyr could gather a hair from his head, nor could the influence of dewy night or genial morn penetrate his more than adamantine panoply. The story of the Seven Sleepers rests on a miraculous interposition—they slept. Mr. Dodsworth did not sleep; his breast never heaved, his pulses were stopped; death had his finger pressed on his lips which no breath might pass. He has removed it now, the grim shadow is vanquished, and stands wondering. His victim has cast from him the frosty spell, and arises as perfect a man as he had lain down an hundred and fifty years before. We have eagerly desired to be furnished with some particulars of his first conversations, and the mode in which he has learnt to adapt himself to his new scene of life. But since facts are denied to us, let us be permitted to indulge in conjecture. What his first words were may be guessed from the expressions used by people exposed to shorter accidents of the like nature. But as his powers return, the plot thickens. His dress had already excited Dr. Hotham's astonishment—the peaked beard—the love locks—the frill, which, until it was thawed, stood stiff under the mingled influence of starch and frost; his dress fashioned like that of one of Vandyke's portraits, or (a more familiar similitude) Mr. Sapio's costume in Winter's Opera of the Oracle, his pointed shoes—all spoke of other times. The curiosity of his preserver was keenly awake, that of Mr. Dodsworth was about to be roused. But to be enabled to conjecture with any degree of likelihood the tenor of his first inquiries, we must endeavor to make out what part he played in his former life. He lived at the most interesting period of English History—he was lost to the world when Oliver Cromwell had arrived at the summit of his ambition, and in the eyes of all Europe the commonwealth of England appeared so established as to endure for ever. Charles I. was dead; Charles II. was an outcast, a beggar, bankrupt even in hope. Mr. Dodsworth's father, the antiquary, received a salary from the republican general, Lord Fairfax, who was himself a great lover of antiquities, and died the very year that his son went to his long, but not unending sleep, a curious coincidence this, for it would seem that our frost-preserved friend was returning to England on his father's death, to claim probably his inheritance—how short lived are human views! Where now is Mr. Dodsworth's patrimony? Where his co-heirs, executors, and fellow legatees? His protracted absence has, we should suppose, given the present possessors to his estate—the world's chronology is an hundred and seventy years older since he seceded from the busy scene, hands after hands have tilled his acres, and then become clods beneath them; we may be permitted to doubt whether one single particle of their surface is individually the same as those which were to have been his—the youthful soil would of itself reject the antique clay of its claimant.

Mr. Dodsworth, if we may judge from the circumstance of his being abroad, was no zealous commonwealth's man, yet his having chosen Italy as the country in which to make his tour and his projected return to England on his father's death, renders it probable that he was no violent loyalist. One of those men he seems to be (or to have been) who did not follow Cato's advice as recorded in the Pharsalia; a party, if to be of no party admits of such a term, which Dante recommends us utterly to despise, and which not unseldom falls between the two stools, a seat on either of which is so carefully avoided. Still Mr. Dodsworth could hardly fail to feel anxious for the latest news from his native country at so critical a period; his absence might have put his own property in jeopardy; we may imagine therefore that after his limbs had felt the cheerful return of circulation, and after he had refreshed himself with such of earth's products as from all analogy he never could have hoped to live to eat, after he had been told from what peril he had been rescued, and said a prayer thereon which even appeared enormously long to Dr. Hotham—we may imagine, we say, that his first question would be: "if any news had arrived lately from England?"

"I had letters yesterday," Dr. Hotham may well be supposed to reply.

"Indeed," cries Mr. Dodsworth, "and pray, sir, has any change for better or worse occurred in that poor distracted country?"

Dr. Hotham suspects a Radical, and coldly replies: "Why, sir, it would be difficult to say in what its distraction consists. People talk of starving manufacturers, bankruptcies, and the fall of the Joint Stock Companies—excrescences these, excrescences which will attach themselves to a state of full health. England, in fact, was never in a more prosperous condition."

Mr. Dodsworth now more than suspects the Republican, and, with what we have supposed to be his accustomed caution, sinks for awhile his loyalty, and in a moderate tone asks: "Do our governors look with careless eyes upon the symptoms of over-health?"

"Our governors," answers his preserver, "if you mean our ministry, are only too alive to temporary embarrassment." (We beg Dr. Hotham's pardon if we wrong him in making him a high Tory; such a quality appertains to our pure anticipated cognition of a Doctor, and such is the only cognizance that we have of this gentleman.) "It were to be wished that they showed themselves more firm—the king, God bless him!"

"Sir!" exclaims Mr. Dodsworth.

Dr. Hotham continues, not aware of the excessive astonishment exhibited by his patient: "The king, God bless him, spares immense sums from his privy purse for the relief of his subjects, and his example has been imitated by all the aristocracy and wealth of England."

"The King!" ejaculates Mr. Dodsworth.

"Yes, sir," emphatically rejoins his preserver; "the king, and I am happy to say that the prejudices that so unhappily and unwarrantably possessed the English people with regard to his Majesty are now, with a few" (with added severity) "and I may say contemptible exceptions, exchanged for dutiful love and such reverence as his talents, virtues, and paternal care deserve."

"Dear sir, you delight me," replies Mr. Dodsworth, while his loyalty late a tiny bud suddenly expands into full flower; "yet I hardly understand; the change is so sudden; and the man—Charles Stuart, King Charles, I may now call him, his murder is I trust execrated as it deserves?"

Dr. Hotham put his hand on the pulse of his patient—he feared an access of delirium from such a wandering from the subject. The pulse was calm, and Mr. Dodsworth continued: "That unfortunate martyr looking down from heaven is, I trust, appeased by the reverence paid to his name and the prayers dedicated to his memory. No sentiment, I think I may venture to assert, is so general in England as the compassion and love in which the memory of that hapless monarch is held?"

"And his son, who now reigns?—"

"Surely, sir, you forget; no son; that of course is impossible. No descendant of his fills the English throne, now worthily occupied by the house of Hanover. The despicable race of the Stuarts, long outcast and wandering, is now extinct, and the last days of the last Pretender to the crown of that family justified in the eyes of the world the sentence which ejected it from the kingdom for ever."

Such must have been Mr. Dodsworth's first lesson in politics. Soon, to the wonder of the preserver and preserved, the real state of the case must have been revealed; for a time, the strange and tremendous circumstance of his long trance may have threatened the wits of Mr. Dodsworth with a total overthrow. He had, as he crossed Mount Saint Gothard, mourned a father—now every human being he had ever seen is "lapped in lead," is dust, each voice he had ever heard is mute.[2] The very sound of the English tongue is changed, as his experience in conversation with Dr. Hotham assures him. Empires, religions, races of men, have probably sprung up or faded; his own patrimony (the thought is idle, yet, without it, how can he live?) is sunk into the thirsty gulf that gapes ever greedy to swallow the past; his learning, his acquirements, are probably obsolete; with a bitter smile he thinks to himself, I must take to my father's profession, and turn antiquary. The familiar objects, thoughts, and habits of my boyhood, are now antiquities. He wonders where the hundred and sixty folio volumes of MS. that his father had compiled, and which, as a lad, he had regarded with religious reverence, now are—where—ah, where? His favorite play-mate, the friend of his later years, his destined and lovely bride, tears long frozen are uncongealed, and flow down his young old cheeks.

But we do not wish to be pathetic; surely since the days of the patriarchs, no fair lady had her death mourned by her lover so many years after it had taken place. Necessity, tyrant of the world, in some degree reconciles Mr. Dodsworth to his fate. At first he is persuaded that the later generation of man is much deteriorated from his contemporaries; they are neither so tall, so handsome, nor so intelligent. Then by degrees he begins to doubt his first impression. The ideas that had taken possession of his brain before his accident, and which had been frozen up for so many years, begin to thaw and dissolve away, making room for others. He dresses himself in the modern style, and does not object much to anything except the neck-cloth and hard-boarded hat. He admires the texture of his shoes and stockings, and looks with admiration on a small Genevese watch, which he often consults, as if he were not yet assured that time had made progress in its accustomed manner, and as if he should find on its dial plate ocular demonstration that he had exchanged his thirty-seventh year for his two hundredth and upwards, and had left A.D. 1654 far behind to find himself suddenly a beholder of the ways of men in this enlightened 19th century. His curiosity is insatiable; when he reads, his eyes cannot purvey fast enough to his mind, and every now and then he lights upon some inexplicable passage, some discovery and knowledge familiar to us, but undreamed of in his days, that throws him into wonder and interminable reverie. Indeed, he may be supposed to pass much of his time in that state, now and then interrupting himself with a royalist song against old Noll and the Roundheads, breaking off suddenly, and looking round fearfully to see who were his auditors, and on beholding the modern appearance of his friend the Doctor, sighing to think that it is no longer of import to any, whether he sing a cavalier catch or a puritanic psalm.

It was an endless task to develop all the philosophic ideas to which Mr.

Dodsworth's resuscitation naturally gives birth. We should like much to converse with this gentleman, and still more to observe the progress of his mind, and the change of his ideas in his very novel situation. If he be a sprightly youth, fond of the shows of the world, careless of the higher human pursuits, he may proceed summarily to cast into the shade all trace of his former life, and endeavor to merge himself at once into the stream of humanity now flowing. It would be curious enough to observe the mistakes he would make, and the medley of manners which would thus be produced. He may think to enter into active life, become whig or tory as his inclinations lead, and get a seat in the, even to him, once called chapel of St. Stephens. He may content himself with turning contemplative philosopher, and find sufficient food for his mind in tracing the march of the human intellect, the changes which have been wrought in the dispositions, desires, and powers of mankind. Will he be an advocate for perfectibility or deterioration? He must admire our manufactures, the progress of science, the diffusion of knowledge, and the fresh spirit of enterprise characteristic of our countrymen. Will he find any individuals to be compared to the glorious spirits of his day? Moderate in his views as we have supposed him to be, he will probably fall at once into the temporizing tone of mind now so much in vogue. He will be pleased to find a calm in politics; he will greatly admire the ministry who have succeeded in conciliating almost all parties—to find peace where he left feud. The same character which he bore a couple of hundred years ago, will influence him now; he will still be the moderate, peaceful, unenthusiastic Mr. Dodsworth that he was in 1647.

For notwithstanding education and circumstances may suffice to direct and form the rough material of the mind, it cannot create, nor give intellect, noble aspiration, and energetic constancy where dullness, wavering of purpose, and groveling desires, are stamped by nature. Entertaining this belief we have (to forget Mr. Dodsworth for awhile) often made conjectures how such and such heroes of antiquity would act, if they were reborn in these times: and then awakened fancy has gone on to imagine that some of them are reborn; that according to the theory explained by Virgil in his sixth Æneid, every thousand years the dead return to life, and their souls endued with the same sensibilities and capacities as before, are turned naked of knowledge into this world, again to dress their skeleton powers in such habiliments as situation, education, and experience will furnish. Pythagoras, we are told, remembered many transmigrations of this sort, as having occurred to himself, though for a philosopher he made very little use of his anterior memories. It would prove an instructive school for kings and statesmen, and in fact for all human beings, called on as they are, to play their part on the stage of the world, could they remember what they had been. Thus we might obtain a glimpse of heaven and of hell, as, the secret of our former identity confined to our own bosoms, we winced or exulted in the blame or praise bestowed on our former selves. While the love of glory and posthumous reputation is as natural to man as his attachment to life itself, he must be, under such a state of things, tremblingly alive to the historic records of his honor or shame. The mild spirit of Fox would have been soothed by the recollection that he had played a worthy part as Marcus Antoninus—the former experiences of Alcibiades or even of the emasculated Steeny of James I. might have caused Sheridan to have refused to tread over again the same path of dazzling but fleeting brilliancy. The soul of our modern Corinna would have been purified and exalted by a consciousness that once it had given life to the form of Sappho. If at the present moment the witch, memory, were in a freak, to cause all the present generation to recollect that some ten centuries back they had been somebody else, would not several of our free thinking martyrs wonder to find that they had suffered as Christians under Domitian, while the judge as he passed sentence would suddenly become aware, that formerly he had condemned the saints of the early church to the torture, for not renouncing the religion he now upheld—nothing but benevolent actions and real goodness would come pure out of the ordeal. While it would be whimsical to perceive how some great men in parish affairs would strut under the consciousness that their hands had once held a scepter, an honest artisan or pilfering domestic would find that he was little altered by being transformed into an idle noble or director of a joint stock company; in every way we may suppose that the humble would be exalted, and the noble and the proud would feel their stars and honors dwindle into baubles and child's play when they called to mind the lowly stations they had once occupied. If philosophical novels were in fashion, we conceive an excellent one might be written on the development of the same mind in various stations, in different periods of the world's history.

But to return to Mr. Dodsworth, and indeed with a few more words to bid him farewell. We entreat him no longer to bury himself in obscurity; or, if he modestly decline publicity, we beg him to make himself known personally to us. We have a thousand inquiries to make, doubts to clear up, facts to ascertain. If any fear that old habits and strangeness of appearance will make him ridiculous to those accustomed to associate with modern exquisites, we beg to assure him that we are not given to ridicule mere outward shows, and that worth and intrinsic excellence will always claim our respect.

This we say, if Mr. Dodsworth is alive. Perhaps he is again no more. Perhaps he opened his eyes only to shut them again more obstinately; perhaps his ancient clay could not thrive on the harvests of these latter days. After a little wonder; a little shuddering to find himself the dead alive—finding no affinity between himself and the present state of things—he has bidden once more an eternal farewell to the sun. Followed to his grave by his preserver and the wondering villagers, he may sleep the true death-sleep in the same valley where he so long reposed. Dr. Hotham may have erected a simple tablet over his twice-buried remains, inscribed—

To the Memory of R. Dodsworth,
An Englishman,
Born April 1, 1617; Died July 16, 18;—Aged 187.

An inscription which, if it were preserved during any terrible convulsion that caused the world to begin its life again, would occasion many learned disquisitions and ingenious theories concerning a race which authentic records showed to have secured the privilege of attaining so vast an age.

NOTES

1. July 1826.
2. This is a quote from *The Passionate Pilgrim*, "It Fell Upon a Day," a poem by William Shakespeare.

Lady Mesmer Circumnavigates the Scientific Imagination in Poe's "The Thousand-and-Second Tale of Scheherazade"

BETH ATKINS

"The Thousand-and-Second Tale of Scheherazade" is one of Edgar Allan Poe's short stories which has received little of the scholarly attention it deserves, and none of the recognition it merits as a work of science fiction. Most of the scholarship it has received has been limited to brief summaries and honorable mentions, usually labeling it either as a parody of 19th century ladies' fashion, or as a work of "popular journalism" documenting scientific advancements (quoted in Denuccio 1990, 365). The former reading is certainly true and worthwhile, as Alexandra Urakova shows in her 2014 essay, "Poe, Fashion, and *Godey's Lady's Book*." However, while the latter reading makes an invaluable point, it also ignores the innumerable possibilities which that point brings to light. Because Poe's sequel to *Arabian Nights* indeed documents so much of science history in its outrageous footnotes, it therefore begs to be analyzed in the context of the 19th century's unique scientific universe. When viewed this way, "The Thousand-and-Second Tale of Scheherazade" can be read as an allegorical journey exploring the 19th century scientific imagination, centering around mesmerism.

Though the 21st century reader may scoff at mesmerism being referred to as "scientific," it is important to understand that mesmerism "wavered on the edge of scientific respectability throughout the nineteenth century" (Burton and Grandy 2004, 185). In the 19th century, the long battle between the old-world occult sciences and the new-world empiricist sciences came to a climax. As Martin Willis shows in *Mesmerists, Monsters, & Machines: Science Fiction & the Cultures of Science in the Nineteenth Century* (2006), the occultist ways of the past did not simply disappear from science overnight to have the materialist ways of the future replace them the next day (4). Instead, the conflicts between occultism and empiricism continued into the 19th century, throughout which scientific practices remained highly unregulated, and the line between "professional" and "amateur" scientist was still incredibly vague. The resulting scientific universe was a Frankenstein-esque conglomerate of "practices and beliefs without strict boundaries or accepted regulations, a melting pot of discordant models of the natural world struggling for supremacy and legitimacy" (Willis 2006, 11). This was a perfect atmosphere for mesmerism to be explored as a science; and it was, abundantly. Mesmerism, also referred to as animal magnetism, remained quite a hot topic throughout the century, and especially during Poe's lifetime.

Thus, even though mesmerism has since been "exiled to the wilderness of the occult" (Burton and Grandy 2004, 185), it was a significant part of the scientific climate in which Poe lived, and its influence can be found in much of his writing. In fact, our heroine, Scheherazade, the most lovable "politic damsel" (Poe 1845a, 61), who seems to somehow exist within both the ancient Eastern world of *Arabian Nights* and the contemporary European world of 19th century America, conspicuously possesses many qualities of a gifted mesmerist. Though Poe never directly states that Scheherazade is an actual mesmerist, her character appears to be inspired by controversies surrounding mesmerism. Poe frequently implanted his stories and characters in this almost subliminal way with scientific topics of his own time. His profound interest in and inspiration from the sciences have been widely discussed by scholars (Scheick 1992, 91), especially his literary experiments with mesmerism (Taylor 2007, 196) and with "fraudulent science" (Willis 2006, 97). In his essay "An Intrinsic Luminosity: Poe's Use of Platonic and Newtonian Optics" (1992), William J. Sheick evinces both how profoundly Poe was interested in the sciences and how deeply his scientific interests influenced his artistic vision. Such influence can be easily seen in Poe's overtly scientific works such as "The Unparalleled Adventure of One Hans Pfaall" (1835), and can be found with a little more effort in his covertly scientific works, such as "Ligeia" (1838) (Scheick 1992, 90, 92, 93). Furthermore, Poe himself was a bit of an amateur scientist who actively followed several scientific disciplines (Scheick 1992), published several scientific hoaxes as short stories, and even wrote his own prose-poem of art-science, *Eureka* (1848). Poe seemed particularly drawn to mesmerism, as Matthew Taylor demonstrates in his essay "Edgar Allan Poe's (Meta)physics: A Pre-History of the Post-Human" (2007): "In addition to writing three explicitly mesmeric tales, Poe reviewed and published the work of other writers on the subject, was acquainted with some of the mesmerist luminaries of his day, and maintained a correspondence with various experts in the field" (198). Therefore, it requires no stretch of the imagination to consider that "The Thousand-and-Second Tale of Scheherazade," like so many of Poe's other stories, might have been influenced by 19th century science and his own ardent fascination with mesmerism.

Poe begins his short story by first claiming to have found another version of the famous work *Arabian Nights* in an obscure publication entitled *Tellmenow Isitsöornot*. This newly-discovered adaptation includes the more widely known aspects of the saga. As retaliation against his unfaithful first wife, "a certain monarch" has been marrying all of "the most beautiful maiden[s]" (Poe 1845a, 61) in his kingdom, in order to execute them the next day. Scheherazade, the daughter of the king's "grand vizier" (Poe 1845a, 61) comes up with a plan to end the king's murderous reign—a plan on which she is willing to bet her life. Scheherazade marries the king and, each night, tells an irresistibly interesting story which she purposely ends on a cliffhanger. His unbearable curiosity induces the king to leave his queen unharmed, so that he may hear the conclusion of the tale the next night. This keeps Scheherazade alive for one thousand and one nights, at which time, traditionally, the king decides not to kill his wife after all; but this is where the *Tellmenow Isitsöornot* differs from other sources. Not only does Poe's source include a thousand-and-second day of Scheherazade's history, but it also injects some 19th-century scientific flair into its narrative. All of Scheherazade's stories up to this point have been based on the mythical, supernatural adventures of Sinbad the sailor. However, on this thousand-and-second night, Scheherazade begins basing her stories, instead, on various facts known to 19th century science, all disguised metaphorically by Scheherazade as additional Sinbad escapades and explained more literally by Poe in his numerous footnotes.

The extensive scientific metaphors and footnotes in the story alone link "The Thousand-and-Second Tale of Scheherazade" to Poe's love of the sciences. But Poe also connects the tale's characters and its narrative to 19th century science by symbolically making his heroine a mesmerist, and her husband her unknowing mesmeric subject. Scheherazade's tyrannical husband is, in fact, the most logical reason for which she might have actually decided to take up the practice of mesmerism. If she could succeed in gaining psychic control over her husband's mind, imposing her peaceful will upon his murderous one, she might thereby "redeem the land from the depopulating tax upon its beauty" (Poe 1845a, 61). Accordingly, Poe bestows Scheherazade with the features essential to any able mesmerist, beginning from his first mention of her. For example, her eyes are her most prominent mesmeric feature. Poe gives almost no physical descriptions of Scheherazade in the story, but makes a point to allude to "her beautiful black eyes" (Poe 1845a, 61) before any of the action of the plot has even happened. Poe's purposeful description of her eyes as "beautiful," "black," and "thoroughly open" (Poe 1845a, 61) endows her with a trait common to many of Poe's characters: a powerful gaze. Scheick (1992), in discussing Poe's relation to optics theories, connects this familiar Poe trope to the Platonic theory that human sight works by means of "light originat[ing] from the eye" and "impact[ing] on objects" (Scheick 1992, 94). According to Scheick, Poe often "adapts" this Platonic theory "to symbolize the sight of a character who represents ideality, especially the artist in possession of an intense imagination" (Scheick 1992, 94). Poe's use of Platonic optics also relates to "medical and optical studies" of his own time which suggested a "subtle capacity of the eye to be a shaper, even a creator of perception" (Scheick 1992, 98). Thus, Scheick recognizes the pattern continued in Scheherazade; Poe's many characters with strange and deep eyes all seem to possess some mysterious power to mold and shape the external world. Yet Poe's preoccupation with his characters' eyes also links to mesmerism. By granting Scheherazade and these other characters their big, beautiful, dark eyes, Poe thereby endows them with the powerful gaze of any gifted mesmerist, whose "piercing eyes" (quoted in Willis 2006, 59) can initiate the trance-state (Willis 2006, 48).

Thus Scheherazade possesses with her striking gaze "a physiognomy similar to Mesmer himself" (Willis 2006, 59). Perhaps she first imposed her mesmeric will upon her husband on their wedding day, when she took his hand and "marr[ied] him […] with her beautiful black eyes as thoroughly open as the nature of the case would allow" (Poe 1845a, 61). But she seems to possess another trait characteristic of any proper mesmerist. Scheherazade is clearly able to penetrate her husband's sleep and control his level of consciousness using only her voice and touch. Throughout the story, when Scheherazade is narrating Sinbad's adventures to her sister (and, indirectly, to her husband), she is always able to bring him out of his deep sleep, into a level of partial consciousness, simply by speaking "in an under-tone" (Poe 1845a, 61), and sometimes with "a pinch or two" (Poe 1845a, 62). Scheherazade's power here intriguingly parallels certain mesmeric definitions outlined by Herbert Mayo, a prominent 19th century scientist who published a book of letters on mesmerism and related theories. In *Popular Superstitions and the Truths Contained Therein with an Account of Mesmerism* (1852), Mayo defines sleep, in contrast to the trance-state, as "the suspension of the attention" (91), while various states of trance seem characterized, instead, by a suspension of the will:

[T]he entranced person displays no will of his own, but his voluntary muscles execute the gestures which his mesmeriser is making, even when standing behind his back. His will takes its guidance from sympathy with the exerted will of the other [Mayo 1852, 177].

With her husband's various grunts, "hums," and "hoos," as well as his "profound interest" (Poe 1845a, 61) in Scheherazade's stories, the king is clearly able to maintain his attention upon his wife's voice. However, his will does not seem to be maintained; though the king does not appear to be mimicking the exact movements of Scheherazade, any control over his voluntary muscles and mental faculties appears to be under his wife's authority. Both of these things indicate that the king is not merely sleeping while Scheherazade is narrating, but is in the impressionable state of a mesmeric trance.

Poe makes Scheherazade's apparent control over the king's level of consciousness and voluntary functions especially evident when he narrates:

> [T]he king having been sufficiently pinched, at length ceased snoring, and finally said "hum!" and then "hoo!" when the queen, understanding these words […] to signify that he was all attention, and would do his best not to snore any more,—the queen […] having arranged these matters to her satisfaction, re-entered thus, at once, into the history of Sinbad the sailor [Poe 1845a, 62].

In this excerpt, Scheherazade is able to "arrange the matters" of her husband's consciousness and individual will "to her satisfaction" with a simple pinch. The king's attention is awakened and focused on Scheherazade's voice, while his will over his body's desire to sleep and to snore is overtaken. Perhaps the most intriguing aspect of this excerpt is the fact that the king's exclamations, "hum!" and "hoo!," appear to convey no meaning at all; yet somehow Scheherazade is certain that these utterances mean the king is at full attention and that he will no longer sleep or snore. This indicates that Scheherazade has some other, more covert way of knowing the king's level of consciousness. Simply, she is the one controlling it.

Scheherazade also appears capable of directing both her husband's attention and his will, not by touch, but by using only her voice. In addition to suspending the king's consciousness in sleep for one thousand and one nights, Scheherazade has also suspended his will to murder her without even a pinch. She wakes her husband each day and keeps him under her spell, so to speak, for nearly three years using only her voice and the wonderment of telling Sinbad's adventures. The strange power of Scheherazade's voice over her husband's will is most clearly evinced by the king's ability to make out Scheherazade's words, even as she speaks indirectly to him and "all in an under-tone" (Poe 1845a, 61). His ability to hear and listen attentively to his wife's whispering voice mimics the mesmerist ("operator")—patient relationship in which the patient "hears the operator alone best, and him [or her] even in a whisper" (Mayo 1852, 169).

After the thousand and one nights have passed, Poe begins reciting from his own "quaint and curious volume of forgotten lore" (Poe 1845b, 112), the

Tellmenow Isitsöornot. This book supposedly holds the never-before-seen continuation of Scheherazade's tale beyond the thousand-and-first night. In this sequel to *Arabian Nights*, Scheherazade tells her sister that she has withheld "the full conclusion of the history of Sinbad the sailor" because, "on the particular night of their narration," Scheherazade was "sleepy" and thus "was seduced into cutting [the stories] short" (Poe 1845a, 62). But Scheherazade assures her sister she will begin narrating "these latter adventures of Sinbad" presently (Poe 1845a, 63). Unfortunately, having already shared one thousand and one nights worth of Sinbad's tales, Scheherazade has told all there is to tell about his many adventures! Her mesmeric powers over her husband seem inherently linked to her daily ritual of storytelling and, if that is so, then she needs access to new information, to knowledge as mystical and awe-inspiring as Sinbad's many fantastical escapades. So our heroine, who, again, seems to somehow exist within both the ancient East and Poe's contemporary America, forms a hypothesis: if someone holds the monopoly over information, such as scientific knowledge, then that someone can make that information seem as mystical and awe-inspiring as is necessary to serve their needs; with this hypothesis, our heroine decides to dictate 19th-century scientific knowledge, disguised in magical language, to her 8th century husband, hoping that it will prolong her hypnotic hold over him.[1]

This tactic devised by our Machiavellian damsel was also common among occult scientists of the late 18th and 19th centuries. In fact, it was one of the primary sources of contention in the battle between nascent empirical science and archaic occult science which characterized the 19th century (Willis, 4). One of the main criticisms of occult scientists was that they "exploit[ed] a supernatural vision of [their] scientific knowledge" (Willis, 32). That is, because non-scientists tended not understand how scientific phenomena worked, they were amazed by scientists who seemed to possess magical secrets. As Dan Burton and David Grandy point out in their 2004 study *Magic, Mystery, and Science*, "secrecy" became a telling "mark of occult systems" because it made occult scientists appear magical:

> A magician, for example, may wish to keep certain ceremonies and formulas from public scrutiny. Why? Often for reasons of power. Certain rites and recipes, it is thought, give one control or influence over the environment and other people. Should mastery of these instruments of power become widespread, the magician loses her advantage [Burton and Grandy 2004, 4].

These secretive practices are exactly what led Franz Mesmer and his science of mesmerism to become irrevocably tied to the occult. Though Mesmer's theories were based in science, his practices were veiled in mystery.[2] For example, Mayo describes in his *Popular Superstitions* a typical session under Franz Mesmer's care:

His patients were received with an air of mystery and studied effect. The apartment, hung with mirrors, was dimly lighted. [...] The patients were seated round a sort of vat, which contained a heterogeneous mixture of chemical ingredients. With this, and with each other, they were placed in relation by means of cords, or jointed rods, or by holding hands; and among them slowly and mysteriously moved Mesmer himself, affecting one by a touch, another by a look, and a third by passes with his hand, a fourth by pointing with a rod.

[...] One person became hysterical, then another; one was seized with catalepsy; others with convulsions; some with palpitations of the heart, perspirations, and other bodily disturbances. [...] The method was supposed to provoke in the sick person exactly the kind of action propitious to his recovery. And it may easily be imagined that many a patient found himself the better after a course of this rude empiricism, and that the effect made by these events passing daily in Paris must have been very considerable. To the ignorant the scene was full of wonderment [Mayo 1852, 157].

Mayo's description is a prime example of the occult aura surrounding Mesmer's practice. This excerpt clearly conveys the mystical atmosphere of Mesmer's sessions and perfectly expresses the melodramatic, hypochondriacal effects their enigmatic mood could have on people. These occult tactics of disguising fact in veils of fiction are ironically what led to both Mesmer's fame and his misfortune; his practice initially thrived but was eventually dismantled. The only reason mesmerism remained scientifically viable after Mesmer's defamation was due to the discovery of the "Odic" force, which offered possible empirical evidence for mesmeric phenomena. Fringe sciences fought for legitimacy in this way, amid the emergent empirical scientific philosophy, by "investigat[ing] the occult in a 'scientific' manner" and by creating "scientific terminology" for their respective disciplines (Burton and Grandy 2004, 185); but mesmerism never could fully shed its occult ties.

Unfortunately Scheherazade, our Lady Mesmer, makes the same fatal mistake as Franz Mesmer himself. In her attempt to keep her husband's murderous impulses at bay, she adopts the occult practice of shrouding science in a mysterious aura of secrecy; she disguises 19th century scientific fact in metaphorical "magical language" (see Willis 2006, 30–32). But as Mesmer's story has taught us, once the thick layers of mystery, magic, and deceit are scraped away from such disguises, only the thin truth remains; you have lost your power. In much the same way, we see our heroine's power over her tyrannical husband slowly disappear after she adopts this occult practice. For the first time in all of Scheherazade's one thousand and one nights of storytelling, on the thousand-and-second night, her husband actually begins to move, respond, and interject when she commences telling of science's future, disguised in metaphor as Sinbad's continued adventures. Her first magical transformation of 19th century science occurs when she narrates that Sinbad has met a race of "men-vermin" who live on the back of a colossal sea-beast with "at least four score of eyes" (Poe 1845a, 62). The men-vermin take Sinbad with them onto the back of the sea-beast, upon which they proceed to "circumnavigat[e] the globe" (Poe 1845a, 63).

At this point in Scheherazade's narration, her husband "turn[s] over from his left side to his right," and says, "It is, in fact, very surprising, my dear queen, that you omitted, hitherto, these latter adventures of Sinbad. Do you know I think them exceedingly entertaining and strange?" (Poe 1845a, 64). The mere fact that her husband has moved and spoken a complete sentence, something he has not done throughout the entire story up to this point, signifies that her husband's will is beginning to emerge from the depths of a thousand-and-one-night trance. Scheherazade's reference to "circumnavigating the globe" is her first allusion to science's future. The phrase garners a dual meaning in the context of this story. First, the allusion is itself a reference to a future scientific discovery. Circumnavigation of the globe is the process by which explorers ultimately revealed that the Earth is round and not flat, a fact not proven until Magellan's 14th century journey, which occurred at least a century after *Arabian Nights* takes place. Scheherazade even describes this specific discovery, immediately following her husband's interjection, as part of Sinbad's adventure: "the beast [...] swam at a prodigious rate through the ocean; although the surface of the latter is, in that part of the world, by no means flat, but round like a pomegranate, so that we went—so to say—either up hill or down hill all the time" (Poe 1845a, 64). Scheherazade's meandering, riddle-like description of the Earth's rounded shape is evidence of her reliance on the occult tactic of disguising science in veils of mystery.

The second meaning of Scheherazade's allusion to "circumnavigating the globe" is that the adventure on which Sinbad and the men-vermin are journeying is allegorically a circumnavigation through the scientific knowledge of the 19th century; but Scheherazade's imagination transforms this scientific knowledge. Inspired by various scientific facts known to Poe's time, the many islands Sinbad and the men-vermin visit all represent those facts metaphorically, and are described by Scheherazade in elaborate, magical language. Her transformation of these scientific facts into mystical fictions is revelatory of how occult scientists like Mesmer could dress simple facts in such extravagant fiction. With each island encountered, Lady Mesmer's metaphors become more and more elaborate, and her husband continues to interrupt with disapproving interjections. With each "Hum!" and "Pshaw!," her husband's will gradually emerges, until finally, he fully awakes from out of Scheherazade's mesmeric control.

Although Lady Mesmer (Scheherazade) designed an ingenious plan to conquer her husband's tyranny through mesmeric control, she ultimately fails due to her use of the occult tactic of veiling science in shrouds of mystery and secrecy. She thus joins her double, Mesmer, and all the others on the long list of scientists whose true accomplishments faded away with the occult practices which condemned them. Did Poe concur with mainstream scientists, then, that science and imagination should remain separate? Being that Poe was such a huge figure in 19th-century science fiction, who clearly enjoyed circumnavigating all the corners of the scientific imagination (and obviously had a lot of fun doing so in the creation of this story), this is doubtful. Instead, Poe appears to be critiquing both the occult sciences and the mainstream sciences of his time, suggesting that these extremes are much too far apart to be productive.

In "Fact, Fiction, Fatality: Poe's 'The Thousand-and-Second Tale of Scheherazade'" (1990), Denuccio focuses on the writer-reader relationship and the connections between fact, fiction, and the reader's ability to suspend disbelief. According to Denuccio, Poe has "establish[ed] a dialectical relationship between the mind's empirical and imaginative operations" wherein "fact and fiction [...] are interdependent, a working partnership" (368). In the proper balance of this "partnership," the writer "opens a space of believability for and interest in the text's enterprise" (Denuccio, 1990, 368–369), thereby making the text "potentially unlimited" (Denuccio 1990, 369), potentially immortal.

In "Mesmeric Revelation: Art as Hypnosis" (2015), Zane Gillespie argues that Poe often utilizes the art of language itself to hypnotize his readers. Poe's uncanny talent at "defamiliarizing, estranging, or alienating" the reader "from casual perception" increases the reader's "suggestibility" and allows Poe to "induce [the reader] to internalize" the ideas he has put forth in his literature (Gillespie 2015, 237–238). This is precisely why "art as hypnosis" works for Poe, but not for Scheherazade. Poe was a master at mingling fact with fiction in his tales. Scheherazade, in the frame of her own story, was not:

> The opposition [...] between fiction and truth, story and actuality, is, Poe suggests, a false dichotomy: fact and fiction partake of each other and are mutually indebted.
>   The success and failure of Scheherazade's tales, therefore, hinge not upon their inherent truth or falsity, but upon their credibility. [...]
>   [...] In relating a tale whose marvels lie outside the compass of the king's experience, Scheherazade effectually abuses her power in the author-reader relationship and, in violating the dictate of verisimilitude, succeeds not only in undermining the king's suspension of disbelief, but also in convincing him that she has played him for a fool [Denuccio 1990, 367, 369].

Thus, just as in the case with Scheherazade, when the fictive aspect of a story exceeds the fact, the story becomes too unbelievable. It destroys itself. It cannot continue without the reader's suspension of disbelief. On the other hand, when observable fact is too strongly relied upon, all imaginative speculation is lost; so, too, is the continuation of scientific discovery and advancement.[3] Therefore, science relies on the potentials of the imagination, and the imagination relies on the potentials of reality. According to these conclusions which cascaded from Poe's own creative philosophies, then, the artist is better off somewhere between the magical and the material, circumnavigating the scientific imagination, floating on the possibilities of fact, riding on a fiction which parallels the truth.

NOTES

1. *Arabian Nights* (aka *The Thousand and One Nights*) is a compilation of Middle Eastern folktales dating roughly from the 8th to 13th centuries.
2. Mesmer held a doctorate in medicine from the University of Vienna with a thesis focused on "the magnetic influence of the planets on humans" (Burton and Grandy 2004, 186).
3. For instance, Einstein's "thought experiments," which uncovered currently-accepted theories that we are still incapable of physically testing, were journeys through the scientific imagination, exploring unknowable but plausible extensions of reality.

BIBLIOGRAPHY

Burton, Dan, and David Grandy. 2004. *Magic, Mystery, and Science.* Indiana UP.
Denuccio, Jerome. 1990. "Fact, Fiction, Fatality: Poe's 'The Thousand-and-Second Tale of Scheherazade.'" *Studies in Short Fiction* 27, no. 3: 365–370.
Gillespie, Zane. 2015. "'Mesmeric Revelation': Art as Hypnosis." *Humanities* 4: 236–249.
Mayo, Herbert. 1852. *Popular Superstitions and the Truths Contained Therein with an Account of Mesmerism.* Lindsay and Blakiston.
Poe, Edgar A. 1845a. "The Thousand-and-Second Tale of Scheherazade." *Godey's Magazine and Lady's Book*, February: 61–67.
Poe, Edgar A. 1902 [1845b]. "The Raven." *The Complete Works of Edgar Allan Poe.* Vol. I. Edited by Charles F. Richardson. Lamp Pub. Co.
Scheick, William J. 1992. "An Intrinsic Luminosity: Poe's Use of Platonic and Newtonian Optics." *The Southern Literary Journal* 24, no. 2: 90–105.
Taylor, Matthew A. 2007. "Edgar Allan Poe's (Meta)Physics: A Pre-History of the Post-Human." *Nineteenth-Century Literature* 62, no. 2: 193–221.
Willis, Martin. 2006. *Mesmerists, Monsters, & Machines: Science Fiction & the Cultures of Science in the Nineteenth Century.* Kent State UP.

"The Thousand-and-Second Tale of Scheherazade" (1845)

EDGAR ALLAN POE

Truth is stranger than fiction.—Old Saying.

Having had occasion, lately, in the course of some Oriental investigations, to consult the Tellmenow Isitsöornot, a work which (like the Zohar of Simeon Jochaides) is scarcely known at all, even in Europe, and which has never been quoted, to my knowledge, by any American—if we except, perhaps, the author of the "Curiosities of American Literature";—having had occasion, I say, to turn over some pages of the first-mentioned very remarkable work, I was not a little astonished to discover that the literary world has hitherto been strangely in error respecting the fate of the vizier's daughter, Scheherazade, as that fate is depicted in the "Arabian Nights"; and that the denouement there given, if not altogether inaccurate, as far as it goes, is at least to blame in not having gone very much farther.

For full information on this interesting topic, I must refer the inquisitive reader to the "Isitsöornot" itself; but, in the mean time, I shall be pardoned for giving a summary of what I there discovered.

It will be remembered, that, in the usual version of the tales, a certain monarch, having good cause to be jealous of his queen, not only puts her to death, but makes a vow, by his beard and the prophet, to espouse each night the most beautiful maiden in his dominions, and the next morning to deliver her up to the executioner.

Having fulfilled this vow for many years to the letter, and with a religious punctuality and method that conferred great credit upon him as a man of devout feelings and excellent sense, he was interrupted one afternoon (no doubt at his prayers) by a visit from his grand vizier, to whose daughter, it appears, there had occurred an idea.

Her name was Scheherazade, and her idea was, that she would either redeem the land from the depopulating tax upon its beauty, or perish, after the approved fashion of all heroines, in the attempt.

Accordingly, and although we do not find it to be leap-year, (which makes the sacrifice more meritorious,) she deputes her father, the grand vizier, to make an offer to the king of her hand. This hand the king eagerly accepts— (he had intended to take it at all events, and had put off the matter from day to day, only through fear of the vizier,)—but, in accepting it now, he gives all parties very distinctly to understand, that, grand vizier or no grand vizier, he has not the slightest design of giving up one iota of his vow or of his privileges. When, therefore, the fair Scheherazade insisted upon marrying the king, and did actually marry him despite her father's excellent advice not to do anything of the kind—when she would and did marry him, I say, will I nill I, it was with her beautiful black eyes as thoroughly open as the nature of the case would allow.

It seems, however, that this politic damsel (who had been reading Machiavelli, beyond doubt,) had a very ingenious little plot in her mind. On the night of the wedding, she contrived, upon I forget what specious pretense, to have her sister occupy a couch sufficiently near that of the royal pair to admit of easy conversation from bed to bed; and, a little before cock-crowing, she took care to awaken the good monarch, her husband, (who bore her none the worse will because he intended to wring her neck on the morrow,)—she managed to awaken him, I say, (although, on account of a capital conscience and an easy digestion, he slept well,) by the profound interest of a story (about a rat and a black cat, I think,) which she was narrating (all in an under-tone, of course,) to her sister. When the day broke, it so happened that this history was not altogether finished, and that Scheherazade, in the nature of things, could not finish it just then, since it was high time for her to get up and be bowstrung—a thing very little more pleasant than hanging, only a trifle more genteel!

The king's curiosity, however, prevailing, I am sorry to say, even over his sound religious principles, induced him for this once to postpone the fulfillment of his vow until next morning, for the purpose and with the hope of hearing that night how it fared in the end with the black cat (a black cat, I think it was) and the rat.

The night having arrived, however, the lady Scheherazade not only put the finishing stroke to the black cat and the rat, (the rat was blue,) but before she well knew what she was about, found herself deep in the intricacies of a narration, having reference (if I am not altogether mistaken) to a pink horse (with green wings) that went, in a violent manner, by clockwork, and was wound up with an indigo key. With this history the king was even more profoundly interested than with the other—and, as the day broke before its conclusion, (notwithstanding all the queen's endeavors to get through with it in time for the bowstringing,) there was again no resource but to postpone that ceremony as before, for twenty-four hours. The next night there happened a similar accident with a similar result; and then the next—and then again the next; so that, in the end, the good monarch, having been unavoidably deprived of all opportunity to keep his vow during a period of no less than one thousand and one nights, either forgets it altogether by the expiration of this time, or gets himself absolved of it in the regular way, or, (what is more probable) breaks it outright, as well as the head of his father confessor. At all events, Scheherazade, who, being lineally descended from Eve, fell heir, perhaps, to the whole seven baskets of talk, which the latter lady, we all know, picked up from under the trees in the garden of Eden; Scheherazade, I say, finally triumphed, and the tariff upon beauty was repealed.

Now, this conclusion (which is that of the story as we have it upon record) is, no doubt, excessively proper and pleasant—but, alas! like a great many pleasant things, is more pleasant than true; and I am indebted altogether to the "Isitsöornot" for the means of correcting the error. "Le mieux," says a French proverb, "est l'ennemi du bien," and, in mentioning that Scheherazade had inherited the seven baskets of talk, I should have added, that she put them out at compound interest until they amounted to seventy-seven.

"My dear sister," said she, on the thousand-and-second night, (I quote the language of the "Isitsöornot" at this point, verbatim,) "my dear sister," said she, "now that all this little difficulty about the bowstring has blown over, and that this odious tax is so happily repealed, I feel that I have been guilty of great indiscretion in withholding from you and the king (who, I am sorry to say, snores—a thing no gentleman would do,) the full conclusion of the history of Sinbad the sailor. This person went through numerous other and more interesting adventures than those which I related; but the truth is, I felt sleepy on the particular night of their narration, and so was seduced into cutting them short—a grievous piece of misconduct, for which I only trust that Allah will forgive me. But even yet it is not too late to remedy my great neglect—and as soon as I have given the king a pinch or two in order to wake him up so far that he may stop making that horrible noise, I will forthwith entertain you (and him if he pleases) with the sequel of this very remarkable story."

Hereupon the sister of Scheherazade, as I have it from the "Isitsöornet," expressed no very particular intensity of gratification; but the king having been sufficiently pinched, at length ceased snoring, and finally said "Hum!" and then "Hoo!" when the queen understanding these words (which are no doubt Arabic) to signify that he was all attention, and would do his best not to snore any more—the queen, I say, having arranged these matters to her satisfaction, re-entered thus, at once, into the history of Sinbad the sailor:

"'At length, in my old age' (these are the words of Sinbad himself, as retailed by Scheherazade)—'at length, in my old age, and after enjoying many years of tranquillity at home, I became once more possessed with a desire of visiting foreign countries; and one day, without acquainting any of my family with my design, I packed up some bundles of such merchandise as was most precious and least bulky, and, engaging a porter to carry them, went with him down to the sea-shore, to await the arrival of any chance vessel that might convey me out of the kingdom into some region which I had not as yet explored.

"Having deposited the packages upon the sands, we sat down beneath some trees, and looked out into the ocean in the hope of perceiving a ship, but during several hours we saw none whatever. At length I fancied that I could hear a singular buzzing or humming sound—and the porter, after listening awhile, declared that he also could distinguish it. Presently it grew louder, and then still louder, so that we could have no doubt that the object which caused it was approaching us. At length, on the edge of the horizon, we discovered a black speck, which rapidly increased in size until we made it out to be a vast monster, swimming with a great part of its body above the surface of the sea. It came towards us with inconceivable swiftness, throwing up huge waves of foam around its breast, and illuminating all that part of the sea through which it passed, with a long line of fire that extended far off into the distance.

"'As the thing drew near we saw it very distinctly. Its length was equal to that of three of the loftiest trees that grow, and it was as wide as the great hall of audience in your palace, O most sublime and munificent of the caliphs. Its body, which was unlike that of ordinary fishes, was as solid as a rock, and of a jetty blackness throughout all that portion of it which floated above the water, with the exception of a narrow blood-red streak that completely begirdled it. The belly, which floated beneath the surface, and of which we could get only a glimpse now and then as the monster rose and fell with the billows, was entirely covered with metallic scales, of a color like that of the moon in misty weather. The back was flat and nearly white, and from it there extended upwards of six spines, about half the length of the whole body.

"'This horrible creature had no mouth that we could perceive; but, as if to make up for this deficiency, it was provided with at least four score of eyes, that protruded from their sockets like those of the green dragon-fly, and were arranged all around the body in two rows, one above the other, and parallel to the blood-red streak, which seemed to answer the purpose of an eyebrow. Two or three of these dreadful eyes were much larger than the others, and had the appearance of solid gold.

"'Although this beast approached us, as I have before said, with the greatest rapidity, it must have been moved altogether by necromancy—for it had neither fins like a fish nor web-feet like a duck, nor wings like the sea-shell which is blown along in the manner of a vessel; nor yet did it writhe itself forward as do the eels. Its head and its tail were shaped precisely alike, only, not far from the latter, were two small holes that served for nostrils, and through which the monster puffed out its thick breath with prodigious violence, and with a shrieking, disagreeable noise.

"'Our terror at beholding this hideous thing was very great; but it was even surpassed by our astonishment, when, upon getting a nearer look, we perceived upon the creature's back a vast number of animals about the size and shape of men, and altogether much resembling them, except that they wore no garments (as men do,) being supplied (by nature, no doubt,) with an ugly, uncomfortable covering, a good deal like cloth, but fitting so tight to the skin, as to render the poor wretches laughably awkward, and put them apparently to severe pain. On the very tips of their heads were certain square-looking boxes, which, at first sight, I thought might have been intended to answer as turbans, but I soon discovered that they were excessively heavy and solid, and I therefore concluded they were contrivances designed, by their great weight, to keep the heads of the animals steady and safe upon their shoulders. Around the necks of the creatures were fastened black collars, (badges of servitude, no doubt,) such as we keep on our dogs, only much wider and infinitely stiffer—so that it was quite impossible for these poor victims to move their heads in any direction without moving the body at the same time; and thus they were doomed to perpetual contemplation of their noses—a view puggish and snubby in a wonderful if not positively in an awful degree.

"'When the monster had nearly reached the shore where we stood, it suddenly pushed out one of its eyes to a great extent, and emitted from it a terrible flash of fire, accompanied by a dense cloud of smoke, and a noise that I can compare to nothing but thunder. As the smoke cleared away, we saw one of the odd man-animals standing near the head of the large beast with a trumpet in his hand, through which (putting it to his mouth) he presently addressed us in loud, harsh, and disagreeable accents, that, perhaps, we should have mistaken for language, had they not come altogether through the nose.

"'Being thus evidently spoken to, I was at a loss how to reply, as I could in no manner understand what was said; and in this difficulty I turned to the porter, who was near swooning through affright, and demanded of him his opinion as to what species of monster it was, what it wanted, and what kind of creatures those were that so swarmed upon its back. To this the porter replied, as well as he could for trepidation, that he had once before heard of this sea-beast; that it was a cruel demon, with bowels of sulphur and blood of fire, created by evil genii as the means of inflicting misery upon mankind;

that the things upon its back were vermin, such as sometimes infest cats and dogs, only a little larger and more savage; and that these vermin had their uses, however evil—for, through the torture they caused the beast by their nibblings and stinging, it was goaded into that degree of wrath which was requisite to make it roar and commit ill, and so fulfil the vengeful and malicious designs of the wicked genii.

"'This account determined me to take to my heels, and, without once even looking behind me, I ran at full speed up into the hills, while the porter ran equally fast, although nearly in an opposite direction, so that, by these means, he finally made his escape with my bundles, of which I have no doubt he took excellent care—although this is a point I cannot determine, as I do not remember that I ever beheld him again.

"'For myself, I was so hotly pursued by a swarm of the men-vermin (who had come to the shore in boats) that I was very soon overtaken, bound hand and foot, and conveyed to the beast, which immediately swam out again into the middle of the sea.

"'I now bitterly repented my folly in quitting a comfortable home to peril my life in such adventures as this; but regret being useless, I made the best of my condition, and exerted myself to secure the good-will of the man-animal that owned the trumpet, and who appeared to exercise authority over its fellows. I succeeded so well in this endeavor that, in a few days, the creature bestowed upon me various tokens of its favor, and, in the end, even went to the trouble of teaching me the rudiments of what it was vain enough to denominate its language; so that, at length, I was enabled to converse with it readily, and came to make it comprehend the ardent desire I had of seeing the world.

"'Washish squashish squeak, Sinbad, hey-diddle diddle, grunt unt grumble, hiss, fiss, whiss,' said he to me, one day after dinner—but I beg a thousand pardons, I had forgotten that your majesty is not conversant with the dialect of the Cock-neighs, (so the man-animals were called; I presume because their language formed the connecting link between that of the horse and that of the rooster). With your permission, I will translate. 'Washish squashish,' and so forth:—that is to say, 'I am happy to find, my dear Sinbad, that you are really a very excellent fellow; we are now about doing a thing which is called circumnavigating the globe; and since you are so desirous of seeing the world, I will strain a point and give you a free passage upon the back of the beast.'"

When the Lady Scheherazade had proceeded thus far, relates the "Isit-söornot," the king turned over from his left side to his right, and said—

"It is, in fact, very surprising, my dear queen, that you omitted, hitherto, these latter adventures of Sinbad. Do you know I think them exceedingly entertaining and strange?"

The king having thus expressed himself, we are told, the fair Scheherazade resumed her history in the following words:—

"Sinbad went on in this manner, with his narrative—'I thanked the man-animal for its kindness, and soon found myself very much at home on the beast, which swam at a prodigious rate through the ocean; although the surface of the latter is, in that part of the world, by no means flat, but round like a pomegranate, so that we went—so to say—either up hill or down hill all the time.'"

"That, I think, was very singular," interrupted the king.

"Nevertheless, it is quite true," replied Scheherazade.

"I have my doubts," rejoined the king; "but, pray, be so good as to go on with the story."

"I will," said the queen. "'The beast,' continued Sinbad, 'swam, as I have related, up hill and down hill, until, at length, we arrived at an island, many hundreds of miles in circumference, but which, nevertheless, had been built in the middle of the sea by a colony of little things like caterpillars.'"[1]

"Hum!" said the king.

"'Leaving this island,' said Sinbad—(for Scheherazade, it must be understood, took no notice of her husband's ill-mannered ejaculation)—'leaving this island, we came to another where the forests were of solid stone, and so hard that they shivered to pieces the finest-tempered axes with which we endeavored to cut them down.'"[2]

"Hum!" said the king, again; but Scheherazade, paying him no attention, continued in the language of Sinbad.

"'Passing beyond this last island, we reached a country where there was a cave that ran to the distance of thirty or forty miles within the bowels of the earth, and that contained a greater number of far more spacious and more magnificent palaces than are to be found in all Damascus and Bagdad. From the roofs of these palaces there hung myriads of gems, like diamonds, but larger than men; and in among the streets of towers and pyramids and temples, there flowed immense rivers as black as ebony, and swarming with fish that had no eyes.'"[3]

"Hum!" said the king.

"'We then swam into a region of the sea where we found a lofty mountain, down whose sides there streamed torrents of melted metal, some of which were twelve miles wide and sixty miles long[4]; while from an abyss on the summit, issued so vast a quantity of ashes that the sun was entirely blotted out from the heavens, and it became darker than the darkest midnight; so that when we were even at the distance of a hundred and fifty miles from the mountain, it was impossible to see the whitest object, however close we held it to our eyes.'"[5]

"Hum!" said the king.

"'After quitting this coast, the beast continued his voyage until we met with a land in which the nature of things seemed reversed—for we here saw a great lake, at the bottom of which, more than a hundred feet beneath the surface of the water, there flourished in full leaf a forest of tall and luxuriant trees."[6]

"Hoo!" said the king.

"'Some hundred miles farther on brought us to a climate where the atmosphere was so dense as to sustain iron or steel, just as our own does feathers."[7]

"Fiddle de dee," said the king.

"'Proceeding still in the same direction, we presently arrived at the most magnificent region in the whole world. Through it there meandered a glorious river for several thousands of miles. This river was of unspeakable depth, and of a transparency richer than that of amber. It was from three to six miles in width; and its banks, which arose on either side to twelve hundred feet in perpendicular height, were crowned with ever-blossoming trees, and perpetual sweet-scented flowers, that made the whole territory one gorgeous garden; but the name of this luxuriant land was the kingdom of Horror, and to enter it was inevitable death.'"

"Humph!" said the king.

"'We left this kingdom in great haste, and, after some days, came to another, where we were astonished to perceive myriads of monstrous animals with horns resembling scythes upon their heads. These hideous beasts dig for themselves vast caverns in the soil, of a funnel shape, and line the sides of them with rocks, so disposed one upon the other that they fall instantly, when trodden upon by other animals, thus precipitating them into the monsters' dens, where their blood is immediately sucked, and their carcasses afterwards hurled contemptuously out to an immense distance from "the caverns of death."'"[8]

"Pooh!" said the king.

"'Continuing our progress, we perceived a district abounding with vegetables that grew not upon any soil, but in the air.[9] There were others that sprang from the substance of other vegetables[10]; others that derived their sustenance from the bodies of living animals[11]; and then, again, there were others that glowed all over with intense fire[12]; others that moved from place to place at pleasure[13]; and what is still more wonderful, we discovered flowers that lived and breathed and moved their limbs at will, and had, moreover, the detestable passion of mankind for enslaving other creatures, and confining them in horrid and solitary prisons until the fulfilment of appointed tasks.'"[14]

"Pshaw!" said the king.

"'Quitting this land, we soon arrived at another in which the bees and the birds are mathematicians of such genius and erudition, that they give daily instructions in the science of geometry to the wise men of the empire. The king of the place having offered a reward for the solution of two very difficult problems, they were solved upon the spot—the one by the bees, and the other by the birds; but the king keeping their solutions a secret, it was only after the most profound researches and labor, and the writing of an infinity of big books, during a long series of years, that the men-mathematicians at length arrived at the identical solutions which had been given upon the spot by the bees and by the birds.'"[15]

"Oh my!" said the king.

"'We had scarcely lost sight of this empire when we found ourselves close upon another, from whose shores there flew over our heads a flock of fowls a mile in breadth, and two hundred and forty miles long; so that, although they flew a mile during every minute, it required no less than four hours for the whole flock to pass over us—in which there were several millions of millions of fowls.'"[16]

"Oh fy!" said the king.

"'No sooner had we got rid of these birds, which occasioned us great annoyance, than we were terrified by the appearance of a fowl of another kind, and infinitely larger than even the rocs which I met in my former voyages; for it was bigger than the biggest of the domes upon your seraglio, oh, most Munificent of Caliphs. This terrible fowl had no head that we could perceive, but was fashioned entirely of belly, which was of a prodigious fatness and roundness, of a soft looking substance, smooth, shining and striped with various colors. In its talons, the monster was bearing away to his eyrie in the heavens, a house from which it had knocked off the roof, and in the interior of which we distinctly saw human beings, who, beyond doubt, were in a state of frightful despair at the horrible fate which awaited them. We shouted with all our might, in the hope of frightening the bird into letting go of its prey; but it merely gave a snort or puff, as if of rage, and then let fall upon our heads a heavy sack which proved to be filled with sand!'"

"Stuff!" said the king.

"'It was just after this adventure that we encountered a continent of immense extent and of prodigious solidity, but which, nevertheless, was supported entirely upon the back of a sky-blue cow that had no fewer than four hundred horns.'"[17]

"That, now, I believe," said the king, "because I have read something of the kind before, in a book."

"'We passed immediately beneath this continent, (swimming in between the legs of the cow,) and, after some hours, found ourselves in a wonderful country indeed, which, I was informed by the man-animal, was his own native land, inhabited by things of his own species. This elevated the man-animal very much in my esteem; and in fact, I now began to feel ashamed of the contemptuous familiarity with which I had treated him; for I found that the man-animals in general were a nation of the most powerful magicians, who lived with worms in their brains,[18] which, no doubt, served to stimulate them by their painful writhings and wrigglings to the most miraculous efforts of imagination.

"Nonsense!" said the king.

"'Among the magicians, were domesticated several animals of very singular kinds; for example, there was a huge horse whose bones were iron and whose blood was boiling water. In place of corn, he had black stones for his usual food; and yet, in spite of so hard a diet, he was so strong and swift that he would drag a load more weighty than the grandest temple in this city, at a rate surpassing that of the flight of most birds.'"[19]

"Twattle!" said the king.

"'I saw, also, among these people a hen without feathers, but bigger than a camel; instead of flesh and bone she had iron and brick; her blood, like that of the horse, (to whom, in fact, she was nearly related,) was boiling water; and like him she ate nothing but wood or black stones. This hen brought forth very frequently, a hundred chickens in the day; and, after birth, they took up their residence for several weeks within the stomach of their mother.'"[20]

"Fal lal!" said the king.

"'One of this nation of mighty conjurors created a man out of brass and wood, and leather, and endowed him with such ingenuity that he would have beaten at chess, all the race of mankind with the exception of the great Caliph, Haroun Alraschid.[21] Another of these magi constructed (of like material) a creature that put to shame even the genius of him who made it; for so great were its reasoning powers that, in a second, it performed calculations of so vast an extent that they would have required the united labor of fifty thousand fleshy men for a year.[22] But a still more wonderful conjuror fashioned for himself a mighty thing that was neither man nor beast, but which had brains of lead, intermixed with a black matter like pitch, and fingers that it employed with such incredible speed and dexterity that it would have had no trouble in writing out twenty thousand copies of the Koran in an hour; and this with so exquisite a precision, that in all the copies there should not be found one to vary from another by the breadth of the finest hair. This thing was of prodigious strength, so that it erected or overthrew the mightiest empires at a breath; but its powers were exercised equally for evil and for good.'"

"Ridiculous!" said the king.

"'Among this nation of necromancers there was also one who had in his veins the blood of the salamanders; for he made no scruple of sitting down to smoke his chibouc in a red-hot oven until his dinner was thoroughly roasted upon its floor.[23] Another had the faculty of converting the common metals into gold, without even looking at them during the process.[24] Another had such a delicacy of touch that he made a wire so fine as to be invisible.[25]

Another had such quickness of perception that he counted all the separate motions of an elastic body, while it was springing backwards and forwards at the rate of nine hundred millions of times in a second."[26]

"Absurd!" said the king.

"'Another of these magicians, by means of a fluid that nobody ever yet saw, could make the corpses of his friends brandish their arms, kick out their legs, fight, or even get up and dance at his will.[27] Another had cultivated his voice to so great an extent that he could have made himself heard from one end of the earth to the other.[28] Another had so long an arm that he could sit down in Damascus and indite a letter at Bagdad—or indeed at any distance whatsoever.[29] Another commanded the lightning to come down to him out of the heavens, and it came at his call; and served him for a plaything when it came. Another took two loud sounds and out of them made a silence. Another constructed a deep darkness out of two brilliant lights.[30] Another made ice in a red-hot furnace.[31] Another directed the sun to paint his portrait, and the sun did.[32] Another took this luminary with the moon and the planets, and having first weighed them with scrupulous accuracy, probed into their depths and found out the solidity of the substance of which they are made. But the whole nation is, indeed, of so surprising a necromantic ability, that not even their infants, nor their commonest cats and dogs have any difficulty in seeing objects that do not exist at all, or that for twenty millions of years before the birth of the nation itself, had been blotted out from the face of creation."[33]

"Preposterous!" said the king.

"'The wives and daughters of these incomparably great and wise magi,'" continued Scheherazade, without being in any manner disturbed by these frequent and most ungentlemanly interruptions on the part of her husband— "'the wives and daughters of these eminent conjurors are every thing that is accomplished and refined; and would be every thing that is interesting and beautiful, but for an unhappy fatality that besets them, and from which not even the miraculous powers of their husbands and fathers has, hitherto, been adequate to save. Some fatalities come in certain shapes, and some in others—but this of which I speak, has come in the shape of a crotchet."

"A what?" said the king.

"'A crotchet,'" said Scheherazade. "'One of the evil genii who are perpetually upon the watch to inflict ill, has put it into the heads of these accomplished ladies that the thing which we describe as personal beauty, consists altogether in the protuberance of the region which lies not very far below the small of the back. Perfection of loveliness, they say, is in the direct ratio of the extent of this hump. Having been long possessed of this idea, and bolsters being cheap in that country, the days have long gone by since it was possible to distinguish a woman from a dromedary—'"

"Stop!" said the king—"I can't stand that, and I won't. You have already given me a dreadful headache with your lies. The day, too, I perceive, is beginning to break. How long have we been married?—my conscience is getting to be troublesome again. And then that dromedary touch—do you take me for a fool? Upon the whole, you might as well get up and be throttled."

These words, as I learn from the Isitsöornot, both grieved and astonished Scheherazade; but, as she knew the king to be a man of scrupulous integrity, and quite unlikely to forfeit his word, she submitted to her fate with a good grace. She derived, however, great consolation, (during the tightening of the bowstring,) from the reflection that much of the history remained still untold, and that the petulance of her brute of a husband had reaped for him a most righteous reward, in depriving him of many inconceivable adventures.

NOTES

1. The coralites.
2. "One of the most remarkable natural curiosities in Texas is a petrified forest, near the head of Pasigno river. It consists of several hundred trees, in an erect position, all turned to stone. Some trees, now growing, are partly petrified. This is a startling fact for natural philosophers, and must cause them to modify the existing theory of petrifaction."—*Kennedy.*

This account, at first discredited, has since been corroborated by the discovery of a completely petrified forest, near the head waters of the Chayenne, or Chienne river, which has its source in the Black Hills of the rocky chain.

There is scarcely, perhaps, a spectacle on the surface of the globe more remarkable, either in a geological or picturesque point of view, than that presented by the petrified forest, near Cairo. The traveller, having passed the tombs of the caliphs, just beyond the gates of the city, proceeds to the southward, nearly at right angles to the road across the desert to Suez, and, after having travelled some ten miles up a low barren valley, covered with sand, gravel, and sea shells, fresh as if the tide had retired but yesterday, crosses a low range of sandhills, which has for some distance run parallel to his path. The scene now presented to him is beyond conception singular and desolate. A mass of fragments of tress, all converted into stone, and when struck by his horse's hoof ringing like cast iron, is seen to extend itself for miles and miles around him, in the form of a decayed and prostrate forest. The wood is of a dark brown hue, but retains its form in perfection, the pieces being from one to fifteen feet in length, and from half a foot to three feet in thickness, strewed so closely together, as far as the eye can reach, that an Egyptian donkey can scarcely thread its way through amongst them, and so natural that, were it in Scotland or Ireland, it might pass without remark for some enormous drained bog, on which the exhumed trees lay rotting in the sun. The roots and rudiments of the branches are, in many cases, nearly perfect, and in some the wormholes eaten under the bark are readily recognisable. The most delicate of the sap vessels, and all the finer portions of the centre of the wood, are perfectly entire, and bear to be examined with the strongest magnifiers. The whole are so thoroughly silicified as to scratch glass and be capable of receiving the highest polish.—*Asiatic Magazine.*

3. The Mammoth Cave of Kentucky.
4. In Iceland, 1783.
5. "During the eruption of Hecla, in 1766, clouds of this kind produced such a degree of darkness that, at Glaumba, which is more than fifty leagues from the mountain, people could only find their way by groping. During the eruption of Vesuvius, in 1794, at Caserta, four leagues distant, people could only walk by the light of torches. On the first of May, 1812, a cloud of volcanic ashes and sand, coming from a volcano in the island of St. Vincent, covered the whole of Barbadoes, spreading over it so intense a darkhess that, at mid-day, in the open air, one could not perceive the trees or other objects near him, or even a

white handkerchief placed at the distance of six inches from the eye."—*Murray*, p. 215, *Phil. edit.*

6. "In the year 1790, in the Caraccas, during an earthquake, a portion of the granite soil sank and left a lake eight hundred yards in diameter, and from eighty to a hundred feet deep. It was a part of the forest of Aripao which sank, and the trees remained green for several months under the water."—*Murray*, p. 221.

7. The hardest steel ever manufactured may, under the action of a blow-pipe, be reduced to an impalpable powder, which will float readily in the atmospheric air.

8. The region of the Niger. See *Simmond's* "*Colonial Magazine.*

9. The *Myrmeleon*—lion-ant. The term "monster" is equally applicable to small abnormal things and to great.

10. The *Epidendron, Flos Aeris*, of the family of the *Orchideæ*, grows with merely the surface of its roots attached to a tree or other object, from which it derives no nutriment—subsisting altogether upon air.

11. The *Parasites*, such as the wonderful *Rafflesia Arnaldii.*

12. *Schouw* advocates a class of plants that grow upon living animals—the *Plantæ Epizoæ*. Of this class are the *Fuci* and *Algæ.*

Mr. J. B. Williams, of Salem, Mass., presented the "National Institute," with an insect from New Zealand, with the following description:—"'*The Hotte,*' a decided caterpillar, or worm, is found growing at the foot of the *Rata* tree, with a plant growing out of its head. This most peculiar and most extraordinary insect travels up both the *Rata* and *Perriri* trees, and entering into the top, eats its way, perforating the trunk of the tree until it reaches the root, it then comes out of the root, and dies, or remains dormant, and the plant propagates out of its head; the body remains perfect and entire, of a harder substance than when alive. From this insect the natives make a coloring for tattooing."

In mines and natural caves we find a species of cryptogamous *fungus* that emits an intense phosphorescence.

13. The orchis, scabius and valisneria.

14. The corolla of this flower (*Aristolochia Clematitis*,) which is tubular, but terminating upwards in a ligulate limb, is inflated into a globular figure at the base. The tubular part is internally beset with stiff hairs, pointing downwards. The globular part contains the pistil, which consists merely of a germen and stigma, together with the surrounding stamens. But the stamens, being shorter than even the germen, cannot discharge the pollen so as to throw it upon the stigma, as the flower stands always upright till after impregnation. And hence, without some additional and peculiar aid, the pollen must necessarily fall down to the bottom of the flower. Now, the aid that nature has furnished in this case, is that of the *Tiputa Pennicornis*, a small insect, which, entering the tube of the corolla in quest of honey, descends to the bottom, and rummages about till it becomes quite covered with pollen; but, not being able to force its way out again, owing to the downward position of the hairs, which converge to a point like the wires of a mouse-trap, and being somewhat impatient of its confinement, it brushes backwards and forwards, trying every corner, till, after repeatedly traversing the stigma, it covers it with pollen sufficient for its impregnation, in consequence of which the flower soon begins to droop, and the hairs to shrink to the side of the tube, effecting an easy passage for the escape of the insect."—*Rev. P. Keith*—"*System of Physiological Botany.*"

15. The bees—ever since bees were—have been constructing their cells with just such sides, in just such number, and at just such inclinations, as it has been demonstrated (in a problem involving the profoundest mathematical principles) are the very sides, in the very number, and at the very angles, which will afford the creatures the most room that is compatible with the greatest stability of structure.

During the latter part of the last century, the question arose among mathematicians— "to determine the best form that can be given to the sails of a windmill, according to their varying distances from the revolving vanes, and likewise from the centres of the revolution." This is an excessively complex problem; for it is, in other words, to find the best possible position at an infinity of varied distances, and at an infinity of points on the arm. There were a thousand futile attempts to answer the query on the part of the most illustrious mathematicians; and when, at length, an undeniable solution was discovered, men found that the wings of a bird had given it with absolute precision, ever since the first bird had traversed the air.

16. He observed a flock of pigeons passing betwixt Frankfort and the Indiana territory, one mile at least in breadth; it took up four hours in passing; which, at the rate of one mile per minute, gives a length of 240 miles; and, supposing three pigeons to each square yard, gives 2,230,272,000 pigeons.—*"Travels in Canada and the United States," by Lieut. F. Hall.*

17. "The earth is upheld by a cow of a blue color, having horns four hundred in number."—*Sale's Koran.*

18. The *Entozoa*, or intestinal worms, have repeatedly been observed in the muscles, and in the cerebral substance of men."—*See Wyatt's Physiology*, p. 143.

19. On the great Western Railway, between London and Exeter, a speed of 71 miles per hour has been attained. A train weighing 90 tons was whirled from Puddington to Didcot (53 miles,) in 51 minutes.

20. The *Eccalobeion*. Vol. I, 7.

21. Maelzel's Automaton Chess-player.

22. Babbage's Calculating Machine.

23. *Chabert*, and, since him, a hundred others.

24. The Electrotype.

25. *Wollaston* made of platinum for the field of views in a telescope, a wire one eighteen-thousandth part of an inch in thickness. It could be seen only by means of the microscope.

26. Newton demonstrated that the retina beneath the influence of the violet ray of the spectrum, vibrated 900,000,000 of times in a second.

27. The Voltaic pile.

28. The Electro Telegraph transmits intelligence instantaneously—at least so far as regards any distance upon the earth.

29. The Electro Telegraph Printing Apparatus.

30. Common experiments in Natural Philosophy. If two red rays from two luminous points be admitted into a dark chamber so as to fall on a white surface, and differ in their length by 0,0000258 of an inch, their intensity is doubled. So also if the difference in length be any whole-number multiple of that fraction. A multiple by 2¼, 3¼, &c., gives an intensity equal to one ray only; but a multiple by 2½, 3½, &c., gives the result of total darkness. In violet rays similar effects arise when the difference in length is 0,0000157 of an inch; and with all other rays the results are the same—the difference varying with a uniform increase from the violet to the red.

Analogous experiments in respect to sound produce analogous results.

31. Place a platina crucible over a spirit lamp, and keep it a red heat; pour in some sulphuric acid, which, though the most volatile of bodies at a common temperature, will be found to become completely fixed in a hot crucible, and not a drop evaporates—being surrounded by an atmosphere of its own, it does not, in fact, touch the sides. A few drops of water are now introduced, when the acid immediately coming in contact with the heated sides of the crucible, flies off in sulphurous acid vapor, and so rapid is its progress, that the caloric of the water passes off with it, which falls a lump of ice to the bottom; by taking advantage of the moment before it is allowed to re-melt, it may be turned out a lump of ice from a red-hot vessel.

32. The Daguerreotype.

33. Although light travels 167,000 miles in a second, the distance of 61 Cygni (the only star whose distance is ascertained,) is so inconceivably great, that its rays would require more than ten years to reach the earth. For stars beyond this, 20—or even 1000 years—would be a moderate estimate. Thus, if they had been annihilated 20, or 1000 years ago, we might still see them to-day, by the light which *started* from their surfaces, 20 or 1000 years in the past time. That many which we see daily are really extinct, is not impossible—not even improbable. The elder Herschel maintains that the light of the faintest nebulæ seen through his great telescope, must have taken 3,000,000 years in reaching the earth. Some, made visible by Lord Ross' instrument must, then, have required at least 20,000,000.

Edward Page Mitchell

Evolution and American Equality

Rob Welch

Since their rediscovery in the 1970s, the short stories of Edward Page Mitchell (1852–1927) have delighted modern readers with their prescient use of still recognizable science fiction tropes.[1] Writing before the advent of cinema, of electric light, of radio, of the automobile or the airplane, Mitchell composed stories about time travel, about teleportation, about astral projection, and about faster-than-light propulsion. "The Senator's Daughter" (1879) includes a laundry list of futuristic inventions: instant, hands-free communication connects people in distant cities, up-to-the-minute news is electronically transmitted to private residences, pneumatic bullet trains traverse the U.S. coast, and hunger has been conquered by chemical engineering. Any of these would certainly make the short story noteworthy. However, "The Senator's Daughter" offers readers much more than a list of innovative technologies. Like much great science fiction, Mitchell's vision of the future in 1937 reflects on the contemporary conditions shared by him and his readers. In particular, with its focus on issues of race, nationalism, and politics, Mitchell's story provokes a social critique of the state of the world in 1879. On the surface, "The Senator's Daughter" is an amusing novelty. Read in the context of its contemporary audience, it is an agent of change.

Edward Page Mitchell worked as a journalist, then editor, for *The Sun*, a leading New York newspaper. *The Sun* published many of his stories throughout the 1870s and 1880s. His stories vary greatly in tone. Many examples of his science fiction are light and comical, featuring science-gone-awry as a comedic element. In "The Man Without a Body" (1877) for instance, Professor Dummkopf undergoes a body transplant as the result of a teleportation experiment gone wrong. Finding himself abandoned in the Natural History museum, he fashions a new body for himself out of found objects

50

from various displays. "The Man Without a Body" is also a satire of technological hype in the invention of the telephone, or "Telepomp," and a reflection
upon the theory of evolution. Some of Mitchell's stories lean toward more
gothic sensibilities. In "The Clock That Went Backward" (1881), a young man
inherits an old, dysfunctional clock, which turns out to be a time-travel
device. In this instance, science takes a backseat to the usual paradoxes that
accompany time travel, and some personal, phantasmagoric paradoxes which
particularly trouble the narrator.

"The Senator's Daughter" takes a middle ground, retaining a tone of
Gothic seriousness punctuated by moments of comedy. The plot is a forbidden romance akin to *Romeo and Juliet.* Two young lovers insist on marrying
despite the opposing views of their families. Mitchell's novel contribution to
this well-worn scenario is the author's combination of race and politics in a
future setting. Mr. Daniel Webster Wanlee is a young American congressman
"of a pure Mongolian ancestry." Clara Newton is the daughter of a Massachusetts senator, from a family whose roots extend back to the mythical founding
of the nation by English settlers. Senator Newton holds strong to an antiquated statute that young men and women of Caucasian and Mongolian
descent are forbidden to marry without the consent of the parents.

The introduction of race as a central component in the conflict of families is extremely provocative for us today, and it was even more so for
Mitchell's contemporary readers. In the mid 19th century, Chinese immigration had been encouraged by the U.S. government as a means of augmenting
the labor force on the west coast of the country (Chin and Tu, 42). Abraham
Lincoln signed the Act to Encourage Immigration in 1864, allowing American
businesses to solicit and sponsor the importation of foreign labor, and on the
west coast, the obvious source for such labor was from across the Pacific.
Official census records between 1840 and 1870 show the Chinese population
of the U.S. as tripling over these decades (Meade). However, as American
migration to California increased and a series of economic depressions
resulted in wide unemployment, immigration became a divisive political
issue, and the Chinese became a favorite target. In part, this was exacerbated
by common views that the Chinese avoided direct government oversight and
that their real population in the U.S. was, perhaps, two to three times what
was recorded in the census (Meade).

By the 1870s the Chinese population in America's west were largely
viewed as undesired alien immigrants (Hing). As Bethany Berger comments,
"Chinese were usually described as permanently unassimilable," meaning
that they would never fulfill the role of common citizen or member of society
(1190). In fact, U.S. law at this time only recognized the possibility of naturalization for citizenship for whites and for those of African descent (thanks
to the recent 14th Amendment). In 1881, two years after the publication of

"The Senator's Daughter," the federal government renegotiated its immigration treaty with China, allowing broad exclusions to be enacted at will, essentially denying further immigration from Asia, a strategy which would not be entirely altered until the Immigration and Naturalization Act of 1965 eliminated country-based quotas from official U.S. policy. As legal scholars, Gabriel Chin and Daniel Tu remark, however, "Chinese workers were not just limited or subject to quotas; instead, they were excluded absolutely on the basis of race" (40). Chinese Americans who resided in the U.S. remained on shaky ground. It was not until the Supreme Court case of United States vs. Wong Kim Ark in 1898 that it became established law that an Asian born on U.S. soil would be recognized as a citizen of the nation. In this atmosphere, Mitchell's selection of Wanlee, a Chinese-American California politician, as his protagonist is particularly daring.

Part of Mitchell's project plays upon his reader's expectations about how assimilable the Chinese, in fact, are. His story opens with Wanlee standing before a mirror, taking in the effect he makes in his elegant, fashionable clothes. Mitchell simply describes his character as being "faultlessly attired." Then, seated in his apartment, Wanlee wiles the time by reading the news of the day, demonstrating the practical application of his "intelligent good sense." At one point during the story, Wanlee muses on his family history, mentioning its humble and recent origins near the Yangtze River. As recently as three generations in the past, his family never cast a thought beyond the land they worked, but Wanlee's parents had come to San Francisco and made a success of their laundry business. In keeping with the American dream, Mitchell's character stands before the reader as a cultured, educated, and public-minded man who has built upon the advances made by his immigrant parents. In the tradition of statesmen of the past, he has made the management of the nation his occupation. His history, his name, Daniel Webster Wanlee, and his devotion to Western fashion, are evidence of his strides toward assimilation.

Yet, Mitchell also plays upon other conceptions of the Asian in contemporary culture. In describing Wanlee, he makes several allusions to the femininity of the figure. In referring to his character's face, Mitchell uses the words "delicate" and "refined," and Wanlee's fingers are tapered, his feet "remarkably small." As Berger indicates, it was typical for Americans to consider the Chinese as effeminate, in part because they were perceived as remaining subservient to arcane, obscure traditions and distant political overlords (1189–90). Chinese in the U.S. were not seen as standing independently or freely. This sense of gendering was a common enough cultural shorthand for establishing hierarchy between races in the 19th century, as Dana Luciano discusses in her study *Arranging Grief* (2007). What is interesting in the case of "The Senator's Daughter" is that Mitchell first introduces this in order to imply negative criticism of his character, but the course of the story contrasts these tokens of physicality, taking pains to show the strength of character which resides within the slight frame of his Asian protagonist.

Mitchell centers the opposition to Wanlee's attempts at positive change in the person of Clara's father, the senator for the state of Massachusetts. Superficially, this might simply be a representation of the tendencies for older generations to retain more conservative views in reaction to the discomfort of adaptation. However, the choice of Boston as the home of Newton has dual significance in relation to the larger themes in "The Senator's Daughter." When Wanlee and Clara decide to confront her father, the young man applies the epithet "little puritan" with affection to his fiancé. This evokes a myriad of connotations about the historic founding of the colony pivotal to American identity, Plymouth, and its subsequent iterations in nearby Boston. The Newtons are associated with early European settlers, establishing them as a kind of aristocracy by virtue of precedence. In a single word, it proclaims them as American, white, and protestant. At the same time, the reference to the pilgrimage of the Puritans in search of certain freedoms identifies that group as merely the first of any number of waves of immigrants in search of the same. Despite all prejudice, this equalizes one group of newcomers with any other. Yet, the term Mitchell uses is puritan. Taken apart from its historic context, the word has mixed connotations, of both idealism and of narrow bigotry. This split is exemplified in the Newtons, father and daughter. Clara is so idealistic and so ready to seek the good that she will martyr herself in the name of her principles. Senator Newton is so set in his determination of what is proper that he will, in turn, willingly require his daughter to martyr herself.

Mitchell's characterization of Senator Newton—his conservative politics and Massachusetts address—are also telling. At the time of the writing of "The Senator's Daughter," Massachusetts had been the focal point for the Radical Republican movement in Congress for the previous two decades, but with the death of Charles Sumner (1811–1874), their tradition of championing civil rights for minorities in the U.S. had also come to a close, along with their struggles over the course of post–Civil War Reconstruction. Senator Newton, sitting in the seat of Sumner, sixty years after that politician's death, and espousing discriminatory policies against a minority in the U.S. provides the reader with some interesting space for reflecting on the nature of progress.

Progress is, after all, what "The Senator's Daughter" exemplifies. The development of civil rights and representation which Wanlee's generation enjoy in the projected 1937 of the story extends the work recently commenced in the real world of Mitchell's readers, in the trauma and change of the American Civil War for African Americans. Looking forward to the future, Mitchell depicts a similar trajectory for Asian Americans. At the same time, Mitchell takes the time to also broaden participation in the heritage which is the American dream, showing how individuals with intelligence, talent, and diligence can prosper in the land of opportunity. Wanlee is living proof of each of these propositions, but, of course, the true star in peering into the future is the wonderful material inventions which will alter the lives of the people to come, and Mitchell does not disappoint on that score from the beginning to the end. In fact, he creates a dichotomy of inventions as both the ultimate problem in "The Senator's Daughter," and its answering solution.

In attempting to break up the Asian Romeo and his Anglo Juliet, Senator Newton employs the threat of law and the threat of a mechanical system of imprisonment. When Wanlee discloses his intention to marry Clara, the Senator brings up "the Suspended Animation Act." This stature upholds the right of parents to object to mixed-race marriage and reads:

> Section 7.391. No male person of Caucasian descent, of or under the age of 25 years, shall marry, or promise or contract himself in marriage with any female person of Mongolian descent without the full written consent of his male parent or guardian, as provided by law; and no female person, either maid or widow, under the age of 30 years, of Caucasian parentage, shall give, promise, or contract herself in marriage with any male person of Mongolian descent...
>
> Section 7.392. Such parents or guardians may, at their discretion ... deliver the offending person of Caucasian descent to the designated officers, and require that his or her consciousness, bodily activities, and vital functions be suspended by the frigorific process known as the Werkomer process...

In essence, the act condemns offenders to multi-year imprisonment in suspended animation. Newton insists he will send his own daughter through this process to prevent her from marrying Wanlee. Part of this threat is not the mere separation and the twelve-year delay it will cause in their union, but the fact that the stasis of the "frigorific process" is not perfect. Those who enter into suspension, more appropriately only hibernate, their bodies continuing to demand nutrients, so that they emerge decrepit, prematurely aged. The threat to the happiness of Wanlee and Clara is therefore doubled.

Handily, Mitchell also sets out a specific answer to the menace of technologically devised discipline, and this comes in the form of yet another advance in science. Peculiarly, however, it is science which adheres nicely to the Asian themes of "The Senator's Daughter." In part one of the story, Wanlee draws a gold box from his waistcoat pocket, full of large grey pastilles (lozenges). He offers one to Walsingham Brown, his friend and lawyer, who announces, "Thus do I satisfy mine hunger." In what has become a classic trope of science fiction, Wanlee and his friend have segued away from eating conventional food and now take their nourishment in pill form. Journalist Mark Novak has traced this trope back to the late 19th century and connected it with first wave feminism, the motif being the liberation of women from food preparation. Yet, for Wanlee and the Mongol/Vegetarian Party which he belongs to, the issue is a more broadly moral one.

Following Buddhist-inspired ethics, the Mongol/Vegetarian Party incorporates a regard for all animal life into its policies. Wanlee, it turns out, is a great radical, even among these reformers; he espouses the rights of all living things, not exclusively animal life. To this end, he has adopted the use of artificial food pills, so that the maintenance of his own existence infringes on no other living thing. As Wanlee explains to Clara: "It is nourishment in its only rational form." Wanlee's championing of the food substitute also bolsters his identity as a scientific-minded progressive. Mitchell introduces the information about the nature of these food pills, something which turns out to be critical to countering the threats of his unwilling father-in-law, in an odd exchange, part comical hyperbole, part philosophical introspection, between Wanlee and Clara. Two young lovers at a social function, worried about their possible future together, their possible happiness, enter into a discussion on the morality of eating. The subject of individual rights is taken to the extreme. Needless to say, however, there are parallels within the story about those who would demand control over others at any cost, and this alters the amusing flavor of the lover's discussion in retrospect.

Mitchell's take on animal rights and vegetable rights is almost certainly meant to be taken lightly by his readers. At the same time, the topic of extending rights where there had previously been none would certainly have struck a chord with his contemporary readers living in the aftermath of the American Civil War. At this time, only recently, male African Americans had been afforded official recognition as citizens, and, of course, campaigns would remain in progress throughout this period to extend similar status to women in general. The question of how far to go with this trend of enfranchisement and equality was a very real consideration for the American public. This becomes overt in the conversation between Clara and Wanlee when she asks if chickens and baboons will be granted the vote as the equal of people. Wanlee responds, rationally, "The right to live and enjoy life is a natural, an inalienable right," but he continues explaining, "The right to vote depends upon conditions of society and of individual intelligence." However, in the name of satire, Mitchell cannot simply stop with that, so Wanlee follows this by expressing his hope that, one day, science and the course of evolution will, indeed, lift these fellow denizens of the U.S., these "voters in embryo" to the side of humankind.

Interestingly, Wanlee expresses the duty he feels towards lesser living things in terms of paternalistic custodianship, a position which immediately corresponds to the views which have previously informed white ownership of other humans and the continued exclusion of women from political agency. Like all great satire, Mitchell amuses, but he also makes the reader think about the subject from novel angles, perhaps inspiring new conclusions about old truths.

Science fiction like that produced by Edward Page Mitchell has always taken advantage of the human impulse to look beyond the years prescribed by mortality. Through it, audiences witness potential epochs where social changes have occurred, providing a speculative view of what we might become. Advances and alterations in the material goods which surround and support life in the storyworld of the future are often an inherent parallel to depictions of the evolution of culture. Predictive fiction is inherently entertaining because of the novelty guaranteed by unknown and unexpected innovations. Part of that entertainment rests on demonstrating logical progressions from existing technology and existing social relationships, so that their potential evolution can be made to seem legitimately possible or even probable. The result is that while audiences look into the future through science fiction, they are putting what is shown into a relationship with the real world. This means that even though science fiction may point beyond the horizon, it is, at the same time, encouraging its audience to consider the here and now, and this gives the genre an awesome capacity to provoke meaningful change. Mitchell seems to have been entirely aware of this aspect of his fiction, and he uses it to amazing effect in "The Senator's Daughter."

NOTE

1. Edward Page Mitchell's stories were originally published anonymously in the *New York Sun*. Sam Moskowitz discovered Mitchell's stories and published them in *The Crystal Man* (Doubleday, 1973).

BIBLIOGRAPHY

Berger, Bethany R. 2016. "Birthright Citizenship on Trial: Elk V. Wilkins and United States V. Wong Kim Ark." *Cardozo Law Review* 37, no. 4: 1185–1258.

Chin, Gabriel J., and Daniel K. Tu. 2016. "Comprehensive Immigration Reform in the Jim Crow Era: Chinese Exclusion and the McCreary Act of 1893." *Asian American Law Journal* 23, no. 1: 39–68.

Hing, Bill Ong. 2013. "Chinese Immigration and Exclusion (US), Nineteenth Century." *Encyclopedia of Race and Racism*, edited by Patrick L. Mason. Gale, 2d ed.

Luciano, Dana. 2007. *Arranging Grief: Sacred Time and the Body in Nineteenth-Century America*. New York UP.

Meade, Edward. 1877. "Chinese Immigration to the United States." Social Science Association of America, 7 Sept., Saratoga, NY, address.

Mitchell, Edward Page. 1973. *The Crystal Man: Stories by Edward Page Mitchell*, edited by Sam Moskowitz. Doubleday.

Novak, Matt. 2014 ."Meal-in-a-pill: A Staple of Science Fiction." *BBC*, 18 Nov., www.bbc.com/future/story/20120221-food-pills-a-staple-of-sci-fi.

Shally-Jensen, Michael. 2014. *Defining Documents in American History: Reconstruction Era*. Salem P.

"The Senator's Daughter" (1879)

E.P. MITCHELL

I. The Small Gold Box

On the evening of the fourth of March, year of grace nineteen hundred and thirty-seven, Mr. Daniel Webster Wanlee devoted several hours to the consummation of a rather elaborate toilet.[1] That accomplished, he placed himself before a mirror and critically surveyed the results of his patient art.

The effect appeared to give him satisfaction. In the glass he beheld a comely young man of thirty, something under the medium stature, faultlessly attired in evening dress. The face was a perfect oval, the complexion delicate, the features refined. The high cheekbones and a slight elevation of the outer corners of the eyes, the short upper lip, from which drooped a slender but aristocratic mustache, the tapered fingers of the hand, and the remarkably small feet, confined tonight in dancing pumps of polished red morocco, were all unmistakable heirlooms of a pure Mongolian ancestry. The long, stiff, black hair, brushed straight back from the forehead, fell in profusion over the neck and shoulders. Several rich decorations shone on the breast of the black broadcloth coat. The knickerbocker breeches were tied at the knees with scarlet ribbons. The stockings were of a flowered silk. Mr. Wanlee's face sparked with intelligent good sense; his figure poised itself before the glass with easy grace.

A soft, distinct utterance, filling the room yet appearing to proceed from no particular quarter, now attracted Mr. Wanlee's attention. He at once recognized the voice of his friend, Mr. Walsingham Brown.[2]

"How are we off for time, old fellow?"

"It's getting late," replied Mr. Wanlee, without turning his face from the mirror. "You had better come over directly."

57

In a very few minutes the curtains at the entrance to Mr. Wanlee's apartments were unceremoniously pulled open, and Mr. Walsingham Brown strode in. The two friends cordially shook hands.

"How is the honorable member from the Los Angeles district?" inquired the newcomer gaily. "And what is there new in Washington society? Prepared to conquer tonight, I see. What's all this? Red ribbons and flowered silk hose! Ah, Wanlee. I thought you had outgrown these frivolities!"

The faintest possible blush appeared on Mr. Daniel Webster Wanlee's cheeks. "It is cool tonight?" he asked, changing the subject.

"Infernally cold," replied his friend. "I wonder you have no snow here. It is snowing hard in New York. There were at least three inches on the ground just now when I took the Pneumatic."

"Pull an easy chair up to the thermo-electrode," said the Mongolian. "You must get the New York climate thawed out of your joints if you expect to waltz creditably. The Washington women are critical in that respect."

Mr. Walsingham Brown pushed a comfortable chair toward a sphere of shining platinum that stood on a crystal pedestal in the center of the room. He pressed a silver button at the base, and the metal globe began to glow incandescently. A genial warmth diffused itself through the apartment. "That feels good," said Mr. Walsingham Brown, extending both hands to catch the heat from the thermo-electrode.

"By the way," he continued, "you haven't accounted to me yet for the scarlet bows. What would your constituents say if they saw you thus—you, the impassioned young orator of the Pacific slope; the thoughtful student of progressive statesmanship; the mainstay and hope of the Extreme Left; the thorn in the side of conservative Vegetarianism; the bete noire of the whole Indo-European gang—you, in knee ribbons and florid extensions, like a club man at a fashionable Harlem hop, or a—"

Mr. Brown interrupted himself with a hearty but goodnatured laugh.

Mr. Wanlee seemed ill at ease. He did not reply to his friend's raillery. He cast a stealthy glance at his knees in the mirror, and then went to one side of the room, where an endless strip of printed paper, about three feet wide, was slowly issuing from between noiseless rollers and falling in neat folds into a willow basket placed on the floor to receive it.[3] Mr. Wanlee bent his head over the broad strip of paper and began to read attentively.

"You take the *Contemporaneous News*, I suppose," said the other.

"No, I prefer the *Interminable Intelligencer*," replied Mr. Wanlee. "The *Contemporaneous* is too much of my own way of thinking. Why should a sensible man ever read the organ of his own party? How much wiser it is to keep posted on what your political opponents think and say."

"Do you find anything about the event of the evening?"

"The ball has opened," said Mr. Wanlee, "and the floor of the Capitol is already crowded. Let me see," he continued, beginning to read aloud: "'The wealth, the beauty, the chivalry, and the brains of the nation combine to lend unprecedented luster to the Inauguration Ball, and the brilliant success of the new Administration is assured beyond all question.'"

"That is encouraging logic," Mr. Brown remarked.

"'President Trimbelly has just entered the rotunda, escorting his beautiful and stately wife, and accompanied by ex–President Riley, Mrs. Riley, and Miss Norah Riley. The illustrious group is of course the cynosure of all eyes. The utmost cordiality prevails among statesmen of all shades of opinion. For once, bitter political animosities seem to have been laid aside with the ordinary habiliments of everyday wear. Conspicuous among the guests are some of the most distinguished radicals of the opposition. Even General Quong, the defeated Mongol-Vegetarian candidate, is now proceeding across the rotunda, leaning on the arm of the Chinese ambassador, with the evident intention of paying his compliments to his successful rival. Not the slightest trace of resentment or hostility is visible upon his strongly marked Asiatic features.'

"The hero of the Battle of Cheyenne can afford to be magnanimous," remarked Mr. Wanlee, looking up from the paper.

"True," said Mr. Walsingham Brown, warmly. "The noble old hoodlum fighter has settled forever the question of the equality of your race. The presidency could have added nothing to his fame."

Mr. Wanlee went on reading: "'The toilets of the ladies are charming. Notable among those which attract the reportorial eye are the peacock feather train of the Princess Hushyida; the mauve—'"

"Cut that," suggested Mr. Brown. "We shall see for ourselves presently. And give me a dinner, like a good fellow. It occurs to me that I have eaten nothing for fifteen days."

The Honorable Mr. Wanlee drew from his waistcoat pocket a small gold box, oval in form. He pressed a spring and the lid flew open. Then he handed the box to his friend. It contained a number of little gray pastilles, hardly larger than peas. Mr. Brown took one between his thumb and forefinger and put it into his mouth. "Thus do I satisfy mine hunger," he said, "or, to borrow the language of the opposition orators, thus do I lend myself to the vile and degrading practice, subversive of society as at present constituted, and outraging the very laws of nature."

Mr. Wanlee was paying no attention. With eager gaze he was again scanning the columns of the *Interminable Intelligencer*. As if involuntarily, he read aloud: "'—Secretary Quimby and Mrs. Quimby, Count Schneeke, the Austrian ambassador, Mrs. Hoyette and the Misses Hoyette of New York, Senator Newton of Massachusetts, whose arrival with his lovely daughter is causing no small sensation—'"

He paused, stammering, for he became aware that his friend was regarding him earnestly. Coloring to the roots of his hair, he affected indifference and began to read again: "'Senator Newton of Massachusetts, whose arrival with his lovely—'"

"I think, my dear boy," said Mr. Walsingham Brown, with a smile, "that it is high time for us to proceed to the Capitol."

II. The Ball at the Capitol

Through a brilliant throng of happy men and charming women, Mr. Wanlee and his friend made their way into the rotunda of the Capitol. Accustomed as they both were to the spectacular efforts which society arranged for its own delectation, the young men were startled by the enchantment of the scene before them. The dingy historical panorama that girds the rotunda was hidden behind a wall of flowers. The heights of the dome were not visible, for beneath that was a temporary interior dome of red roses and white lilies, which poured down from the concavity a continual and almost oppressive shower of fragrance. From the center of the floor ascended to the height of forty or fifty feet a single jet of water, rendered intensely luminous by the newly discovered hydroelectric process, and flooding the room with a light ten times brighter than daylight, yet soft and grateful as the light of the moon. The air pulsated with music, for every flower in the dome overhead gave utterance to the notes which Ratibolial, in the conservatoire at Paris, was sending across the Atlantic from the vibrant tip of his baton.

The friends had hardly reached the center of the rotunda, where the hydroelectric fountain threw aloft its jet of blazing water, and where two opposite streams of promenaders from the north and the south wings of the Capitol met and mingled in an eddy of polite humanity, before Mr. Walsingham Brown was seized and led off captive by some of his Washington acquaintances.

Wanlee pushed on, scarcely noticing his friend's defection. He directed his steps wherever the crowd seemed thickest, casting ahead and on either side of him quick glances of inquiry, now and then exchanging bows with people whom he recognized, but pausing only once to enter into conversation. That was when he was accosted by General Quong, the leader of the Mongol Vegetarian party and the defeated candidate for President in the campaign of 1936. The veteran spoke familiarly to the young congressman and detained him only a moment. "You are looking for somebody, Wanlee," said General Quong, kindly. "I see it in your eyes. I grant you leave of absence."

Mr. Wanlee proceeded down the long corridor that leads to the Senate chamber, and continued there his eager search. Disappointed, he turned back, retraced his steps to the rotunda, and went to the other extremity of the Capitol. The Hall of Representatives was reserved for the dancers. From the great clock above the Speaker's desk issued the music of a waltz, to the rhythm of which several hundred couples were whirling over the polished floor.

Wanlee stood at the door, watching the couples as they moved before him in making the circuit of the hall. Presently his eyes began to sparkle. They were resting upon the beautiful face and supple figure of a girl in white satin, who waltzed in perfect form with a young man, apparently an Italian. Wanlee advanced a step or two, and at the same instant the lady became aware of his presence. She said a word to her partner, who immediately relinquished her waist.

"I have been expecting you this age," said the girl, holding out her hand to Wanlee. "I am delighted that you have come."

"Thank you, Miss Newton," said Wanlee.

"You may retire, Francesco," she continued, turning to the young man who had just been her partner. "I shall not need you again."

The young man addressed as Francesco bowed respectfully and departed without a word.

"Let us not lose this lovely waltz," said Miss Newton, putting her hand upon Wanlee's shoulder. "It will be my first this evening."

"Then you have not danced?" asked Wanlee, as they glided off together.

"No, Daniel," said Miss Newton, "I haven't danced with any gentlemen."

The Mongolian thanked her with a smile.

"I have made good use of Francesco, however," she went on. "What a blessing a competent protectional partner is! Only think, our grandmothers, and even our mothers, were obliged to sit dismally around the walls waiting the pleasure of their high and mighty-"

She paused suddenly, for a shade of annoyance had fallen upon her partner's face. "Forgive me," she whispered, her head almost upon his shoulder. "Forgive me if I have wounded you. You know, love, that I would not-"

"I know it," he interrupted. "You are too good and too noble to let that weigh a feather's weight in your estimation of the Man. You never pause to think that my mother and my grandmother were not accustomed to meet your mother and your grandmother in society—for the very excellent reason," he continued, with a little bitterness in his tone, "that my mother had her hands full in my father's laundry in San Francisco, while my grandmother's social ideas hardly extended beyond the cabin of our ancestral san-pan on the Yangtze Kiang. *You* do not care for that. But there are others—"

They waltzed on for some time in silence, he, thoughtful and moody, and she, sympathetically concerned.

"And the senator; where is he tonight?" asked Wanlee at last.

"Papa!" said the girl, with a frightened little glance over her shoulder.

"Oh! Papa merely made his appearance here to bring me and because it was expected of him. He has gone home to work on his tiresome speech against the vegetables."

"Do you think," asked Wanlee, after a few minutes, whispering the words very slowly and very low, "that the senator has any suspicion?"

It was her turn now to manifest embarrassment. "I am very sure," she replied, "that Papa has not the least idea in the world of it all. And that is what worries me. I constantly feel that we are walking together on a volcano. I know that we are right, and that heaven means it to be just as it is; yet, I cannot help trembling in my happiness. You know as well as I do the antiquated and absurd notions that still prevail in Massachusetts, and that Papa is a conservative among the conservatives. He respects your ability, that I discovered long ago. Whenever you speak in the House, he reads your remarks with great attention. I think," she continued with a forced laugh, "that your arguments bother him a good deal."

"This must have an end, Clara," said the Chinaman, as the music ceased and the waltzers stopped. "I cannot allow you to remain a day longer in an equivocal position. My honor and your own peace of mind require that there shall be an explanation to your father. Have you the courage to stake all our happiness on one bold move?"

"I have courage," frankly replied the girl, "to go with you before my father and tell him all. And furthermore," she continued, slightly pressing his arm and looking into his face with a charming blush, "I have courage even beyond that."

"You beloved little Puritan!" was his reply.

As they passed out of the Hall of Representatives, they encountered Mr. Walsingham Brown with Miss Hoyette of New York. The New York lady spoke cordially to Miss Newton, but recognized Wanlee with a rather distant bow. Wanlee's eyes sought and met those of his friend. "I may need your counsel before morning," he said in a low voice.

"All right, my dear fellow," said Mr. Brown. "Depend on me." And the two couples separated.

The Mongolian and his Massachusetts sweetheart drifted with the tide into the supper room. Both were preoccupied with their own thoughts. Almost mechanically, Wanlee led his companion to a corner of the supper room and established her in a seat behind a screen of palmettos, sheltered from the observation of the throne.

"It is nice of you to bring me here," said the girl, "for I am hungry after our waltz."

Intimate as their souls had become, this was the first time that she had ever asked him for food. It was an innocent and natural request, yet Wanlee shuddered when he heard it, and bit his under lip to control his agitation.

He looked from behind the palmettos at the tables heaped with delicate viands and surrounded by men, eagerly pressing forward to obtain refreshment for the ladies in their care. Wanlee shuddered again at the spectacle. After a momentary hesitation he returned to Miss Newton, seated himself beside her, and taking her hand in his, began to speak deliberately and earnestly.

"Clara," he said, "I am going to ask you for a final proof of your affection. Do not start and look alarmed, but hear me patiently. If, after hearing me, you still bid me bring you a *pâté*, or the wing of a fowl, or a salad, or even a plate of fruit, I will do so, though it wrench the heart in my bosom. But first listen to what I have to say."

"Certainly I will listen to all you have to say," she replied.

"You know enough of the political theories that divide parties," he went on, nervously examining the rings on her slender fingers, "to be aware that what I conscientiously believe to be true is very different from what you have been educated to believe."

"I know," said Miss Newton, "that you are a Vegetarian and do not approve the use of meat. I know that you have spoken eloquently in the House on the right of every living being to protection in its life, and that that is the theory of your party. Papa says that it is demagogy—that the opposition parade an absurd and sophistical theory in order to win votes and get themselves into office. Still, I know that a great many excellent people, friends of ours in Massachusetts, are coming to believe with you, and, of course, loving you as I do, I have the firmest faith in the honesty of your convictions. You are not a demagogue, Daniel. You are above pandering to the radicalism of the rabble. Neither my father nor all the world could make me think the contrary."

Mr. Daniel Webster Wanlee squeezed her hand and went on:

"Living as you do in the most ultra-conservative of circles, dear Clara, you have had no opportunity to understand the tremendous significance and force of the movement that is now sweeping over the land, and of which I am a very humble representative. It is something more than a political agitation; it is an upheaval and reorganization of society on the basis of science and abstract right. It is fit and proper that I, belonging to a race that has only been emancipated and enfranchised by the march of time, should stand in the advance guard—in the forlorn hope, it may be—of the new revolution."

His flaming eyes were now looking directly into hers. Although a little troubled by his earnestness, she could not hide her proud satisfaction in his manly bearing.

"We believe that every animal is born free and equal," he said. "That the humblest polyp or the most insignificant mollusk has an equal right with you or me to life and the enjoyment of happiness. Why, are we not all brothers? Are we not all children of a common evolution? What are we human animals but the more favored members of the great family? Is Senator Newton of Massachusetts further removed in intelligence from the Australian bushman, than the Australian bushman or the Flathead Indian is removed from the ox which Senator Newton orders slain to yield food for his family? Have we a right to take the paltriest life that evolution has given? Is not the butchery of an ox or of a chicken murder—nay, fratricide—in the view of absolute justice? Is it not cannibalism of the most repulsive and cowardly sort to prey upon the flesh of our defenseless brother animals, and to sacrifice their lives and rights to an unnatural appetite that has no foundation save in the habit of long ages of barbarian selfishness?"

"I have never thought of these things," said Miss Clara, slowly. "Would you elevate them to the suffrage—I mean the ox and the chicken and the baboon?"

"There speaks the daughter of the senator from Massachusetts," cried Wanlee. "No, we would not give them the suffrage—at least, not at present. The right to live and enjoy life is a natural, an inalienable right. The right to vote depends upon conditions of society and of individual intelligence. The ox, the chicken, the baboon are not yet prepared for the ballot. But they are voters in embryo; they are struggling up through the same process that our own ancestors underwent, and it is a crime, an unnatural, horrible thing, to cut off their career, their future, for the sake of a meal!"

"Those are noble sentiments, I must admit," said Miss Newton, with considerable enthusiasm.

"They are the sentiments of the Mongol-Vegetarian party," said Wanlee. "They will carry the country in 1940, and elect the next President of the United States."

"I admire your earnestness," said Miss Newton after a pause, "and I will not grieve you by asking you to bring me even so much as a chicken wing. I do not think I could eat it now, with your words still in my ears. A little fruit is all that I want."

"Once more," said Wanlee, taking the tall girl's hand again, "I must request you to consider. The principles, my dearest, that I have already enunciated are the principles of the great mass of our party. They are held even by the respectable, easygoing, not oversensitive voters such as constitute the bulk of every political organization. But there are a few of us who stand on ground still more advanced. We do not expect to bring the laggards up to our line for years, perhaps in our lifetime. We simply carry the accepted theory to its logical conclusions and calmly await ultimate results."

"And what is your ground, pray?" she inquired. "I cannot see how anything could be more dreadfully radical—that is, more bewildering and generally upsetting at first sight—than the ground which you just took."

"If what I have said is true, and I believe it to be true, then how can we escape including the Vegetable Kingdom in our proclamation of emancipation from man's tyranny? The tree, the plant, even the fungus, have they not individual life, and have they not also the right to live?"

"But how—"

"And indeed," continued the Chinaman, not noticing the interruption, "who can say where vegetable life ends and animal life begins? Science has tried in vain to draw the boundary line. I hold that to uproot a potato is to destroy an existence certainly, although perhaps remotely akin to ours. To pluck a grape is to maim the living vine; and to drink the juice of that grape is to outrage consanguinity. In this broad, elevated view of the matter it becomes a duty to refrain from vegetable food. Nothing less than the vital principal itself becomes the test and tie of universal brotherhood. 'All living things are born free and equal, and have a right to existence and the enjoyment of existence.' Is not that a beautiful thought?"

"It is a beautiful thought," said the maiden. "But—I know you will think me dreadfully cold, and practical, and unsympathetic—but how are *we* to live? Have *we* no right, too, to existence? Must we starve to death in order to establish the theoretical right of vegetables not to be eaten?"

"My dear love," said Wanlee, "that would be a serious and perplexing question, had not the latest discovery of science already solved it for us."

He took from his waistcoat pocket the small gold box, scarcely larger than a watch, and opened the cover. In the palm of her white hand he placed one of the little pastilles.

"Eat it," said he. "It will satisfy your hunger."

She put the morsel into her mouth. "I would do as you bade me," she said, "even if it were poison."

"It is not poison," he rejoined. "It is nourishment in the only rational form."

"But it is tasteless; almost without substance."

"Yet it will support life for from eighteen to twenty-five days. This little gold box holds food enough to afford all subsistence to the entire Seventy-sixth Congress for a month."

She took the box and curiously examined its contents.

"And how long would it support my life—for more than a year, perhaps?"

"Yes, for more than ten—more than twenty years."

"I will not bore you with chemical and physiological facts," continued Wanlee, "but you must know that the food which we take, in whatever form, resolves itself into what are called proximate principles—starch, sugar, oleine, flurin, albumen, and so on. These are selected and assimilated by the organs of the body, and go to build up the necessary tissues. But all these proximate principles, in their turn, are simply combinations of the ultimate chemical elements, chiefly carbon, nitrogen, hydrogen, and oxygen. It is upon these elements that we depend for sustenance. By the old plan we obtained them indirectly. They passed from the earth and the air into the grass; from the grass into the muscular tissues of the ox; and from the beef into our own persons, loaded down and encumbered by a mass of useless, irrelevant matter. The German chemists have discovered how to supply the needed elements in compact, undiluted form—here they are in this little box. Now shall mankind go direct to the fountainhead of nature for his aliment; now shall the old roundabout, cumbrous, inhuman method be at an end; now shall the evils of gluttony and the attendant vices cease; now shall the brutal murdering of fellow animals and brother vegetables forever stop—now shall all this be, since the new, holy cause has been consecrated by the lips I love!"

He bent and kissed those lips. Then he suddenly looked up and saw Mr. Walsingham Brown standing at his elbow.

"You are observed—compromised, I fear," said Mr. Brown, hurriedly. "That Italian dancer in your employ, Miss Newton, has been following you like a hound. I have been paying him the same gracious attention. He has just left the Capitol post haste. I fear there may be a scene."

The brave girl, with clear eyes, gave her Mongolian lover a look worth to him a year of life. "There shall be no scene," she said; "we will go at once to my father, Daniel, and bear ourselves the tale which Francesco would carry."

The three left the Capitol without delay. At the head of Pennsylvania Avenue they entered a great building, lighted up as brilliantly as the Capitol itself. An elevator took them down toward the bowels of the earth.[4] At the fourth landing they passed from the elevator into a small carriage, luxuriously upholstered. Mr. Walsingham Brown touched an ivory knob at the end of the conveyance. A man in uniform presented himself at the door.

"To Boston," said Mr. Walsingham Brown.

III. The Frozen Bride

The senator from Massachusetts sat in the library of his mansion on North Street at two o'clock in the morning. An expression of astonishment and rage distorted his pale, cold features. The pen had dropped from his fingers, blotting the last sentences written upon the manuscript of his great speech—for Senator Newton still adhered to the ancient fashion of recording thought. The blotted sentences were these:

"The logic of events compels us to acknowledge the political equality of those Asiatic invaders—shall I say conquerors?—of our Indo-European institutions. But the logic of events is often repugnant to common sense, and its conclusions abhorrent to patriotism and right. The sword has opened for them the way to the ballot box; but, Mr. President, and I say it deliberately, no power under heaven can unlock for these aliens the sacred approaches to our homes and hearts!"

Beside the senator stood Francesco, the professional dancer. His face wore a smile of malicious triumph.

"With the Chinaman? Miss Newton—my daughter?" gasped the senator. "I do not believe you. It is a lie."

"Then come to the Capitol, Your Excellency, and see it with your own eyes," said the Italian.

The door was quickly opened and Clara Newton entered the room, followed by the Honorable Mr. Wanlee and his friend.

"There is no need of making that excursion, Papa," said the girl. "You can see it with your own eyes here and now. Francesco, leave the house!"

The senator bowed with forced politeness to Mr. Walsingbam Brown. Of the presence of Wanlee he took not the slightest notice.

Senator Newton attempted to laugh. "This is a pleasantry, Clara," he said; "a practical jest, designed by yourself and Mr. Brown for my midnight diversion. It is a trifle unseasonable."

"It is no jest," replied his daughter, bravely. She then went up to Wanlee and took his hand in hers. "Papa," she said, "this is a gentleman of whom you already know something. He is our equal in station, in intellect, and in moral worth. He is in every way worthy of my friendship and your esteem. Will you listen to what he has to say to you? Will you, Papa?"

The senator laughed a short, hard laugh, and turned to Mr. Walsingham Brown. "I have no communication to make to the member of the lower branch," said he. "Why should he have any communication to make to me?"

Miss Newton put her arm around the waist of the young Chinaman and led him squarely in front of her father. "Because," she said, in a voice as firm and clear as the note of a silver bell "-because I love him."

In recalling with Wanlee the circumstances of this interview, Mr. Walsingham Brown said long afterward, "She glowed for a moment like the platinum of your thermo-electrode."

"If the member from California," said Senator Newton, without changing the tone of his voice, and still continuing to address himself to Mr. Brown, "has worked upon the sentimentality of this foolish child, that is her misfortune, and mine. It cannot be helped now. But if the member from California presumes to hope to profit in the least by his sinister operations, or to enjoy further opportunities for pursuing them, the member from California deceives himself."

So saying he turned around in his chair and began to write on his great speech.

"I come," said Wanlee slowly, now speaking for the first time, "as an honorable man to ask of Senator Newton the hand of his daughter in honorable marriage. Her own consent has already been given."

"I have nothing further to say," said the Senator, once more turning his cold face toward Mr. Brown. Then he paused an instant, and added with a sting, "I am told that the member from California is a prophet and apostle of Vegetable Rights. Let him seek a cactus in marriage. He should wed on his own level."

Wanlee, coloring at the wanton insult, was about to leave the room. A quick sign from Miss Newton arrested him.

"But I have something further to say," she cried with spirit. "Listen, Father; it is this. If Mr. Wanlee goes out of the house without a word from you—a word such as is due him from you as a gentleman and as my father—I go with him to be his wife before the sun rises!"

"Go if you will, girl," the senator coldly replied. "But first consult with Mr. Walsingham Brown, who is a lawyer and a gentleman, as to the tenor and effect of the Suspended Animation Act."

Miss Newton looked inquiringly from one face to another. The words had no meaning to her. Her lover turned suddenly pale and clutched at the back of a chair for support. Mr. Brown's cheeks were also white. He stepped quickly forward, holding out his hands as if to avert some dreadful calamity.

"Surely you would not—" he began. "But no! That is an absolute low, an inhuman, outrageous enactment that has long been as dead as the partisan fury that prompted it. For a quarter of a century it has been a dead letter on the statute books."

"I was not aware," said the senator, from between firmly set teeth, "that the act had ever been repealed."

He took from the shelf a volume of statutes and opened the book. "I will read the text," he said. "It will form an appropriate part of the ritual of this marriage." He read as follows:

"Section 7.391. No male person of Caucasian descent, of or under the age of 25 years, shall marry, or promise or contract himself in marriage with any female person of Mongolian descent without the full written consent of his male parent or guardian, as provided by law; and no female person, either maid or widow, under the age of 30 years, of Caucasian parentage, shall give, promise, or contract herself in marriage with any male person of Mongolian descent without the full written and registered consent of her male and female parents or guardians, as provided by law. And any marriage obligations so contracted shall be null and void, and the Caucasian so contracting shall be guilty of a misdemeanor and liable to punishment at the discretion of his or her male parent or guardian as provided by law.

"Section 7.392. Such parents or guardians may, at their discretion and upon application to the authorities of the United States District Court for the district within which the offense is committed, deliver the offending person of Caucasian descent to the designated officers, and require that his or her consciousness, bodily activities, and vital functions be suspended by the frigorific process known as the Werkomer process, for a period equal to that which must elapse before the offending person will arrive at the age of 25 years, if a male, or 30 years, if a female; or for a shorter period at the discretion of the parent or guardian; said shorter period to be fixed in advance."

"What does it mean?" demanded Miss Newton, bewildered by the verbiage of the act, and alarmed by her lover's exclamation of despair.

Mr. Walsingbam Brown shook his head, sadly. "It means," said he, "that the cruel sin of the fathers is to be visited upon the children."

"It means, Clara," said Wanlee with a great effort, "that we must part."

"Understand me, Mr. Brown," said the senator, rising and motioning impatiently with the hand that held the pen, as if to dismiss both the subject and the intruding party. "I do not employ the Suspended Animation Act as a bugaboo to frighten a silly girl out of her lamentable infatuation. As surely as the law stands, so surely will I put it to use."

Miss Newton gave her father a long, steady look which neither Wanlee nor Mr. Brown could interpret and then slowly led the way to the parlor. She closed the door and locked it. The clock on the mantel said four.

A complete change had come over the girl's manner. The spirit of defiance, of passionate appeal, of outspoken love, had gone. She was calm now, as cold and self-possessed as the senator himself. "Frozen!" she kept saying under her breath. "He has frozen me already with his frigid heart."

She quickly asked Mr. Walsingham Brown to explain clearly the force and bearings of the statute which her father had read from the book. When he had done so, she inquired, "Is there not also a law providing for voluntary suspension of animation?"

"The Twenty-seventh Amendment to the Constitution," replied the lawyer, "recognizes the right of any individual, not satisfied with the condition of his life, to suspend that life for a time, long or short, according to his pleasure. But it is rarely, as you know, that any one avails himself of the right—practically never, except as the only means to procure divorce from uncongenial marriage relations."

"Still," she persisted, "the right exists and the way is open?" He bowed. She went to Wanlee and said:

"My darling, it must be so. I must leave you for a time, but as your wife. We will arrange a wedding"—and she smiled sadly—"within this hour. Mr. Brown will go with us to the clergyman. Then we will proceed at once to the Refuge, and you yourself shall lead me to the cloister that is to keep me safe till times are better for us. No, do not be startled, my love! The resolution is

taken; you cannot alter it. And it will not be so very long, dear. Once, by accident, in arranging my father's papers, I came across his Life Probabilities,
drawn up by the Vital Bureau at Washington. He has less than ten years to
live. I never thought to calculate in cold blood on the chances of my father's
life, but it must be. In ten years, Daniel, you may come to the Refuge again
and claim your bride. You will find me as you left me."

With tears streaming down his pale cheeks, the Mongolian strove to dis-
suade the Caucasian from her purpose. Hardly less affected, Mr. Walsingham
Brown joined his entreaties and arguments.

"Have you ever seen," he asked, "a woman who has undergone what you
propose to undergo? She went into the Refuge, perhaps, as you will go, fresh,
rosy, beautiful, full of life and energy. She comes out a prematurely aged,
withered, sallow, flaccid body, a living corpse—a skeleton, a ghost of her former self. In spite of all they say, there can be no absolute suspension of animation. Absolute suspension would be death. Even in the case of the most
perfect freezing there is still some activity of the vital functions, and they
gnaw and prey upon the existence of the unconscious subject. Will you risk,"
he suddenly demanded, using the last and most perfect argument that can
be addressed to a woman "-will you risk the effect your loss of beauty may
have upon Wanlee's love after ten years' separation?"

Clara Newton was smiling now. "For my poor beauty," she replied, "I
care very little. Yet perhaps even that may be preserved."

She took from the bosom of her dress the little gold box which the Chinaman had given her in the supper room of the Capitol, and hastily swallowed
its entire contents.

Wanlee now spoke with determination: "Since you have resolved to sacrifice ten years of your life my duty is with you. I shall share with you the
sacrifice and share also the joy of awakening."

She gravely shook her head. "It is no sacrifice for me," she said. "But you
must remain in life. You have a great and noble work to perform. Till the
oppressed of the lower orders of being are emancipated from man's injustice
and cruelty, you cannot abandon their cause. I think your duty is plain."

"You are right," he said, bowing his head to his breast.

In the gray dawn of the early morning the officials at the Frigorific
Refuge in Cambridgeport were astonished by the arrival of a bridal party.
The bridegroom's haggard countenance contrasted strangely with the elegance
of his full evening toilet, and the bright scarlet bows at his knees seemed a
mockery of grief. The bride, in white satin, wore a placid smile on her lovely
face. The friend accompanying the two was grave and silent.

Without delay the necessary papers of admission were drawn up and
signed and the proper registration was made upon the books of the estab-
lishment. For an instant husband and wife rested in each other's arms. Then

she, still cheerful, followed the attendants toward the inner door, while he, pressing both hands upon his tearless eyes, turned away sobbing.

A moment later the intense cold of the congealing chamber caught the bride and wrapped her close in its icy embrace.

NOTES

1. Mitchell uses "toilet" here as a verb in the outdated use, to mean "toil" or "groom."

2. Mitchell indicates that Wanlee and Brown are speaking over telephone. Wanlee is in Los Angeles and Brown is in New York. It takes Brown "a very few minutes" to cross the country on the "Pneumatic" bullet train.

3. The technology described here resembles a domestic telegraph configured to receive the latest news, something like an on-call newspaper printed in the home.

4. The elevator ride taken here by the three main characters indicates an additional form of transportation, something like a long-distance taxi-style subway service connecting Washington, D.C., to Boston.

"Runaway Cyclone," Or: The First Bengali Science Fiction Story[1]

Christin Hoene

According to *The Encyclopedia of Science Fiction*'s entry on Bengal, the "most significant work of sf, and undoubtedly one of the best works of Bangla sf in the formative stage, is the highly subversive attack on colonial repression, 'Niruddesher Kahini' ('The Story of the Missing One') by 'Acharya' Jagadish Chandra Bose (1858–1937)." Born in British India, Bose was an internationally renowned scientist, public intellectual, and polymath who was mostly known for his work as a physicist and his research on electromagnetic (millimeter) waves (then called Hertzian waves) until his contributions were curiously forgotten. He became known instead for his work on the physiology of plants. Bose was also the president of the Academy of Bengali Literature for several years; he delivered the Presidential address at the literary conference held at Mymensing on 14 April 1911 (Bose 1986, 139). In 1896 he wrote what is arguably the first Bengali science fiction story.

Bose wrote "Niruddesher Kahini" as an entry for a short story competition that was organized, somewhat peculiarly, by an Indian hair oil company (Bhattacharya 2006; Menon and Singh 2013). The condition for all entries was that the stories had to make reference to the company's most prominent product, Kuntal Keshari (Kuntaline in the 1896 version). Bose features Kuntal Keshari prominently as the *deus ex machina* that saves Calcutta from an approaching cyclone. Bose's story won that competition. Twenty-five years later, in 1921, he published an expanded version under the new title "Palatak Toofan" (Menon and Singh 2013). In 2013, the story was finally translated into English by Bodhisattva Chattopadhyay, as "Runaway Cyclone," and published in the online magazine *Strange Horizons*.[2]

The story is about a cyclone that threatens Calcutta. Newspapers warn of the impending catastrophe, citing the latest readings by the Meteorological Department. But on the appointed day, the cyclone fails to appear, much to the astonishment of the newspapers, the Meteorological Department, and western scientists. It is only in the second part of the story that the mystery is lifted by a personal account of a balding man, who is on a ship in the middle of the cyclone shortly before it makes landfall. Thinking that his last moment has come, he remembers that his daughter has packed him a bottle of Kuntal Keshari. He also remembers a scientific article that he recently read that describes how a film of oil on water calms the surface. The man throws the bottle of hair oil overboard, which immediately calms the waters. The cyclone disappears, and disaster is avoided.

Several things are remarkable about this story when we look at it as a work of science fiction, on the one hand, and as a work of colonial literature on the other. The story consists of two parts. Part one mainly charts the arrival and sudden disappearance of the cyclone as described through the lens of Western scientists and English-language newspaper articles. Everyone is equally puzzled. In part two we learn about the real cause of the cyclone's disappearance: the bottle of hair oil.

What is striking is that this resolution seems scientifically sound and completely improbable at the same time: one single bottle of hair oil to calm a cyclone? After all, the protagonist had just read about the effects of oil on water in a scientific journal. This adds a supernatural dimension to the scientific one.

The 1921 version adds the origin story of the hair oil, which extends the supernatural elements of the story. An English circus director once travelled to India, but upon arrival his lion lost its mane due to sea-sickness. In dire straits, the man prays at the feet of a Sanyasi, who in turn offers him a bottle of Kuntal Keshari and says that the formula had come to him in a dream. The hair oil cures the lion and makes its mane grow back within the week.

This origin story complicates our reading of "Runaway Cyclone" as a work of science fiction; it does not add to the scientific element of the story. The origin story further mystifies the hair oil and renders "Runaway Cyclone" a peculiar hybrid of science fiction and magical realism. The science fictional elements include the cyclone (a natural phenomenon), expert meteorologists, and the chemical effects of oil on water. The magical realist elements include the circus, the bald lion, and the circus director praying at the feet of a Sanyasi, who in turn offers him a hair oil whose formula came to him in a dream.

The 1921 version integrates both elements, which become mutually dependent rather than mutually exclusive. The Western scientists quoted in the story fail in their ability to account for the cyclone's sudden disappearance, and their failure is one of the imagination. As far as they know, there simply cannot be a rational explanation for the phenomenon. Strictly speaking, there is none. The properties of the hair oil are as much scientific in their effect as they are supernatural in their origin. The Western scientists' narrow view thus hinders them from seeing the bigger picture.

One might read Bose's choice to alternate between Western and native perspectives as an attack on Western science. In fact, the East-West dichotomy echoes throughout Bose's non-fictional writings, particularly in the numerous speeches that he delivered from the 1910s to the 1930s at the inaugurations of universities, the opening of his own research institute in Calcutta, and on other occasions. Bose was an interdisciplinary scientist from India and worked at a time when neither interdisciplinarity nor scientists from India were particularly highly regarded in the west (Bose in Geddes 1920, 229). Throughout his life, Bose had to battle the colonial prejudice that Indians were inept at the natural sciences because of their predisposition towards the metaphysical (*ibid.*). Bose proved the prejudice wrong by sheer success.

In his speeches, Bose also rhetorically undermines the validity of the premise that a vivid imagination is bad for scientific pursuit, by first acknowledging that this "burning imagination" is indeed intrinsic to the Indian mind, and by then arguing that it is beneficial rather than detrimental for scientific thought, because it opens up the mind for a "clear vision" of what is possible (1986, 69). "The excessive specialisation in the West," on the other hand, "has led to the danger of our losing sight of the fundamental truth that there are not sciences but a single science that includes all" (45). Thus, the scientists' inability to account for the runaway cyclone is not a failure of science as such; it is a failure of the western approach to science.

NOTES

1. This article was first published in *Decolonising Speculative Fiction*, PSA Newsletter (#21), 13–15.
2. According to the editors, Anil Menon and Vandana Singh, and the translator, Bodhisattva Chattopadhyay, this is the first translation of Bose's story into English.

BIBLIOGRAPHY

"Bengal." *The Encyclopedia of Science Fiction*. http://www.sf-encyclopedia.com/entry/bengal. Accessed 13 Apr. 2018.
Bhattacharya, Arupratan. 2006. *Bangalir Bigyanbhabana O Sadhana*. Dey's Publishing.
Bose, Jagadish Chandra. 1920. "The Dedication," in *An Indian Pioneer of Science: The Life and Work of Sir Jagadis C. Bose* by Patrick Geddes. Longmans, Green, and Co.
Bose, Jagadish Chandra. 1986. *Bose Speaks*. Edited by Dibakar Sen and Ajoy Kumar Chakraborty. Puthipatra.
Bose, Jagadish Chandra. 2009 [1921]. *Abyakto: A Collection of Popular Science of Jagadish Chandra Bose Articles and Other Essays*. Dey's Publishing.
Bose, Jagadish Chandra. 2013. "Runaway Cyclone." Trans. Bodhisattva Chattopadhyay. *Strange Horizons*, 30 September. http://strangehorizons.com/fiction/runaway-cyclone/. Accessed 13 Apr. 2018.

Deb, Anish, ed. 2007. *Sera Kalpabigyan* (*Best Science Fiction*). Ananda Publishers Limited.
Menon, Anil, and Vandana Singh. 2013. "Introduction to 'Runaway Cyclone' and 'Sheesha Ghat.'" *Strange Horizons*, 30 September. http://strangehorizons.com/fiction/introduc
tion-to-runaway-cyclone-and-sheesha-ghat/. Accessed 6 Nov. 2018.

"Runaway Cyclone"
(1896/1921)[1]

JAGADISH CHANDRA BOSE

Translated by BODHISATTVA CHATTOPADHYAY

Part I—A Scientific Mystery

A few years ago a supernatural event was observed which rocked the scientific communities of America and Europe. A number of articles were published in various scientific journals to explain the phenomenon. But till now no explanation of the event has been found satisfactory.

On 28 September the leading English daily of Calcutta[2] published the following news received from Shimla: *Shimla Meteorological Office, 27 September: A cyclone in the Bay of Bengal is imminent.*[3]

On 29 September the aforementioned daily published the following news: *Meteorological Office, Alipore: A tremendous cyclone is about to strike Bengal in two days. A Danger-Signal has been put up on Diamond Harbour.*

On the 30th the news was extremely frightening: *The Barometer fell two inches in the last half hour. By ten o'clock tomorrow Calcutta will face the worst and most dangerous cyclone in years.*[4]

No one slept that night in Calcutta. The timorous souls stayed awake in fear of their uncertain future.

On 1 October the sky remained cloudy, and a few drops of rain fell during the day. It remained dark throughout the day, but about four in the evening the sky suddenly became clear without a trace of the cyclone.

The next day the Meteorological Department sent the following news to the newspaper office: *The cyclone that was to strike Calcutta has left the Bay of Bengal and has probably gone off in another direction in the Indian Ocean.*

76

However, despite the attempts of many scientists to follow the trail of the cyclone, no one was able to discover the cyclone's new direction.

The leading English daily[5] published the following news: *Now it is certain that scientific knowledge is completely false.*

Another daily[6] published the following: *If science is false then why should the taxpayers be burdened by the totally unreliable Meteorological department?*

Various other dailies[7] joined as chorus: *Let it go! Scrap it!*

The government was in a fix. A few days ago new equipment worth over one lakh Rupees had been purchased for the Meteorological Department. Now those items would not even sell for the price of broken glass bottles. Besides, where would one transfer the Chief Officer of the Meteorological Department?

In dire straits the government appealed to the Calcutta Medical College: "We wish to appoint a new Chair at the Medical College. Lectures would be delivered on the following topic: 'On the Effect of Variation of Barometric Pressure on the Human System.'" The principal of the Medical College wrote back:

> *A wonderful suggestion. A decrease in air pressure enhances blood circulation in the human body. This would undoubtedly help rejuvenate the body. However, the citizens of Calcutta are under the following pressures at the moment:*
>
> *1st—Air. Pressure per square inch: 15 pounds.*
> *2nd—Malaria. Pressure per square inch: 20 pounds.*
> *3rd—Patented medicines. Pressure per square inch: 30 pounds.*
> *4th—University. Pressure per square inch: 50 pounds.*
> *5th—Income tax. Pressure per square inch: 80 pounds.*
> *6th—Municipal tax. Pressure per square inch: 1 tonne.*
>
> *The relief of a few inches of air pressure would be like a handful of twigs on an already heavy load. Thus starting this Chair in Calcutta might not have particularly beneficial or noticeable effects on the residents of this city. In the hills of Shimla the air pressure as well as other pressures is comparatively much less. Hence it would be better if the said Chair was appointed at Shimla because the effects would be more noticeable there.*

The government remained silent on the issue after this. The meteorological department managed to survive this particular crisis.

The issue of the cyclone however remained unresolved.

A scientist published an article in *Nature* once. His theory was that the cyclone was dispersed by the gravitational pull of an invisible comet. These are all mere guesses.[8]

Even now the issue raises cycloney debates in the scientific community. At the British Association convention at Oxford, a German professor presented an erudite paper on the "runaway cyclone" phenomenon which astounded his peers. According to the Professor, "A cyclone is merely a form of the atmosphere. Let us first examine how the atmosphere came into being. When the Earth was simply molten metallic matter which had come out of the sun, it did not have an atmosphere. How oxygen, nitrogen, and hydrogen came together out of this molten matter is still one of the mysteries of creation. Even more mysterious and fascinating is the evolution of life. Let us assume that the atmosphere somehow came into being. What is an even greater problem is how this atmosphere does not dissolve and vanish into space. This is because of Earth's gravitational pull. Gravity works according to relative mass. That which is heavier is subject to more gravitational force and is therefore relatively tied to its own position on the earth. The lighter object is less influenced by gravity and is therefore relatively free. This is why when we mix oil and water, the lighter oil generally floats to the surface. Hydrogen being lighter tries to escape the Earth's atmosphere—however it is not completely free of the gravitational pull. However we doubt if the truth of relative mass is applicable to areas other than physics. For instance, in the country called India, the men are heavier and relatively free, the women who are relatively light are tied to the domestic space. In any case, only matter remains attached to the Earth by virtue of its gravity. After the death of matter it is free of the Earth. When man gives up his ghost the force of gravity no longer restricts his movement. Some people say that even in death man is not free of Earth, because even ghosts have to move under the commands of the Theosophical society. In the case of matter however it is incorrect to say that it attains five states—because we see only three. When bombarded with radium matter breaks down into three states—alpha, beta, and gamma. Thus when matter is broken down the non-matter escapes into an unknown space. While living however, it is impossible to escape the force of gravity."

While the professor did provide a scientific explanation of why matter does not escape into space, he failed to point out why the cyclone suddenly disappeared in the Bay of Bengal.

The truth of the matter is known to only one person in this world—me. In the next part I will give a detailed explanation of the phenomenon.

Part II

I fell extremely ill some years ago. I was in bed for almost a month. The doctor said that a sea journey was absolutely necessary; without it I would not survive another spell of the illness. So I decided to journey to Ceylon.

The illness had taken its toll on my once abundant hair. One day my eight-year-old daughter came up to me and asked: "Daddy, what is an island?" Before I could answer she took hold of the few locks of hair left on my otherwise smooth head surface and said: "Here are the islands." After a while she said: "I have put a bottle of 'Kuntal Keshari' in your bag. Use it every day during your voyage; otherwise in the salty sea-water even these few islands would vanish."

The story of how "Kuntal Keshari" was invented is very interesting. A British Sahib came to India with his circus troupe. The star attraction of the circus was a lion with a huge and lustrous black mane. By a stroke of misfortune the lion lost its thick hair during the voyage to India because of a microbial disease. When the ship landed one could not see much difference between the lion and a hairless street dog. The helpless circus manager prostrated himself before a Sanyasi, touched his feet, and with folded hands asked for a solution. A Christian, and an Englishman at that! The Sanyasi was impressed with the man's devotion and as blessing gave him a bottle of oil whose formulae had come to the Sanyasi in a dream. This is the same oil which later became famous as "Kuntal Keshari." By applying this oil the lion got its mane back within a week. For all bald men and their partners this oil holds a special fascination. This news was published for the public good in all the newspapers of the country. The leading monthly magazine even featured the news on its cover.

On 28 September I set sail on the *Chusan*. The first two days were uneventful and pleasant. On the 1st however the sea assumed a strange and hostile form and the sea-breeze stopped completely. Even the surface of the sea remained taut. We were all struck by the sad look on the Captain's face. He told us that very soon an extremely violent cyclone would crash upon us. Being far from the coast, our future was now in God's hands.

Soon thereafter the sky became overcast with thick black clouds. It became dark almost instantly and some strong winds from afar came and struck our ship several times. I have only a faint idea of what happened thereafter. All of a sudden it was as if the angry giants of yore had returned and come to destroy the earth. The sounds of the cyclone winds mixed with the sounds of the angry sea and made the music of destruction all around us. Waves upon waves hit our boat and rocked it from all sides. A huge wave took away our mast and life-boat with it. Our last day was upon us.

One remembers one's loved ones when his final moments are near. I remembered my loved ones, and strangely, even my daughter's joke about my sparse hair:

"Daddy, I have put a bottle of 'Kuntal Keshari' in your bag."

Suddenly I remembered what I had read recently in a scientific journal about the effects of oil on water waves. I remembered that oil calms the surface of moving water. I took out my bottle of "Kuntal Keshari" that very moment from my bag and with great difficulty climbed up to the deck. I saw that a gigantic mountain-like wave was coming to strike us down.

I abandoned all hope, opened the cap of the "Kuntal Keshari" bottle and threw it at the sea. Like magic the sea became calm, and the wonderful cooling oil even calmed the entire atmosphere. The sun came up in a second. Thus we were spared from a certain death and it is for this reason the cyclone never reached Calcutta. How many thousands were saved from an untimely death simply by this one bottle of hair oil, who can say?[9]

*   *   *

Six months after this story the following scientific explanation was published by *Scientific American.*

The Solution of a Mystery

The vanished cyclone of Calcutta remained so long a mystery to vex the soul of meteorologists. We are now glad to be able to offer an explanation of this seeming departure from all known laws that govern atmospheric disturbances. It would appear that a passenger on board the *Chusan* threw overboard a bottle of KUNTALINE while the vessel was in the Bay of Bengal and the storm was at its height. The film of oil spread rapidly over the troubled waters, and produced a wave of condensation, thus counteracting the wave of rarefaction to which the cyclone was due. The superincumbent atmosphere being released from its dangerous tension, subsided into a state of calm. Thus by the merest chance, a catastrophe was averted.

NOTES

1. The author wrote the story twice—once in 1896, when it was called *The Story of the Missing One (Niruddesher Kahini)*, and then rewrote it for a collection (*Abyakto* or *The Unsaid*) in 1921, when it was renamed to *Runaway Cyclone (Palatak Toofan)*. The source text for translation of both the 1896 and 1921 versions of the story was taken from *Sera Kalpabigyan (Best Science Fiction)*, ed. Anish Deb (Kolkata: Ananda Publishers Limited, 2007). The 1921 version has been cross-checked against the reprinted *Abyakto: A collection of popular science of Jagadish Chandra Bose articles and other essays* by Jagadish Chandra Bose (Kolkata: Dey's Publishing, 2009 [1921]). The translation was previously published in the science fiction magazine *Strange Horizons* in September 2013.
2. 1896: *Englishman.*
3. Cyclones have been common phenomena in Bengal. There were four major cyclones in the Bay of Bengal in the 19th century alone. Of these, a particularly destructive one had been the great Calcutta cyclone of 1864 in which over 50,000 lives were lost. The Meteorological Department in Kolkata was established after this cyclone. According to the *Encyclopaedia of Hurricanes, Typhoons and Cyclones:*
   Aghast at the Great Calcutta Cyclone's economic and human scope, the British East India Company subsequently established the continent's first weather service, the Indian Meteorological Department. Symbolically headquartered in a rebuilt Calcutta, the service was tasked with tracking threatening Bay of Bengal cyclones through shipping reports and then telegraphing that information to vulnerable coastal areas via a comprehensive network of warning stations [David Longshore, *Encyclopaedia of Hurricanes, Typhoons and Cyclones*, New York: Facts on File, 2008, pp. 257–58].

4. At this point a number of significant lines of the 1896 version have been left out, most significantly the line reported by the Reuters agent to the *Times*: "The Capital of our Indian Empire is in danger." By the time the story was republished with the new title, Calcutta was no longer the capital city.

5. 1896: *Englishman.*

6. 1896: *Daily News.*

7. 1896: *Daily News.*

8. 1896: *Pioneer, Civil and Military Gazette, Statesman.*

9. The 1896 version ended with the italicized section that follows, which has been restored to this combined version here. It was also originally in English.

Thomas Edison's Hypnotizing Machine

Technology, Science Fiction and "Progress"

Ivy Roberts

In 1890, American writer and journalist George Parsons Lathrop approached Thomas Alva Edison, famed inventor and electrician, with an advance contract for a science fiction novel. Lathrop and Edison collaborated casually over the course of the next year. Edison eventually delivered to Lathrop a 30-page manuscript of notes for a novel called "Progress." But Edison's preoccupation with other projects brought the novel "Progress" to a standstill. "Progress" was never published.

Seven years later, Lathrop negotiated a new contract, and "In the Deep of Time" appeared in Sunday editions of American newspapers from December 1896 to February 1897. Pre-release ads described "In the Deep of Time" as "a serial story ... a thrilling novel of a future controlled by electricity." There are many similarities between "Progress" and "In the Deep of Time," in which Edison receives credit as a "collaborator."

One episode stands out. Towards the end, the antagonist attacks the hero with "Nothing Less Than a Hypnotizing Machine!" Is it a blank sheet? A bright light? A weapon? For his climactic battle, Lathrop pits villain against hero, using a symbol of the cinema as a weapon. As a science-fictional weapon or mode of attack, the hypnotizing machine relays contemporary fears of technological progress and spectacle. The hypnotizing machine is a reflection of early cinema culture in general and Edison's vitascope in particular. In this episode, Lathrop speculates on how the cinema will shape the future: as a mind control device.

The relationship between hypnosis and cinema has been well established in film scholarship. Take the psychoanalytic film theory of Metz (1977), Bellour (1979), and Comolli (1980), for instance. Metz theorizes the relationship between film viewing and the state of dreaming. Bellour posits that the cinema itself in technological allegory for hypnotism. Comolli postulates that the cinematic apparatus is an ideology machine. More recently, German literature scholar Stefan Andriopoulos (2014) examined the correlations between late 19th century German culture, cinema, and Mesmerism.

I would like to take a different route. My approach to literature and technology will take us through a cultural history of science fiction. Roger Luckhurst describes just such an approach in his 2005 book: "A cultural history of science fiction will saturate texts … as part of a constantly shifting network that ties together science, technology, social history, and cultural expression with different emphases at different times" (6). Luckhurst's contextual approach acknowledges that science fiction literature exists within a cultural milieu. Ideas flow both ways: from the culture into the literature and vice versa.

Seeing as how Edison chose the loaded term "progress" as the title of his novel, it should already be clear that power and control were important themes for the authors. Lathrop and Edison's articulation of "future controlled by electricity" promotes a vision of progress based on the assumption of technological determinism. The scholarship of historian of technology Leo Marx can also help us out here. In *The Machine in the Garden* (1964), Marx explores the complicated character of technological progress in 19th century America, drawing associations between nature, history, psychology, and national pride. For example, Marx compares the popular idea of the "annihilation of time and space" with the promise that through technology we can gain control over nature: "The extravagance of this sentiment [the annihilation of time and space] apparently is felt to match the sublimity of technological progress" (194). Therefore, according to Marx (and by extension Edison), technological progress defines man's ability to control over the historical path of civilization, and exact power in society.

Edison's "Progress" (1890)

By today's standards, you might call George Parsons Lathrop an Edison groupie. Lathrop was a freelance journalist who frequented Edison's Menlo Park lab. Lathrop's 1890 *Harper's* interview, "Talks with Edison," establishes themes of science-fictionality and technological power through social control that would recur in both "Progress" and "In the Deep of Time." Their conversation described in this article indicates just how closely science fiction and invention are entangled in the technological imagination. During the interview, Edison pulls out a sketchpad, which he describes as his "novel." It contains notes for inventions that he has yet to build. This gesture insinuates the ways in which creativity, invention, and science fiction flow from literature to culture and back.

In that same interview, Lathrop recounts an odd conversation in which Edison describes a truly science-fictional concept—not a technology per se, but a kind of superhuman ability. What if man could control individual atoms? He explained: "I could say to one particular atom in me—call it atom number 4320—go and be part of the rose for a while.... They could be called together again, they would bring back their experiences while they were parts of those different substances, and I should have the benefit of the knowledge." Here, Lathrop relay's Edison's apparent obsession with control and power through the use of technology. All these themes would resurface in the vision of the future "controlled by electricity" described in "Progress" and "In the Deep of Time."

By August of 1891, Edison's commitment to other projects (such as ore mining, phonography, and the invention of the kinetograph) brought his collaboration with Lathrop to an end. For about a year, the collaborators had been passing notes back and forth. The 30-page manuscript, which consists mostly of scattered notes and suggestions for futuristic inventions, is all that remains of the novel "Progress." Some highlights from the manuscript include ocean telegraphy between ships at sea, a fascination with the classical ideal of beauty, and new applications for recording and transmitting information.

Lathrop's "In the Deep of Time" (1896–7)

In 1896, Lathrop secured a new contract for his Edison collaboration. Irving Bacheller's newspaper syndicate, a company that licensed stories and sold them to papers across the country. Five installments appeared in Sunday morning papers beginning in December 1896. "In the Deep of Time" also appears in a UK edition published in *English illustrated* in March/April 1897, with a different set of images. The first part begins with a disclaimer written by Lathrop:

> This story is the result of conversations with Thomas A. Edison, the substance of which he afterwards put into the form of notes written for my use. His suggestions as to inventions and changed mechanical, industrial and social conditions in the future, here embodied, I understand to be simply hints as to what might possibly be accomplished. Mr. Edison assumes no further responsibility for them. For the story itself I alone am responsible.

"In the Deep of Time" opens on the last days of the 19th century: "Near the close of the nineteenth century, the Society of Futurity was formed for scientific experimentation on a grand scale." The hero of the story is Gerald Bemis. Heartbroken after being rejected by his true love, Eva Pryor, Bemis signs on as test subject for a scientific experiment in "vivification": "a scheme for prolonging life by freezing." Bemis wakes up 300 years later to a technological utopia governed by the Society of Futurity.

The Society for Futurity matches Bemis with a new love interest, Electra: "She bowed graciously, and came forward with a smile so absolutely sincere that I could not recall having beheld the like of it before…." It's love at first sight. Bemis is immediately dumbstruck by her beauty and grace. Lathrop continues: "She was exquisite, serene, commanding, and absolutely without humbug." Electra represents the pinnacle of Classical beauty.

Now, every story needs an antagonist. Hammerfleet is "a tall man, black bearded, almost forbidding in his gravity," "patronizing," sinister, and threatening. Since Electra and Hammerfleet are betrothed, Bemis makes it a love triangle. Electra describes to Bemis how both she and Hammerfleet are "Children of the State": "persons of unusual physical and mental endowments were permitted to become at the age of forty, after passing through examinations and inspection, and having their internal condition carefully ascertained by X-rays. They were then suitably mated in marriage to someone of equal standard, with a view to perpetuating and increasing the elements of the race." Electra insinuates that her marriage to Hammerfleet was prearranged; the government designated them as a matched pair based on physical and mental aptitudes.

"'This is Electra,' Said Our Guardian" from "In the Deep of Time." *English Illustrated* 16, 1896/1897.

"Improved Conditions"

The opening of part 6, entitled "Improved Conditions," describes a future society transformed by science and technology while enriched by traditional American values. Technology can make life easier, but it can't replace human ingenuity: "No machinery, however ingenious, and no amount of invention, however marvelous, will ever take the place of will-power and character." For Lathrop, entertainment and communication technologies create a future in which privileged access facilitates a lifestyle of both solitude and connectivity. He peppers the story with kinetoscopes, vitascopes, telephones, and telegraphs. Lathrop's ideal future society operates by remote, so that individuals need not mingle in crowds or rub shoulders with the disadvantaged.

The narrative constructs a frame from which to view the future as an outcome of mastery over nature through scientific control. Lathrop's story features three separate scientific societies: the Society of Futurity, the Darwinian Society of Para, and the Society of Harmonic Curves. Each serve different purposes in the story, and their storylines do not overlap or intersect. Repeatedly placing the reader in contact with elite scientific societies suggests the rigidity of class structure in Lathrop's technocratic society. In this universe, technology supports the autonomy of the individual. But the elitism of the societies suggests that many individuals are restricted from access to such a lifestyle.

The Darwinian Society of Para and the Society of Harmonic Curves both manifest directly from Edison's *Progress* notes. Both societies represent the power of the scientific elite to control population. Progress includes a note concerning the Darwinian society, offering it as a suggestion to Lathrop for further development. He wrote: "the 80th generation would equal in intelligence and beauty the Bushmen tribe of Africa" (Edison 1890, 3). From Edison's notes, Lathrop described a method of social Darwinism and artificial selection by which apes became a slave class. Lathrop describes the Society of Harmonic Curves, also from Edison's notes, that developed a formula for the perfect human being. Bemis narrates a story of scientific progress emphasizing the spectacular power of technology to build a better future. But in the process, Lathrop constructs a society in which technological infrastructure has created the necessity for social stratification. The scientific elite engineer subaltern classes in contrast to their superior human beings.

Chapter 8, "Sea Signaling—The Final Flight," which is anthologized in this volume, opens with a practical demonstration of an advanced communications technology (i.e., cloud telegraphy) working alongside science-fictional transportation technologies (i.e., air ships). Lathrop intersperses speculative social advancements as well. Casual references to English as the universal language and Christianity as the preferred religion indicate overtones of American Imperialism. The belief in the superiority of industrialized nations aligns with underlying themes of eugenics, Classical aesthetics, and government control apparent elsewhere in Lathrop's story.

Through a scattered narrative peppered with globetrotting and disconnected subplots, "In the Deep of Time" reads as a dramatic backdrop for the promotion of experimental technologies. Haven woken from "vivification" in New York, Bemis travels by electric rail to Chicago to view "the impressive ruins of various world's fairs," to Buffalo, and then to various European capitals "and other parts of the globe." Mentions are also made of Mars and South America.

A Hypnotizing Machine

Bemis' circumnavigation serves mainly for the purpose of explaining futuristic transportation technologies. All the while, Hammerfleet pursues Bemis and his entourage with murderous intent. When they land in exotic Norway, Bemis decides to sightsee the fjords. This will be Hammerfleet's perfect opportunity! Lathrop identifies the hypnotizing machine explicitly as a weapon and as a regulated medical device: "He [Hammerfleet] unrolled in front of me a peculiar glittering curtain that uncurled from a rod in his hand, dropping thence to the ground…. I gazed helplessly at the glittering thing; and it was evident that my enemy was putting it in operation. The next moment I lost all consciousness of myself, as myself…."

The hypnotizing machine appears in Edison's "Progress" (1890) as a passing thought. It is just a note for future exploration, indicating many possible applications and interpretations. "Progress" is peppered with notes for all sorts of instruments: practical, industrial, and entertaining. The hypnotizing machine could have been a tool for mind control or perhaps an instrument for the measurement of psychological acuity.

The purpose to which Lathrop applies the hypnotizing machine is multifaceted. In one sense, as the above passage indicates, it is a weapon. In another, the hypnotizing machine is a tool for medical use: "These machines are used medically, for

"Nothing Less Than a Hypnotizing Machine" from "In the Deep of Time." Bacheller Syndicate. January 1897.

the investigation of nervous disorders and weak organisms; and they are also applied officially to the examination of candidates for the civil service and for high office; but the laws of the world and all the nations forbid their use in any other way." In a third sense, the visual representations of the hypnotizing machine in both U.S. and UK versions of the story bear little resem-

"A Hypnotizing Machine" from "In the Deep of Time." *English Illustrated* 17, 1897.

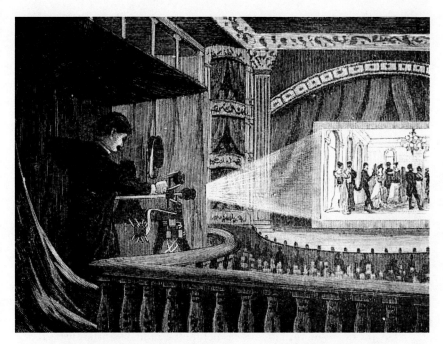

"The Kinetoscope Stereopticon," *Scientific American* (October 31, 1896): 325.

blance to a medical instrument. The hypnotizing machine by far resembles an entertainment device in the manner of a theatrical curtain or screen projection. Early cinema machines such as the kinetograph and kinetoscope are discussed in both "Progress" and "In the Deep of Time." But by 1897, the vitascope was on its way to superseding the kinetoscope. The kinetoscope (later the nickelodeon) was a single-viewer novelty. The vitascope enabled mass entertainment by making it possible to project scenes onto a screen hung in a vaudeville auditorium. Lathrop mentions the vitascope several times in "In the Deep of Time" as a 23rd century entertainment technology. If you can imagine yourself as a 19th century contemporary reader, such references indicate that the cinema will become a key public and home venue in the future.

This illustration of the vitascope from *Scientific American* (1896) for instance bears peculiar resemblance. In this sense, one could make the analogy between Hammerfleet as the projectionist and Bemis as the stunned, "astonished" spectator, to borrow the phraseology of cinema historian Tom Gunning (1989). In "An Aesthetic of Astonishment," Gunning discusses the reports and subsequent mythology about the audience who ran screaming from the early projections of the Lumiere film, *The Arrival of a Train at the Station* (*L'arrivée d'un train en gare de La Ciotat*, 1895). Gunning shows how early film projections stunned their audiences, and how a culture of "aston-ishment" grew up around the image of the cinema as a result. Hammerfleet's hypnotizing machine consists of "a peculiar glittering curtain." As Bemis narrates: "I gazed helplessly at the glittering thing.... The next moment I lost all consciousness of myself, as myself.... His [Hammer-fleet's] object had been to hypnotise me back to the nineteenth century ... then seclude me personally and keep me permanently hypnotized under this delusion." During the initial promotion of the Vitascope in 1896–7, editorial commentary in newspapers had yet to settle on a conventional language of the cinema. Was it a sheet? A screen? A canvas? In any case, the promotional rhetoric foregrounded just how lifelike the cinematic images were. The *New York Journal* commented: "For two hours dancing girls and groups of figures, all of life size, seemed to exist as realities on the big white screen..." (*New York Journal* 4 April 1896. quoted in Musser 2002, 14). The *New York Times* wrote: "When the hall was darkened last night a buzzing and whirring were heard in the turret, and an unusually bright light fell on the screen" ("Edison's Vitascope Cheered: Projecting Kinetoscope Exhibited for First Time at Koster & Bial's." *New York Times* April 24, 1896). Exhibitors took a more practical approach, identifying the screen as a sheet or canvas: "When the machine is started by the operator, the bare canvas before the audience instantly becomes a stage, upon which living beings move about...." (Raff and Gammon, Vitas-cope, 2. Quoted in Musser 2002, 15; See also diagram in Musser 1991, 127).

Imagine yourself as a contemporary reader. In a way, the cinema resem-bles a magnificently bright light with the potential of blinding, or mesmer-izing its unwary audience. Not only are the movies an astonishing spectacle; they are also a bright light shining into a rapidly closing decade, heralding a 20th century ruled by electricity.

BIBLIOGRAPHY

Andriopoulos, Stefan. 2008. *Possessed: Hypnotic Crimes, Corporate Fiction, and the Invention of Cinema*. U of Chicago P.
Bergstrom, Janet. 1979. "Alternation, Segmentation, Hypnosis: Interview with Raymond Bel-lour." *Camera Obscura* 3, no. 4: 71–103.
Carlson, W. Bernard, and Michael E. Gorman. 1990. "Understanding Invention as a Cognitive Process: The Case of Thomas Edison and Early Motion Pictures, 1888–91." *Social Studies of Science* 20, no. 3: 387–430.
Collins, Theresa, Lisa Gitelman, and Gregory Jankunis. 2002. *Thomas Edison and Modern America: A Brief History with Documents*. Palgrave Macmillan.
Csicsery-Ronay, Istvan. 2008. *The Seven Beauties of Science Fiction*. Wesleyan UP.
Gunning, Tom. 1989/2004. "An Aesthetic of Astonishment: Early Film and the (in) Credulous Spectator." *Film Theory: Critical Concepts in Media and Cultural Studies* 3: 76–95.
Luckhurst, Roger. 2005. *Science Fiction*. Polity.
Luckhurst, Roger. 2012. "Laboratories for Global Space-Time: Science-Fictionality and the World's Fairs, 1851–1939." *Science Fiction Studies* 39.3: 385–400.
Marx, Leo. 1964. *The Machine in the Garden: Technology and the Pastoral Ideal in America*. Oxford UP.

Marx, Leo. 1987. "Does Improved Technology Mean Progress." *Technology Review* 90, no. 1: 33–41.

Moore, Paul S. 2012. "Advance Newspaper Publicity for the Vitascope and the Mass Address of Cinema's Reading Public." *A Companion to Early Cinema*: 381–397.

Musser, Charles. 1994. *The Emergence of Cinema: The American Screen to 1907*. Vol. 1. U of California P.

Perschon, Mike D. 2012. "The Steampunk Aesthetic: Technofantasies in a Neo-Victorian Retrofuture." PhD. Diss. U of Alberta.

Smith, Merritt Roe, and Leo Marx, eds. 1994. *Does Technology Drive History?: The Dilemma of Technological Determinism*. MIT Press.

"In the Deep of Time" (1896–7), Synopsis and Chapter VIII (of VIII): "Sea Signaling—The Final Flight"

GEORGE PARSONS LATHROP

The story, as told by the author, is the result or conversation with Thomas A. Edison, the substance of which Mr. Edison afterwards put into the form of notes written for the author's use. Mr. Edison's suggestions as to inventions, etc., are understood to be simply hints as to what might possibly be accomplished. For the story itself the author is responsible.

Synopsis

Gerald Bemis, at the end of the nineteenth century, having been unsuccessful in his suit for the hand or Eva Pryor, allows himself to be "vivificated" by the Society of Futurity. By a newly-discovered process, animation is suspended, and Bemis is placed in a hermetically sealed cylinder. Three centuries later the cylinder is opened by the chiefs of the society then in control and Bemis is revived. Among many wonderful discoveries he finds that telegraphic communication with the planet Mars has been established. Word comes from Mars that one Bronson, who had started for that planet in an anti-gravity machine, has not arrived there, and later that a messenger from Mars is on his way to the earth. Meanwhile Bemis discovers that Eva Pryor, who really loved him, was also "vivificated." He meets her and finds that his love for her has vanished. He falls in love with Electra, a beautiful twenty-second century girl, who is in turn loved by Hammerfleet, a man of her own period. The messenger from Mars, Zorlin, arrives with Bronson, and all travel in an airship to Chicago. There Bemis proposes to Electra. She explains that she is a "Child of the State," and has been affianced to Hammerfleet. The latter overhears the conversation, but represses his jealousy. He unites with Bemis to make an excursion with him to see the country, and lures him into a vast plant of moving machinery near Buffalo. Hammerfleet then escapes, leaving Bemis in great danger in the midst of a network of wheels, levers and cranks. Bemis is rescued by Zorlin and Electra, who stop the machinery, and Hammerfleet is banished from Electra's presence. Bemis again urges Electra to marry him. She will not consent to this, but agrees to take a trip with Zorlin and Bemis in an airship around the world. After they have started from Fire Island, Bemis discovers that Eva Pryor has been smuggled aboard by Electra.

Chapter VIII
Sea Signaling—The Final Flight.

We had noticed at times when the sky was cloudy, both by day and by night, certain periodic flashes of light appearing on the clouds in quick succession. Electra told me that these were caused by the system of cloud-telegraphy now in use, and to anyone familiar with the Morse alphabet, as I was, it was easy to read the messages so flashed about the heavens, though I could not understand those which were in cipher. Most of them were of a general nature, and had nothing to do with us. But at intervals we observed that telegraphic inquiries were being made on the clouds about our party, and that certain persons whom we were not able to identify— most of them signing their communications with numerals instead of names—were answering those inquiries. I may as well jot down in this place the information I gathered as to the mode of signaling by cloud-flash and by other new methods.

Powerful electric rays are, by means of lenses, brought to thin pen-

"Cloud Telegraphy" from "In the Deep of Time." Bacheller Syndicate. January 1897.

cils of intense light. A single one of these is then projected upward against a cloud. A controlling shutter in the path of the beam of light interrupts it at will, so that it may be made to show long or short flashes on the clouds. Words are thus illuminated in the sky, and made to shine in the zenith repeatedly, until an answering reflection is obtained. The chief use of this cloud telegraph is, of course, on the sea, between ships and "steamers"—as they are still called, notwithstanding that they do not use steam—or for airboats. Conversation may be carried on in this way between vessels many miles apart, and a message received by one can be transmitted to others, so that inquiries and replies fly all around the globe and to remote parts of the ocean. The system was found useful in those later voyages to the North Pole, which have not been followed up since a general exploration of the open Arctic Sea was effected. It has also saved many lives, prevented collisions and caught many fugitive criminals. Sailing vessels are provided with a water paddle to drive the necessary electric generating mechanism for signaling when the ship is in motion.

In some of the much-traveled sea regions, another method of communication is used for the daytime. A sailcloth woven with metallic wires is hung between the tips or two masts, and is connected to a special electric generating apparatus producing waves of extreme sharpness and great intensity, that follow each other at the rate of 700 per second. An electric stress thus propagated to infinite distance is, at moderate distances, strong enough to be collected by the metalized sail of another vessel. One ship, for example, wishes to know whether there is another within the area of signaling, but out of sight. The musical note formed by electric inductive waves is set going, and by means of a key is stopped and started again at will. Other vessels in the area have watchers, who, at intervals, listen to an exquisitely sensitive telephone made selectively sensitive to waves of exactly 700 per second. This is brought about by a tuning fork attachment to the diaphragm, tuned exactly to respond to waves at that rate; hence, although the part of the waves collected by the sail cloth is many million times less than could be gathered if it were close to the signaling ship, yet the tuning fork collects successive waves until the amplitude of vibration is sufficient to cause audibility. The signaling current is continuous for several seconds. Then the transmitting vessel stops it, and connects the sail with its receiving apparatus, to listen for a return wave. After the preliminary signals have been exchanged, conversation is carried on in the usual way. It is slow, or course, owing to the time necessary for the successive impulses to rise to the point of audibility; but the method is very accurate and reliable in all but foggy or rainy weather.

For foggy weather signaling, there is still another ingenious device. A circular hole is cut in the vessel below the water line, about two feet in diameter and closed by a circular steel plate or diaphragm one-eighth of an inch thick. On the inner side there is a thick iron chamber, completely inclosing [*sic*] the space behind the diaphragm, and here is placed a small, shrill whistle worked by compressed air or steam and controllable by a valve or key. Alongside of this apparatus is another diaphragm made like the first, but there extends from the center of it a very short, fine steel wire, highly stretched, the other end of which is connected to a sensitive diaphragm from which tubes lead to both ears of the signalman. By an adjustable attachment, this steel wire can be regulated to greater or less tension, as a violin string is, and it is tuned to respond to the note given out by the whistles on other steamers, which are all of precisely the same pitch. In fogs, the signalman alternately sounds the whistle and listens for a return; his receiving apparatus not being responsive to any other sound than that to which it is tuned—beyond the rippling or dashing of water on the sides of the vessel, and the movement of the propelling shutter machinery, which are continuous, and do not interfere with the signalman's hearing a periodic musical sound. The sound waves or the whistle are communicated to the water by the steel diaphragm in front, and travel through the sea just as in air, but much farther, since the conductivity of water for sound is greater than that of air. One of the most important uses of this machine on large passenger ships is to ascertain the direction of approaching vessels with exactness, and for this purpose they have two sets of diaphragms on opposite sides of the ship, connected telephonically.

Still another contrivance for preventing collisions, or giving notice of the nearness of icebergs or of derelicts, impresses me. This is "the automatic pilot," a small cigar-shaped copper vessel some fifteen feet long and twenty-four inches at its greatest diameter, having within it an electric motor, which drives a screw propeller at its end. From the masthead a reel passes two insulated wires, which run from the ship's dynamo electric engine down to the cigar-shaped "pilot," to which they are joined side by side, about two feet apart. They not only carry electricity to the motor of the pilot, but also cause the pilot to move in harmony with the steamer's course. As soon as a fog appears the "pilot" is launched; and the current passing to it through the wires from the masthead revolves the motor in the little pilot-craft and sends her shooting ahead of the ship or steamer. If the pilot tends to veer from a straight line, one of the wires becomes more taut than the other and so affects the steering apparatus as to bring the copper boat back to the right course. I forgot to say that these wires or cables, although having only about the thickness of a knitting-needle, are twisted together from a number of very fine steel wire; and, as the speed of the pilot is greater than the ship's and keeps her about half a mile ahead of the latter, the wires always tend to become taut. If the pilot strikes any obstacle, the fact becomes known at once to the man at the dynamo, and the engine is stopped and reversed without loss of time. Many serious accidents have been avoided by this precaution.

The automatic pilot boat is taken on board again, of course, when the fog clears.

It will be evident to anyone who reads this little sketch of my first experiences and impressions that, with such means of cloud flashes and sea signaling—besides which, it must be mentioned, the construction of ocean cables was now very cheap and great numbers of private cable lines were in use—it would not be possible for our party to escape indefinitely from vigilant and determined pursuers. A good pursuer, by means of the omnipresent telegraph wires and signal systems, could tap the whole earth as a wood pecker taps a tree for his prey; and, moreover, the French Submarine Society for mapping the bottom of the sea had its under-water boats and observers in all parts of the world, liable to bob up to the surface of the deep anywhere, so that, if these were to be utilized, one of them might locate our position on or over the ocean at any instant.

However, we led our friends and enemies a pretty good chase, and kept it up many weeks. On our return from the Antarctic Commonwealth to Patagonia (now an important manufacturing country), we ascertained that Hammerfleet had survived his cyclone wreck—having, in feet, been picked up by a submarine geographical boat—and that he was using the wires, the clouds and metalized sail telegraph to trace us. We therefore concluded to run quickly over to China and Japan, and were well repaid by the evidences of immense progress which we saw there, the same improvements that I have already described having been introduced in those countries. English, now the universal language, has been pretty well domesticated in China, though it still cuts some pigeon wings in the dance of rustic lips. What interested Eva and me greatly, among other things, was the simple plan of making ice here, as in India and all hot countries, by hoisting balloons which carry watertanks 20,000 feet into the air, freeze the water and bring it down again, a constant relay of balloons steadily renewing the supply.

As we passed on through Turkey, a peaceful, flourishing Christian country, through strong and rehabilitated Greece and Italy, to German and France and England, we were pleased to observe the wonderful effects obtained by the particular societies, each devoted to a specific fruit or flower, which now produced fruits of a lusciousness beyond belief, and had so changed flowers that the mysterious something in them called harmonic grouping gave us an indescribable sensation of beauty totally wanting in the flowers known to the ancients. In art, also, the Society of Harmonic Curves has brought about great changes. The human form, in this day, is—through wise cultivation—much more beautiful than the average of old times, besides which, painters and sculptors, owing to an improved knowledge of curve harmony, develop from the living model an idea of loveliness and perfection formerly approached only by the Greeks and even by them approached but partially.

This development of beauty seems to have come from a radically altered, more restful mode of life, a purer application of supernatural religion to existence, and a better realization of the laws of natural science as in accord with religion. So, too, and from similar causes, the great changes in manufacturing systems have benefited the race. Owing to systems for the electric distribution of power over great areas, the industrial economy of very early times has been restored. Now among the countless homes of the people, those of the mechanics are each provided with its little workshop where only one operation in any particular manufacture is carried out. A single part of any machine is passed from house to house until finished, and is then returned to the great assembling shop to be gathered into the complete machine. The profound change in the moral, mental, and social condition of the working people effected by a return once more to occupation in the home, instead of the promiscuous association in large factories, has been one of the most potent agents in improving the state of the population, lessening crime, drunkenness, and other evils; stimulating true education, and restoring to labor its natural poetry and idyllic character.

Thanks to the plastic process of building, even the poorest worker has his own home. With the children of mechanics learning their trade at home from the earliest years, highly trained workmen have been developed, who produce mechanisms and fabrics once thought to be impossible and of a cheapness that is surprising. In those branches of the mechanic arts where labor cannot be subdivided, great factories still hold their place. But they are automatic—like that in which Hammerfleet had tried to entrap me—and need the attendance of only one watcher; so perfected are the science and art of automatic action, by the higher type of intellect of the modern mechanic and artisan.

There are many other things of which I would like to speak, but I must bring this memorandum to a close before leaving earth, as I am about to do, for a voyage and an absence which may be permanent.

With all the improvements in machinery, inventions and modes of life, human nature, also, has somewhat improved, but it has not radically altered. Its passions, good and bad, remain much the same, together with its weakness, fickleness and treachery. Noting this, and having seen so much of the world even in our rapid journeys, I began to grow a trifle tired of it all and to yearn for something new and for a rest. Moreover, Zorlin had stirred up so much controversy by his private and public talks wherever he went, regarding his large cosmic views in religion, philosophy and science, that he, also, longed for return to his native planet.

It was when we had arrived at this state of mind that Graemantle suddenly came up with us, just as we alighted from an airship in Norway. After getting us under thorough observation by a number of emissaries, he had obtained from the World Committee of Twenty an order for Electra, as an American "Child of the State," to return with him; and he now put her under a mildly paternal sort of arrest. A day or two later Hammerfleet arrived; surprising me while I was taking a walk in a quiet spot outside of Christiania. He looked haggard, vindictive and terrible. I nerved myself to resist whatever attack he might make; but I was not prepared for the particular weapon he produced. He unrolled in front of me a peculiar glittering curtain that uncurled from a rod in his hand, dropping thence to the ground; and in a moment l recognized that it was something I had heard of but had not seen before—nothing less than a hypnotizing machine! These machines are used medically, for the investigation of nervous disorders and weak organisms; and they are also applied officially to the examination of candidates for the civil service and for high office; but the laws of the world and all the nations forbid their use in any other way.

I gazed helplessly at the glittering thing; and it was evident that my enemy was putting it in operation. The next moment I lost all consciousness of myself, as my self. What would have happened, I do not know; for I came almost immediately back to myself, and found that Graemantle, Zorlin, and Electra had come to my rescue in the nick of time; having been guided by Zorlin, whose Kurol mind had enabled him to divine from a little distance what was going on.

This episode settled Hammerfleet's fate. He was promptly sent back to the United States in irons, and isolated in one of the penal districts. His merely using the hypnotizing machine was sufficient reason for this, and when he saw the game was up he confessed that his object had been to hypnotize me back into the nineteenth century, into my glass chrysalis in Gladwin's laboratory, then seclude me personally and keep me permanently hypnotized under this delusion, which would have been practically the same as death, for this world.

All through our journeyings, I had been more and more impressed with Eva Pryor's gentleness and winning qualities; and, from wondering at first whether I had not made a mistake as to my real feeling toward her, I came to the positive conclusion that I had done so. Now that we had completed our globe voyage, and Zorlin was pining for his home on Kuro, or Mars, I had a candid little conversation with her and wound up by asking her: "How would you like to carry out actually what you once said you would do—go to Mars with me? The Kurols don't marry; and we can act with entire consistency, by being brother and sister, up there."

"Delightful," she cried, grasping my hand. "Will Zorlin take us?"

A Stellar express car was ordered immediately; and I have barely time now to jot down here that we are about to depart. Whether I shall ever come back I do not know; but my mind is quite made up that I will not come back alone.

Postscript by the Editor

A.D. 2201.

Bemis has returned to earth, and married Eva. "It is worth while," he says, "to have been vivificated for three hundred years and to have gone to Mars, in order to find out a woman's mind—and my own.

The Emotional Birth of AI in "Moxon's Master"

Rob Welch

While the concept of human-like robots can be traced over an extended period of cultural history, the idea of artificial intelligence is a relatively recent one. In 1899, Ambrose Bierce published a short story containing the kernel of this extraordinary advance in the pages of the *San Francisco Examiner*. The story, "Moxon's Master," focuses on what separates self-conscious, biological life from machine replications of that life. "Moxon's Master" (1899) belongs to a distinct trend in thinking about artificial intelligence that erupted in late 19th century American fiction. Bierce's work contributed to a nascent conversation in science fiction and popular science about artificial intelligence.

Before science fiction authors began contemplating the human-robot relationship, the space between animate and inanimate had been explored throughout mythology and folklore. In classical myth, many characters transform; Daphne becomes a tree and Philomela becomes a nightingale. Alternatively, objects can also transform into living things. Ovid relays the legend of Pygmalion, in which a marble figure becomes a living woman. In Jewish folklore, the golem, another inanimate figure, is given the power of motion only to remain a tool for the one who controls it. These examples establish a distinction that would continue to play out in the pages of science fiction. The artificial creature in Shelley's *Frankenstein* (1818) is fully cognizant and, in modern terms, self-programmed. By comparison, the automaton in E.T.A Hoffman's "The Sandman" (1816) is more a working model of the human, not a replacement for it. The tradition of human-like robots continues in science fiction cinema. In *Forbidden Planet* (1956), Robby the Robot appears humanoid in design, but remains golem-like, under the command of humans around him, in particular his master, Dr. Morbius. In *Solo: A Star Wars Story* (2018),

Lando Calrissian's droid co-pilot, L3-37, is independent and sassy, while also considering "herself" in a complicated emotional relationship with her human partner. This distinction between implement and individual is not precisely one of linear development through time, but rather a consistent dichotomy.

The representation of robots in late 19th century American fiction tended to focus on specialized machines with limited functionality and no potential for self-control.

One noteworthy example can be found in Edward Ellis' *The Steam Man of the Prairies* (1868). Ellis' invention is a steam engine in the shape of a person. The representation of the human-like robot in this case is significant for the fact that the character has no other special abilities apart from being able to do what a steam engine does. Ellis' characters overcome difficulties throughout the plot by having access to this handy, personal locomotive—a machine in the shape of a large man. Yet, in "Moxon's Master" Bierce upends the trend of representing the robot as a mindless tool by re-introducing the problematics of investing the artificial with intelligence, will, and emotion. The inclusion of emotion into the equation of self-consciousness is the real groundbreaking contribution Bierce makes to the genre of science fiction.

Ambrose Bierce

Ambrose Bierce was a prolific writer with a career spanning nearly half a century, and characterizing his work as functioning through a single method or with a sole purpose would be misleading. Besides historical, war-related fiction and early contributions to science fiction, Bierce also wrote several stories which capitalize on the late Victorian interest in the occult. His "ghost stories" are noteworthy for their reserve in employing the kind of reversals which are otherwise typical for much of Bierce's work.

In "The Damned Thing," for instance, testimony is given of a man who has been killed by an invisible creature. The limitation of the human senses and the triumph of human ingenuity provide consistent themes in "The Damned Thing." The narrator insists that the invisible being's exterior must fall outside the range of visual spectrum available to human sight. Bierce draws on hard science to inform a narrative that would otherwise be a straightforward ghost story. In his criticism of Bierce's work, Matthew A. Taylor argues that the themes of science and the supernatural in "The Damned Thing" reflects a change typical of the time. Advancement in knowledge and societal shifts due to industrialization caused people to reassess what they knew about the world. Taylor explains: "The mid- to late nineteenth century ghosts and materialist science were mutually possessed, each haunted by the other" (416). Historian Minsoo Kang also notes shifts during the 19th century in ideas about machines coming to life. At first, such stories are related to the occult, about the possession of objects by animating, supernatural spirits. Later, life is associated with machines as they are seen more and more as equal (or superior) replacements for the human (2011, 225). A similar sort of questioning about the symbiosis of human and machine are evident in "Moxon's Master."

"Moxon's Master"

"Moxon's Master" is split into two movements, both strongly flavored by gothic sensibilities. The story opens on a stormy night, with Moxon and the narrator conversing about metaphysics and philosophy in a parlor room before a crackling fire. A noise from Moxon's private workroom disrupts their conversation. Moxon goes to investigate, and returns with a freshly wounded face. The narrator stifles his curiosity, and their discussion continues as they contemplate the nature of life, machine, and autonomy. The second part of the story consists of the narrator returning home, still deep in thought. Along the way, he is inspired enough by his reflections on their talk to return to Moxon's house to share a fresh perspective. Through the machine-shop window, the narrator observes Moxon and a mysterious stranger playing chess. Bierce describes the strange chess-player:

> He was apparently not more than five feet in height, with proportions suggesting those of a gorilla—tremendous breadth of shoulders, thick, short neck and broad, squat head, which had a tangled growth of black hair and was topped by a crimson fez. A tunic of the same color, belted tightly to the waist, reached the seat—apparently a box—upon which he sat; his legs and feet were not seen. His left forearm appeared to rest in his lap; he moved his pieces with his right hand, which seemed disproportionately long [Bierce 1910, 100].

The narrator's curiosity stuns him into silent observation of the game. When Moxon announces checkmate, the "automaton chess-player" goes berserk. In a fit of rage, the machine murders its master.

The Metaphysical Discussion: Part One

In Bierce's story, the two friends differ on the matter of consciousness, debating whether independent control is a necessary extension of what separates the human from anything else. Throughout the conversation in the first part, Moxon goes to great lengths to posit that organization for purposeful ends equates to thought; in this view, a vining plant that reaches for a higher point to grasp might be defined as sentient. Moxon's allegory sets the stage for the reader to consider life beyond the boundaries of the human. The question of whether a human is a machine, or if a machine could be human, has real significance in the context of the changes that were taking place at the turn of the century: factory time, Taylorism, and eugenics in particular.

Bierce's callback to a perspective associated with the Enlightenment is particularly pertinent to the author and his audience. As Moxon and his guest chat through the first segment of the story, the inventor defers to philosophical and scientific sources to support his contention about how narrow are our definitions for intelligent life. He paraphrases Herbert Spencer and John Stuart Mill. Moxon's premise, however, resembles a metaphor drawn by a much earlier philosopher, Thomas Hobbes. "Moxon's Master" begins with the narrator posing the question, "Do you really think a machine thinks?" The gist of the inventor's reply might be taken directly from Hobbes' *Leviathan*: "For seeing life is but a motion of limbs, the begining [*sic*] whereof is in some principall [*sic*] part within; why may we not say, that all automata (engines that move by themselves by springs and wheeles [*sic*] as doth a watch) have an artificiall [*sic*] life?" (3). Moxon concludes, just as Hobbes does, by answering the question with another: "Is not a man a machine?" (88).

In his studies on the imagery of automata, Minsoo Kang points to shifts which occurred between the early and late Enlightenment which, even then, altered the valence of the question from inherently positive to dubious, at best. In the early Enlightenment, in the days of Hobbes, the human ideal represents the social, productive, and reasonable: an integrated part of society. In this scenario, each individual is a perfect machine designed by a benign creator to work in harmony with other perfect machines. Early Enlightenment philosophy such as this presumes that everyone is made to fill the place they occupy. In the late Enlightenment, the ideal shifts to one of progress, the subtexts of progress being that neither the individual machine nor the machine of society are perfect. In order to achieve this goal, the later Enlightenment privileges genius and individuality.

Nineteenth century philosophy follows a similar arc, emphasizing community over individuality. Utilitarianism, evidenced in "Moxon's Master" by the presence of Mill, operates on the premise that the good of the many determines the inherently moral course. In this view, the responsibility of the individual to the self is served by considering that self as a part of a larger whole. By mid-century, with the crush of industrialization and the depersonalization of people into "labor," a real sense of polarization develops where the benefits earned by the social group practically accrue to an extremely limited few. Kang relates: "The image of the industrial machine as an irrational, terrifying, destructive, and superhuman entity was envisioned by those who felt that the progress of industrialization had taken on a life of its own beyond human interest and control" (243). In the prefatory discussion of the difference between human and machine in "Moxon's Master," Bierce, a contemporary of both Marx and Nietzsche, explores his age's struggle to understand the nature of the industrial machine.

The Mechanical Turk and the Automaton Chess-Player: Part Two

Bierce's reputation for reversals and unexpected twists in his short stories, demonstrated most famously in "Occurrence at Owl Creek Bridge" (1890), suggests a mystery beneath the surface of the plot in "Moxon's Master." Bierce's stories often conclude with the revelation of key information that requires the reader to re-evaluate the story from the beginning. Bierce expert E.F. Bleiler admits that what goes on in the story must be the subject of personal interpretation because "Bierce obviously intended uncertainty by leaving so much for the reader either to imagine or reconstruct" (1988, 388). Bleiler and other critics have engaged spiritedly in such imagining and reconstructing. For instance, according to Daniel Canty (1996), the chess game and the revealing of the machine is part of an elaborate prank, which Moxon has staged with his conversation in the first part of the story.

In "Moxon's Master," the robot is described as wearing "a crimson fez" and a belted tunic of the same color, giving it a suggestively foreign appearance (Bierce 1910, 100). The physical appearance of the robot and its ability to play chess is taken by both Bleiler and Canty to constitute a multi-faceted allusion to Maelzel's chess-player. This famous automaton originated in eighteenth-century Vienna. It was subsequently shown across Europe and the United States into the mid 19th century. The chess-player was popularly known as the Mechanical Turk because it was attired in clothes reminiscent of the Ottoman Empire. Johann Maelzel was the proprietor of this exhibition at the time when Edgar Allan Poe wrote an aggressively detailed expose on the automaton as a hoax in 1836.

In "Who Was Moxon's Master?" (1985), Bleiler posits the theory that Moxon's chess-playing machine resemblance to Maezel's automaton should be viewed as a cue to understand Moxon's machine similarly as a hoax. Bleiler offers: "Bierce's linking of Moxon's device to Maelzel's, with the Turkishness, which is not demanded by story logic, conveys a built-in suggestion of falseness" (186). Viewing the chess-player as a puppet means, however, that whoever is operating the machine commits murder in Bierce's story, and this unknown character must then be accounted for. Bleiler points to the moment

in the story when the sound
from the next-door workshop
interrupts the conversation;
Bierce's narrator conjectures
that the inventor has secreted
a woman in that room. When
Moxon returns from checking
on the disturbance, the narrator sees evidence for this theory in the wound on his
friend's face, interpreting the
marks to look very like those
made by a woman's nails.
Bleiler suggests that accepting
the narrator's original surmise
solves the mystery: Moxon's

Wolfgang von Kempelen, The Turkish Chess
Player (The Mechanical Turk) (1783).

unknown mistress executes further violence by operating the chess-player,
mastering her lover through the technology he has created. Alternatively, in
"Who Was Really Moxon's Master?" (1988), Franz Rottensteiner argues that
the more logical outcome is that a third, minor character murdered Moxon:
Haley, who visits the narrator in the hospital during the story's coda. Bierce
describes Haley as "Moxon's confidential workman" (105). Haley quizzes the
narrator rather cryptically about the events of that night, and his motivation
for doing so does cast some doubt on the character.

All of these conjectures about who is behind the murderous machine,
however, rely on the premise that Bierce has offered a vital clue about the
falseness of his chess-player. This is, by no means, an established fact. The
inclusion of the "clue" might, in fact, be rather too obvious to be taken at face
value. Bierce was an accomplished and prolific author, and given his penchant
for twists, connecting Moxon's creation to a famous hoax might be precisely
nothing more than a red herring. Yet, this unsolvable debate might be beside
the point when considering Maelzel's Turk in a metaphorical context. In her
book on the popular imagery of artificial life, Gaby Wood (2002) speaks of
Maelzel and the legacy of his chess-player as a piece of theater posing as science. The appeal of that historical fraud is in its blurring the boundaries
between machine and human. Wood suggests the mood of the audience wit-
nessing the mechanical wonder: "Mixed in with the magic and the marvel is
a fear: that we can be replaced all too easily, and that we are uncertain now
of what it is that makes us human" (xlv). Sitting for a show with Maelzel's
chess-player becomes a space for personal reflection for the audience members to contemplate their own humanity in the presence of a not-man-not-
machine. The effect for this audience is the same whether the machine is

really independent or not; their belief in the possibility of what they are seeing is what matters. Wood suggests that the result is, metaphysically, playing with fire (82). In "Moxon's Master," Bierce replicates this experience for his reader, amplifying it by ambiguities inherent in the discourse of narration, making the audience utterly dependent on finite words to gather all available data.

Bierce also settles wisely and suggestively on the meeting place between man and machine, in the game of chess. For a large part of the 20th century, engineers have used the game of chess as a benchmark for measuring artificial intelligence. Interactivity, as displayed in a game of chess, is intellectual, but the impulse to design and engage in such a game as chess is an extension of human sociality which depends less on intellect and more upon emotion and ethics. The practice of playing, for the human, is one of pleasure, and the rules are not merely limiting directions for play, but part of a formula for fair interchange in competition with another person. In Bierce's story, the machine's ability to play chess reads as a display of rational thought. As Wood's commentary suggests, observing artificial life in the process of strategizing enables the witness to empathize with the machine. The result is a sense of compatibility profound enough to provoke a feeling of sympathy. Yet, that feeling must be tinged with a level of anxiety because the approximation of a portion of humanness is not accompanied by evidence of other tempering, qualifying elements of humanness. The anxiety of the narrator as he observes the progress of the game in Bierce's story mirrors this conflicted empathy exactly.

"Moxon's Master," however, goes beyond the theater piece of Maezel's hoax by adding a dimension to considering the possibility of a machine operating through functional rationality. Bierce's chess-player demonstrates a key variation from his forebear, the Turk. Its display of emotional engagement, its fury at losing to Moxon, indicates that the machine is doing more than logically strategizing; it is experiencing feelings about the game. In other words, Bierce shows this artificial creation experiencing its world in multiple valences, thinking in a way which parallels human intelligence where understanding is shaped as much by feeling as it is by fact.

In "Moxon's Master," Bierce blazes the trail for future representations of self-controlling machines in science fiction. Distinct from the 19th century tendency to portray human-like robots as mindless machines, Bierce's emotional robot anticipates the contemplations of AI that would later appear in such works as *Bladerunner* (1982) and *Westworld* (2016). More philosophical in nature, works such as these revolve around issues resulting from the introduction of emotions into artificial humans and the difficulties these beings have in responding to feelings without a lifetime of growing into them. Moxon's machine is in precisely this position, created to think and feel like a human, and this thinking entails its emotional connection to its world, the workroom around it, the chessboard before it, and, particularly, the opponent who defeats it.

BIBLIOGRAPHY

Bierce, Ambrose. 1910. "Moxon's Master." *The Collected Works of Ambrose Bierce: Can Such Things Be?* Neale, 88–105.
Bleiler, E.F. 1985. "Who Was Moxon's Master?" *Extrapolation* 26, no. 3 (Fall): 181–9.
Bleiler, E.F. 1988. "More on 'Moxon's Master.'" *Science Fiction Studies* 15, no. 3: 386–91.
Bleiler, E.F. 1997. "Remastering Moxon." *Science Fiction Studies* 24, no. 1 (Mar.): 184–5.
Canty, Daniel. 1996. "The Meaning of 'Moxon's Master.'" *Science Fiction Studies* 23, no. 3 (Nov.): 538–41.
Hobbes, Thomas. 1950. *Leviathan.* E.P. Dutton.
Jackson, Tony E. 2017. "Imitative Identity, Imitative Art, and AI: Artificial Intelligence." *Mosaic* 50, no. 2 (June): 47–64.
Kang, Minsoo. 2011. *Sublime Dreams of Living Machines: The Automaton in the European Imagination.* Harvard UP.
Kang, Minsoo. 2012. "From the Man-Machine to the Automaton-Man: The Enlightenment Origins of the Mechanistic Imagery of Humanity." *Vital Matters: Eighteenth Century Views of Conception, Life, and Death,* edited by Helen Deutsch and Mary Terrall, U of Toronto P, 148–73.
Rottensteiner, Franz. 1988. "Who Was Really Moxon's Master?" *Science Fiction Studies* 15, no. 1: 107–12.
Taylor, Matthew A. 2013. "Ghost-Humanism; Or, Spectors of Materialism." *J19* 1, no. 2 (Fall): 416–22.
Wallach, Wendell, and Colin Allen. 2009. *Moral Machines: Teaching Robots Right from Wrong.* Oxford UP.
Wood, Gaby. 2002. *Edison's Eve: A Magical History of the Quest for Mechanical Life.* Anchor.

"Moxon's Master" (1899)

AMBROSE BIERCE

"Are you serious?—do you really believe a machine thinks?"

I got no immediate reply; Moxon was apparently intent upon the coals in the grate, touching them deftly here and there with the fire-poker till they signified a sense of his attention by a brighter glow. For several weeks I had been observing in him a growing habit of delay in answering even the most trivial of commonplace questions. His air, however, was that of preoccupation rather than deliberation: one might have said that he had "something on his mind."

Presently he said:

"What is a 'machine'? The word has been variously defined. Here is one definition from a popular dictionary: 'Any instrument or organization by which power is applied and made effective, or a desired effect produced.' Well, then, is not a man a machine? And you will admit that he thinks—or thinks he thinks."

"If you do not wish to answer my question," I said, rather testily, "why not say so?—all that you say is mere evasion. You know well enough that when I say 'machine' I do not mean a man, but something that man has made and controls."

"When it does not control him," he said, rising abruptly and looking out of a window, whence nothing was visible in the blackness of a stormy night. A moment later he turned about and with a smile said:

"I beg your pardon; I had no thought of evasion. I considered the dictionary man's unconscious testimony suggestive and worth something in the discussion. I can give your question a direct answer easily enough: I do believe that a machine thinks about the work that it is doing."

That was direct enough, certainly. It was not altogether pleasing, for it tended to confirm a sad suspicion that Moxon's devotion to study and work in his machine-shop had not been good from him. I knew, for one thing, that he suffered from insomnia, and that is no light affliction. Had it affected his mind? His reply to my question seemed to me then evidence that it had; perhaps I should think differently about it now. I was younger then, and among the blessings that are not denied to youth is ignorance. Incited by that great stimulant to controversy, I said:

"And what, pray, does it think with—in the absence of a brain?"

The reply, coming with less than his customary delay, took his favorite form of counter-interrogation:

"With what does a plant think—in the absence of a brain?"

"Ah, plants also belong to the philosopher class! I should be pleased to know some of their conclusions; you may omit the premises."

"Perhaps," he replied, apparently unaffected by my foolish irony, "you may be able to infer their convictions from their acts. I will spare you the familiar examples of the sensitive mimosa and those insectivorous flowers and those whose stamens bend down and shake their pollen upon the entering bee in order that he may fertilize their distant mates. But observe this. In an open spot in my garden I planted a climbing vine. When it was barely above the surface I set a stake into the soil a yard away. The vine at once made for it, but as it was about to reach it after several days I removed it a few feet. The vine at once altered its course, making an acute angle, and again made for the stake. This manoeuver was repeated several times, but finally, as if discouraged, the vine abandoned the pursuit and ignoring further attempts to divert it traveled to a small tree, further away, which it climbed.

"Roots of the eucalyptus will prolong themselves incredibly in search of moisture. A well-known horticulturist relates that one entered an old drainpipe and followed it until it came to a break, where a section of the pipe had been removed to make way for a stone wall that had been built across its course. The root left the drain and followed the wall until it found an opening where a stone had fallen out. It crept through and following the other side of the wall back to the drain, entered the unexplored part and resumed its journey."

"And all this?"

"Can you miss the significance of it? It shows the consciousness of plants. It proves they think."

"Even if it did—what then? We were speaking, not of plants, but of machines. They may be composed partly of wood—wood that has no longer vitality—or wholly of metal. Is thought an attribute also of the mineral kingdom?"

"How else do you explain the phenomena, for example, of crystallization?"

"I do not explain them."

"Because you cannot without affirming what you wish to deny, namely, intelligent cooperation among the constituent elements of the crystals. When soldiers form lines, or hollow squares, you call it reason. When wild geese in flight take the form of a letter V you say instinct. When the homogenous atoms of a mineral, moving freely in solution, arrange themselves into shapes mathematically perfect, or particles of frozen moisture into the symmetrical and beautiful forms of snowflakes, you have nothing to say. You have not even invented a name to conceal your heroic unreason."

Moxon was speaking with unusual animation and earnestness. As he paused I heard in an adjoining room known to me as his "machine-shop," which no one but himself was permitted to enter, a singular thumping sound, as of some one pounding upon a table with an open hand. Moxon heard it at the same moment and, visibly agitated, rose and hurriedly passed into the room whence it came. I thought it odd that any one else should be in there, and my interest in my friend—with doubtless a touch of unwarrantable curiosity—led me to listen intently, though, I am happy to say, not at the key-hole. There were confused sounds, as of a struggle or scuffle; the floor shook. I distinctly heard hard breathing and a hoarse whisper which said "Damn you!" Then all was silent, and presently Moxon reappeared and said, with a rather sorry smile:

"Pardon me for leaving you so abruptly, I have a machine in there that lost its temper and cut up rough."

Fixing my eyes steadily upon his left cheek, which was traversed by four parallel excoriations showing blood, I said:

"How would it do to trim its nails?"

I could have spared myself the jest; he gave it no attention, but seated himself in the chair that he had left and resumed the interrupted monologue as if nothing had occurred:

"Doubtless you do not hold with those (I need not name them to a man of your reading) who have taught that all matter is sentient, that every atom is a living, feeling, conscious being. *I* do. There is no such thing as dead, inert matter: it is all alive; all instinct with force, actual and potential; all sensitive to the same forces in its environment and susceptible to the contagion of higher and subtler ones residing in such superior organisms as it may be brought into relationship with, as those of man when he is fashioning it into an instrument of his will. It absorbs something of his intelligence and pur-pose—more of them in proportion to the complexity of the resulting machine and that of his work.

"Do you happen to recall Herbert Spencer's definition of 'Life'? I read it thirty years ago. He may have altered it afterward, for anything I know, but in all that time I have been unable to think of a single word that could prof-itably be changed or added or removed. It seems to me not only the best defi-nition, but the only possible one.

"'Life,' he says, 'is a definite combination of heterogeneous changes, both simultaneous and successive, in correspondence with external coexistences and sequences.'"

"That defines the phenomenon," I said, "but gives no hint of its cause."

"That," he replied, "is all that any definition can do. As Mill points out, we know nothing of effect except as a consequent. Of certain phenomena, one never occurs without the other, which is dissimilar: the first in point of time we call the cause, the second, the effect. One who had many times seen a rabbit pursued by a dog, and had never seen rabbits and dogs otherwise, would think the rabbit the cause of the dog.

"But I fear," he added, laughing naturally enough, "that my rabbit is leading me a long way from the track of my legitimate quarry: I'm indulging in the pleasure of the chase for its own sake. What I want you to observe is that in Herbert Spenser's definition of 'life' the activity of a machine is included—there is nothing in the definition that is not applicable to it. According to this sharpest of observers and deepest of thinkers, if a man during his period of activity is alive, so is a machine when in operation. As an inventor and constructor of machines I know that to be true."

Moxon was silent for a long time, gazing absently into the fire. It was growing late and I thought it time to be going, but somehow I did not like the notion of leaving him in that isolated house, all alone except for the presence of some person whose nature my conjectures could go no further than that it was unfriendly, perhaps malign. Leaning toward him and looking earnestly into his eyes while making a motion with my hand through the door of his workshop, I said:

"Moxon, whom do you have in there?"

Somewhat to my surprise he laughed lightly and answered without hesitation:

"Nobody; the incident that you have in mind was caused by my folly in leaving a machine in action with nothing to act upon, while I undertook the interminable task of enlightening your understanding. Do you happen to know that Consciousness is the creature of Rhythm?"

"O bother them both!" I replied, rising and laying hold of my overcoat. "I'm going to wish you good night; and I'll add the hope that the machine which you inadvertently left in action will have her gloves on the next time you think it needful to stop her."

Without waiting to observe the effect of my shot I left the house.

Rain was falling, and the darkness was intense. In the sky beyond the crest of a hill toward which I groped my way along precarious plank sidewalks and across miry, unpaved streets I could see the faint glow of the city's lights, but behind me nothing was visible but a single window of Moxon's house. It glowed with what seemed to me a mysterious and fateful meaning. I knew it was an uncurtained aperture in my friend's "machine-shop," and I had little doubt that he had resumed the studies interrupted by his duties as my instructor in mechanical consciousness and the fatherhood of Rhythm. Odd, and in some degree humorous, as his convictions seemed to me at that time, I could not wholly divest myself of the feeling that they had some tragic relation to his life and character—perhaps to his destiny—although I no longer entertained the notion that they were the vagaries of a disordered mind. Whatever might be thought of his views, his exposition of them was too logical for that. Over and over, his last words came back to me: "Consciousness is the creature of Rhythm." Bald and terse as the statement was, I now found it infinitely alluring. At each recurrence it broadened in meaning and deepened in suggestion. Why, here (I thought) is something upon which to found a philosophy. If consciousness is the product of rhythm all things *are* conscious, for all have motion, and all motion is rhythmic. I wondered if Moxon knew the significance and breadth of his thought—the scope of this momentous generalization; or had he arrived at his philosophic faith by the tortuous and uncertain road of observation?

That faith was then new to me, and all Moxon's expounding had failed to make me a convert; but now it seemed as if a great light shone about me, like that which fell upon Saul of Tarsus; and out there in the storm and darkness and solitude I experienced what Lewes calls "The endless variety and excitement of philosophic thought." I exulted in a new sense of knowledge, a new pride of reason. My feet seemed hardly to touch the earth; it was as if I were uplifted and borne through the air by invisible wings.

Yielding to an impulse to seek further light from him whom I now recognized as my master and guide, I had unconsciously turned about, and almost before I was aware of having done so found myself again at Moxon's door. I was drenched with rain, but felt no discomfort. Unable in my excitement to find the doorbell I instinctively tried the knob. It turned and, entering, I mounted the stairs to the room that I had so recently left. All was dark and silent; Moxon, as I had supposed, was in the adjoining room—the "machine shop." Groping along the wall until I found the communicating door I knocked loudly several times, but got no response, which I attributed to the uproar outside, for the wind was blowing a gale and dashing the rain against the thin walls in sheets. The drumming upon the shingle roof spanning the unceiled room was loud and incessant.

I had never been invited into the machine-shop—had, indeed, been denied admittance, as had all others, with one exception, a skilled metal worker, of whom no one knew anything except that his name was Haley and his habit silence. But in my spiritual exaltation, discretion and civility were alike forgotten and I opened the door. What I saw took all philosophical speculation out of me in short order.

Moxon sat facing me at the farther side of a small table upon which a single candle made all the light that was in the room. Opposite him, his back toward me, sat another person. On the table between the two was a chessboard; the men were playing. I knew little about chess, but as only a few pieces were on the board it was obvious that the game was near its close. Moxon was intensely interested—not so much, it seemed to me, in the game as in his antagonist, upon whom he had fixed so intent a look that, standing though I did directly in the line of his vision, I was altogether unobserved. His face was ghastly white, and his eyes glittered like diamonds. Of his antagonist I had only a back view, but that was sufficient; I should not have cared to see his face.

He was apparently not more than five feet in height, with proportions suggesting those of a gorilla—tremendous breadth of shoulders, thick, short neck and broad, squat head, which had a tangled growth of black hair and was topped by a crimson fez. A tunic of the same color, belted tightly to the waist, reached the seat—apparently a box—upon which he sat; his legs and feet were not seen. His left forearm appeared to rest in his lap; he moved his pieces with his right hand, which seemed disproportionately long.

I had shrunk back and now stood a little to one side of the doorway and in shadow. If Moxon had looked farther than the face of his opponent he could have observed nothing now, excepting that the door was open. Something forbade me either to enter or retire, a feeling—I know not how it came— that I was in the presence of imminent tragedy and might serve my friend by remaining. With a scarcely conscious rebellion against the indelicacy of the act I remained.

The play was rapid. Moxon hardly glanced at the board before making his moves, and to my unskilled eye seemed to move the piece most convenient to his hand, his motions in doing so being quick, nervous and lacking in precision. The response of his antagonist, while equally prompt in the inception, was made with a slow, uniform, mechanical and, I thought, somewhat theatrical movement of the arm, that was a sore trial to my patience. There was something unearthly about it all, and I caught myself shuddering. But I was wet and cold.

Two or three times after moving a piece the stranger slightly inclined his head, and each time I observed that Moxon shifted his king. All at once the thought came to me that the man was dumb. And then that he was a machine—an automaton chessplayer! Then I remembered that Moxon had once spoken to me of having invented such a piece of mechanism, though I did not understand that it had actually been constructed. Was all his talk about the consciousness and intelligence of machines merely a prelude to eventual exhibition of this device—only a trick to intensify the effect of its mechanical action upon me in my ignorance of its secret?

A fine end, this, of all my intellectual transports—my "endless variety and excitement of philosophic thought!" I was about to retire in disgust when something occurred to hold my curiosity. I observed a shrug of the thing's great shoulders, as if it were irritated: and so natural was this—so entirely human—that in my new view of the matter it startled me. Nor was that all, for a moment later it struck the table sharply with its clenched hand. At that gesture Moxon seemed even more startled than I: he pushed his chair a little backward, as in alarm.

Presently Moxon, whose play it was, raised his hand high above the board, pounced upon one of his pieces like a sparrowhawk and with an exclamation "checkmate!" rose quickly to his feet and stepped behind his chair. The automaton sat motionless.

The wind had now gone down, but I heard, at lessening intervals and progressively louder, the rumble and roll of thunder. In the pauses between I now became conscious of a low humming or buzzing which, like the thunder, grew momentarily louder and more distinct. It seemed to come from the body of the automaton, and was unmistakably a whirring of wheels. It gave me the impression of a disordered mechanism which had escaped the repressive and regulating action of some controlling part—an effect such as might be expected if a pawl should be jostled from the teeth of a ratchet-wheel. But before I had time for much conjecture as to its nature my attention was taken by the strange motions of the automaton itself. A slight but continuous convulsion appeared to have possession of it. In body and head it shook like a man with palsy or an ague chill, and the motion augmented every moment until the entire figure was in violent agitation. Suddenly it sprang to its feet and with a movement almost too quick for the eye to follow shot forward across table and chair, with both arms thrust forward to their full length— the posture and lunge of a diver. Moxon tried to throw himself backward out of reach, but he was too late: I saw the horrible thing's hands close upon his throat, his own clutch its wrists. Then the table was overturned, the candle thrown to the floor and extinguished, and all was black dark. But the noise of the struggle was dreadfully distinct, and most terrible of all were the raucous, squawking sounds made by the strangled man's efforts to breathe. Guided by the infernal hubbub, I sprang to the rescue of my friend, but had hardly taken a stride in the darkness when the whole room blazed with a blinding white light that burned into my brain and heart and memory a vivid picture of the combatants on the floor, Moxon underneath, his throat still in the clutch of those iron hands, his head forced backward, his eyes protruding, his mouth wide open and his tongue thrust out; and—horrible contrast!— upon the painted face of the assassin an expression of tranquil and profound thought, as in the solution of a problem in chess! This I observed, then all was blackness and silence.

Three days later I recovered consciousness in a hospital. As the memory of that tragic night slowly evolved in my ailing brain I recognized in my attendant Moxon's confidential workman, Haley. Responding to a look he approached, smiling.

"Tell me about it," I managed to say, faintly—"all about it."

"Certainly," he said; "you were carried unconscious from a burning house—Moxon's. Nobody knows how you came to be there. You may have to do a little explaining. The origin of the fire is a bit mysterious, too. My own notion is that the house was struck by lightning."

"And Moxon?"

"Buried yesterday—what was left of him."

Apparently this reticent person could unfold himself on occasion. When imparting shocking intelligence to the sick he was affable enough. After some moments of the keenest mental suffering I ventured to ask another question:

"Who rescued me?"

"Well, if that interests you—I did."

"Thank you, Mr. Haley, and may God bless you for it. Did you rescue, also, that charming product of your skill, the automaton chess-player that murdered its inventor?"

The man was silent a long time, looking away from me. Presently he turned and gravely said:

"Do you know that?"

"I do," I replied; "I saw it done."

That was many years ago. If asked today I should answer less confidently.

The Science Fiction Worlds of Edgar Rice Burroughs[1]

Jessie F. Terrell, Jr.

Edgar Rice Burroughs (1875–1950) was one of the "most popular, prolific, and influential scientific writers of all time, a figure to stand with Verne, Wells, and a few others as an all-time master of scientific romance" (Lupoff, 3). His science fiction stories, beginning with *A Princess of Mars,* published in 1912 in *All-Story* magazine, defined the "planetary romance" genre (Madison, 34–35). Reflecting on the impact of *A Princess of Mars,* science fiction historian Sam Moskowitz said, "Burroughs turned the entire direction of science fiction from prophesy and sociology to romantic adventure, making the major market for such work the all-fiction pulp magazines, and became the major influence on the field through to 1934" (291).

Regarding his influences from the works of fiction, Burroughs stated, "To Mr. Kipling as to Mr. Haggard I owe a debt of gratitude for having stimulated my youthful imagination and this I greatly acknowledge but Mr. Wells I have never read and consequently his stories could not have influenced me in any way" (Porges, 214). Burroughs' father, a former Union officer, was also a major influence. Major George Burroughs served in the Civil War and raised his children on military principles. Courage, skill, and honor appear prominently in Burroughs' stories.

By his mid-thirties, Edgar Rice Burroughs had failed at 18 jobs and had pawned "Mrs. Burroughs' jewelry and my watch … to buy food" for his wife and two young children (Schneider, 149–150). The desire for success as well as the demands of a growing family nurtured a concern for the human struggle in the progressive era when mankind was coming to grips with problems posed by industrialization, urbanization, immigration, and corruption. Filling his idle time reading the pulp magazines, Burroughs realized the stories from his own imagination "were just as good if not better" (Lupoff, 7).

The universal appeal of Burroughs' heroes was based on the chivalry of 18th century romanticism where country living, or a natural lifestyle, provided relief from the disease, filth, noise, and confusion of the city (Madison, 18). His stories offer escapism so that the hero could take the reader to a primitive world where one can be unencumbered and free from the rules of civilization. Burroughs provided a lush, colorful landscape with mystery and danger stimulating both mind and spirit.

Writing in the preface to *Tanar of Pellucidar*, Paul Cook (2006) noted Burroughs' prose and exact word choices: "Burroughs' style owes a great deal to the languorous prose of late Victorian writers, particularly Robert Lewis Stevenson and Rudyard Kipling. He also owes something to Henry James in his use of long, complex sentences and Jack London for his compact narrative detail" (viii). Burroughs' style is descriptive, with a prose that is nearly poetic in presenting vivid images or a dire situation. He ties the characters and setting together with action to describe an event including the effects upon the senses and psyche.

The hero's journey is a theme found throughout the stories of Edgar Rice Burroughs. In *The Hero with a Thousand Faces* (1949), popular mythologist Joseph Campbell describes the hero's journey: "A hero ventures forth from the world of common day into a region of supernatural wonder: fabulous forces are there encountered, and a decisive victory is won: the hero comes back from this mysterious adventure with the power to bestow boons on his fellow man" (23). The hero of a Burroughs' story traverses a savage or alien world to confront fierce creatures, villains, and impossible odds to find love and save the day. Burroughs' heroes are like knights from King Arthur's Round Table: men of high principles espousing courage, chivalry, leadership, honor, and duty (Madison, 40). The heroines, too, are strong of spirit, high-minded, outspoken, fearless, and capable of defending themselves. Romantic frustrations are known to occur, though the hero is often naïve or confused by the heroine's misleading signals. The Burroughs hero may survive battle, captivity, and escape. But the coming together of two people from different worlds with their own customs and traditions make for an awkward courtship where scorn is a barrier to be overcome by the story's end. Like adventure, romance is a given, but successful romance is never certain.

Worlds with exotic civilizations, technologies, and creatures serve as the stage for exploration. The Burroughs universe includes the fictional Barsoom (Mars), Amtor (Venus), a dystopian London, Va-Nah (the interior of the Moon), the subterranean jungle of Pellucidar, the lost continent of Caprona, and its interior called Caspak. World building provides Burroughs with the means to tell stories on multiple levels. At the surface level there is hero, heroine, and the hero's journey. But at a deeper level lies the opportunity to explore questions of race, environment, religion, and cooperation between nations.

With each setting, Burroughs reflects on a different social issue. On Barsoom, his *Mars* stories address social issues, including the scarcity of resources. On Caspak, *The Land that Time Forgot* (1924) examines Darwin's theory of evolution. *The Monster Men* (1929) questions the ethics of improving the human species. Dramas on Va-nah in *The Moon Maid* (1926) play out the impact of repression imposed by a communist-like government. What direction should a visitor take on Pellucidar in *At the Earth's Core* (1922), where compasses do not work and a wrong turn could be your last? *At the Earth's Core* provides a forum for basic survival stories of mankind versus mankind and mankind versus nature. The "hollow earth" story permits Burroughs to consider themes of back to nature and a natural lifestyle forsaking the complications and rigidity of modern society.

Edgar Rice Burroughs was thorough in his research, using scientific theories current for the early 20th century. He drew upon the astronomical theories of Percival Lowell, the evolution theory of Charles Darwin, the social evolution theories of Henry Lewis Morgan, and the eugenics work of Francis Galton to name but a few. His technology was based on the best available scientific information, providing just enough details to spur the imagination (Reid, 27; Roy, 17).

Barsoom

John Carter plays protagonist in the first three Barsoom stories (*Princess of Mars, Gods of Mars,* and *Warlord of Mars*). Carter is a professional soldier whose childhood is a mystery; he doesn't even know his own age. He arrives on a fantasy version of Mars, named Barsoom, where he finds a detailed geography, mythology, history, flora, creatures, and people of multiple colors (Lupoff, 11). "ERB [Edgar Rice Burroughs] was a master storyteller. The worlds that Burroughs created, his Mars, with all its lands and peoples, would remain the true star of the series, from the first to the last" (Martin, xv). Barsoom is dying, with dried up seabeds, vanishing vegetation, and sparse water. As the land became barren and water disappeared, so did the population. Survivors abandoned some cities and retreated to a few functioning outposts (Brady, 33–34).

The layout of Barsoom provides a means to present a multi-racial society. For instance, Burroughs disrupts accepted 20th century American norms of racial color in *Gods of Mars* (1918). People of a given "color" tend to congregate together. The white Holy Therns are most evil of Barsoom's humanoids; They maintain "secret temples ... hidden in the heart of every community." The black race is described as having "marvelous beauty" (Burroughs 1917). Slavery exists on Barsoom, but it is not based on color: "It is not by race but by organization of power that the good people of Mars are distinguishable from the evil ones" (Flautz, 268). All people of Barsoom are concerned with the scarcity of resources, raising questions of survival that lead to violence, wars and subterfuge ranging from city-states to tribes to the individual (Reid, 44).

When Carter first arrives on Barsoom, tribes are segregated racially and geographically. Carter first encounters a tribe of green Martians called Tharks. The green Martians stand twelve to fifteen feet tall, weigh about four hundred pounds, and sport an extra set of arms about the mid-section. They are cruel and warlike, brandishing both projectile rifles and sometimes multiple swords with their extra limbs. The green Martian race is both tribal and nomadic, similar to the Apache (Roy, 58). Barsoom's remaining humanoids have two arms and two legs, but they also come in a variety of colors, including black, white, yellow, and red. The black race are the first from which all other races sprang. Also known as the "First Born," they are a proud race standing six feet or more in height with skin of "polished ebony" (Burroughs 1918).

John Carter, the career soldier, aspires to a military code of honor based on principles, including loyalty, chivalry, duty, integrity, honor, service and respect for all persons. A similar code of honor exists on Barsoom. Once Carter learns the language and the people, he adapts in heroic fashion (Brady, 61). The green Martians befriend Carter. Then Carter falls in love and weds a red woman, the Princess of Mars. The couple eventually delivers a multi-racial son and daughter. Carter goes on to unite several of the warring races.

Caspak

Burroughs' *The Land That Time Forgot* (1924) first appeared in three installments in *Blue Book* magazine in 1918. The second installment was named *People That Time Forgot*, which was followed by *Out of Time's Abyss*. In 1924, all three stories were published together in the first hardback edition as *The Land That Time Forgot*. During the paperback boom of the sixties and seventies the three installments were published separately as the Caspak trilogy. Two movies based on the trilogy were produced by Amicus in 1975 and 1977 (Zeuschner, 156, 161).

The Land That Time Forgot provides a fictional laboratory (the island of Caspak) to witness the stages of evolution in an accelerated time period (Reid, 194–195). Survival of the fittest is a constant concern on Caspak, where wild and hungry creatures run rampant. Much like Pellucidar in *At the Earth's Core*, Caspak includes dinosaurs but also an array of beasts from different time periods and continents. Marine Plesiosaurs from the Mesozoic era live side by side with modern reptiles and snakes. Jurassic-era Allosaurs and Diplodocus battle Cretaceous-era Tyrannosaurs and Pterodactyls for territory.

Dinosaurs cohabitate with bison from North America, aurochs from Asia, bears from Europe, Asian tiger, and African leopards. The island also provides a home to mammoths, mastodons, rhinoceros, sabre-tooth tigers, deer, monkeys, lions, panthers, lynx, cows, goats, and wolves.

Residents of Caspak use the phrase "up from the beginning" to describe their "evolution in a lifetime": "If an egg survives it goes through all the stages of development that man has passed through during the unthinkable eons since life first moved upon the earth's face" (Burroughs 1924, 208). The women of Caspak bathe in a "birthing pool" where they deposit an egg. The egg becomes a tadpole that makes its way downstream into the sea. Those tadpoles become fish, reptiles, or amphibians. For some, the development process continues until they become baboons and apes (Lupof, 69–70). If the creature can survive the dangers of Caspak, and if its genes are inclined, the ape (or *Ho-Lu*) could evolve through seven stages of mankind (Brady, 116).

While the majority of life forms on Caspak use the birthing pool to procreate, some Galu women deliver with a live human birth. The all-male Wieroo race are unable to reproduce on their own. Thus, they are obsessed with learning the Galu secret of live birth: "From the beginning of time jealousy has existed between the Wieroo and the Galus as to which would eventually dominate the world" (Burroughs 1924, 131). The Wieroos abduct Galu women to bear their children. Therefore, Wieroos can only be borne by Galu mothers who are capable of a live birth.

Burroughs presents the Galu and the Wieroo as two possible directions for humanity. The Galus resemble humankind in its present form. They have the potential to continue the development of the human race as we know it (Reid, 218). Reinforced by their hideous appearance and practices, the Wieroo disregard honor, courage, and virility. The Wieroo emphasize mental discipline that leads to cruelty.

In some respects, the Wieroos are the opposite of the reptilian Mahars that dominate the world of Pellucidar in *At the Earth's Core*. Both Wieroos and Mahars depend on captive human females, but for the Wieroo the captive is a mating partner. For the Mahar, the captive is dinner. The Wieroos are all male while the Mahars are all female.

Va-Nah

Burroughs biographer Richard Lupoff calls *The Moon Maid* a "masterpiece of science fiction and a too-often overlooked pioneer work of the modern school of social extrapolation in science fiction" (80). After some revisions, *The Moon Maid* was published in *All-Story* magazine in 1923 with two follow-up installments in 1925. The hardcover first edition appeared in 1926.

In *The Moon Maid*, Earth's first manned mission to Barsoom is sabotaged. They are forced to land on the moon instead. There, the astronauts discover a civilization in the interior of the moon. The villains of this story, the Kalkars, arose as a secret society opposing the class system and capitalism. The Kalkars maintain control by instilling ignorance: "no learning is better than a little" (Brady, 171).

Enslaved by the Kalkars, the Va-Gas can speak and reason but are warlike cannibals who crave meat (McWhorter, 414). The Va-Gas, sometimes depicted as centaurs, pose a strange sight: three-toed quadrupeds with human-like faces. The Va-Gas can stand on two legs or all four legs. When standing on their hind legs, their front legs serve as arms. They can clutch a spear even while running on all fours. The Moon's lesser gravity enables them to jump 100 feet into the air.

The rise of communism in Russia in 1918 inspired Burroughs to offer insightful social commentary still relevant in today's world where dictators and political strongmen force their will on a helpless populace. Ironically, the repression and fear instilled by a political dictator is similar to the Mahar's hypnotic control that spreads terror through all of Pellucidar in *At the Earth's Core*.

Pellucidar

The machine devised for the journey to the world inside the Earth (Pellucidar) is a wonder of science and engineering. The Iron Mole is a steel cylinder 100 feet long and jointed to twist and turn through rock formations. It burrows into the crust using a drill that can generate "more power to the cubic inch than any other engine did to the cubic foot" (Burroughs 1922, 6).

Without a vehicle, the protagonist of adventure fiction has no means to make the journey. Burroughs' "Iron Mole" ranks with Verne's rocket and H.G. Wells' Time Machine as extraordinary feats of engineering that make the story possible. Vehicles both deliver the hero to the world of adventure and provide the means for escape.

Inventor Abner Perry conceived of a drilling machine to burrow in search of minerals and ore. The "mechanical subterranean prospector" was Perry's life work (Burroughs 1922, 5). David Innes, the owner of a mining company, intrigued by Perry's design, invested heavily in the construction of this full-size prospector, or "Iron Mole." Neither Perry nor Innes were adventurers. Neither was either looking for a world to conquer. Once in Pellucidar and caught up in the drama between indigenous humans and the predator Mahars, both Innes and Perry rise to the occasion. Innes is a natural leader with vision. Perry's inventions furnish the technology to first wage war, and then build a society.

The first journey in the Iron Mole to Pellucidar is as great a risk for Innes and Perry as space travel is for astronauts. Problems develop immediately on the maiden voyage. The exterior temperature, speed, and direction are of constant concern. At a speed of seven miles per hour, the Iron Mole burrows out of control, with the basics of air, food, water, and fuel in short supply. Stranded five hundred miles inside the Earth is a real possibility.

"The Iron Mole" by Tom Floyd (2006).

For the passengers of the Iron Mole, the "noise is deafening," as vibrations force our heroes to hold on for dear life (Burroughs 1922, 8). At a depth of 700 feet, they realize steering has failed. One mile into the Earth, the exterior temperature is 110 degrees. At four miles, the outside temperature rises to 140 degrees. Uncertain as to their fate, Perry reviews the scientific theories speculating on the thickness and composition of the Earth's crust. After twelve hours, they are 84 miles inside the Earth with the exterior temperature of 153 degrees Fahrenheit. At a depth of five hundred miles, they come to a stop. Then the real adventure begins.

Once in the "hollow earth" world of Pellucidar, Innes leads the fight against a reptilian race called Mahars who enslave and devour human Pellucidarians. Mahars possess a hypnotic ability to control people's minds. Under Innes' leadership, people unite in a common cause to seek a better way of life. It is not colonialism but a free democracy that springs to life in Pellucidar. Perry contributes books and ideas to the revolution, building a printing press and helping the Pellucidarians build schools to teach reading and writing. It is the power of Edgar Rice Burroughs' words that brings Pellucidar to life for us.

Jules Verne's *Journey to the Center of the Earth* (1864) inspired *At the*

At the Earth's Core, **paperback cover design by J. Allen St. John (1922). Copyright © Edgar Rice Burroughs, Inc. (In specific countries) All rights reserved.**

Earth's Core and other subterranean tales of Pellucidar, such as *Tanar of Pellucidar* (1929), *Back to the Stone Age* (1937), and *Land of Terror* (1944). Written in 1864, *Journey to the Center of the Earth* describes a huge underground cave in which explorers discover living dinosaurs. Despite Burroughs' homage to one of the most famous works of classic science fiction, the differences between the novels are vast. The greatest similarity between the novels comes down to the concept: a lost world within the hollow Earth.

While Verne spends 13 chapters laying the groundwork for the journey, Burroughs' journey begins immediately in chapter 1 aboard the Iron Mole. Verne's exposition emphasizes the history and science of his adventure. The protagonist, Professor Lidenbrock, along with the help of his nephew, Axel, decipher an ancient runic manuscript that leads them to Iceland and the passageway into the Earth. Burroughs uses technology and engineering to solve the problem of passage.

Verne's journey is one of scientific discovery of the natural world. While Verne's Professor and Axel are compelled to enter the cave for the purposes of scientific discovery, Burroughs' protagonists are motivated by profit. Axel, who is fearful of the adventure, unsuccessfully uses scientific theories to discourage his uncle. Despite the risk, Perry and Innes enthusiastically embark on the journey with the intent to make both men "fabulously wealthy" (Burroughs 1922, 6).

Axel's fears are realized when they find an oversized human skull. Upon this first indication of human habitants in the cave, the Professor and Axel opt to avoid an encounter with the twelve-foot tall prehistoric humans. Innes and Perry show no such reluctance. Much to the contrary, Burroughs' journey leads Innes and Perry into a great war between a lost civilization and its reptilian enemies. They push forward to see what is over the next hill. Their reaction to oppression is to confront and challenge it. Innes and Perry interact with many people in their wonderings through Pellucidar. Perry and Innes visit five tribes of Pellucidar. At least six individuals are introduced by name and two figure prominently in the plot: Diane the Beautiful and Hooja the Sly One. The determination to move forward without fear is a recurring theme throughout Burroughs stories. There may be discussion as to the proper direction or approach, but no hesitation and no conflict as to the desired end result. The quintessential Burroughs hero answers the call to action without reluctance or hesitation.

Jules Verne's *Journey* hinted at the wonders of exploring a subterranean fiction. But Edgar Rice Burroughs devised a more complex world with adventures and discoveries for both his heroes and readers. *At the Earth's Core* presents a much larger and more developed world than Verne's cavern, having a variety of countries to explore with people to meet, animals to observe and an evil to confront.

The adventure begins with the Iron Mole as described in Burroughs' *At the Earth's Core*. The first chapter of *At the Earth's Core* illustrates Edgar Rice Burroughs' timeless ability to entertain with a thrilling adventure, enhance the imagination, present social issues for examination, and espouse the virtues of a hero who rises to the occasion.

NOTE

1. Trademarks PELLUCIDAR® and EDGAR RICE BURROUGHS® Owned by Edgar Rice Burroughs, Inc., and Used by Permission.

WORKS CITED

Brady, Clark A. 1996. *The Burroughs Cyclopaedia*. McFarland.
Burroughs, Edgar Rice. 1917. *A Princess of Mars*, A.C. McClurg & Co.
Burroughs, Edgar Rice. 1918. *The Gods of Mars*, A.C. McClurg & Co.
Burroughs, Edgar Rice. 1919. *The Warlord of Mars*, A.C. McClurg & Co.

Burroughs, Edgar Rice. 1920. *Thuvia, Maid of Mars*, A.C. McClurg & Co.
Burroughs, Edgar Rice. 1922. *At the Earth's Core*, A.C. McClurg & Co.
Burroughs, Edgar Rice. 1923. *Pellucidar*, A.C. McClurg & Co.
Burroughs, Edgar Rice. 1924. *Land That Time Forgot*, A.C. McClurg & Co.
Burroughs, Edgar Rice. 1926. *The Moon Maid*, A.C. McClurg & Co.
Burroughs, Edgar Rice. 1929. *The Monster Men*, A.C. McClurg & Co.
Burroughs, Edgar Rice. 1955. *Beyond Thirty*, A.C. McClurg & Co., Lloyd A. Esbach.
Burroughs, Edgar Rice. 2006 [1930]. *Tanar of Pellucidar*. U of Nebraska Press.
Burroughs, Edgar Rice. 2009. "Entertainment Is Fiction's Purpose." In *Edgar Rice Burroughs Tells All*, edited by Jerry L. Schneider. Pulpville Press.
Campbell, Joseph. 1949. *The Hero with a Thousand Faces*. Pantheon.
Flautz, J.T. 1967. "An American Demagogue in Barsoom." *The Journal of Popular Culture* 1, no. 3: 263–275.
Lupoff, Richard A. 2005. *Master of Adventure*. University of Nebraska Press.
Madison, Charles A. 2015. "The First Popular Planetary Romance." In *Edgar Rice Burroughs: The Master of Pulp Storytelling*, edited by Charles A. Madison. ERBGRAPHICS.
Moskowitz, Sam. 1970. "The Discovery of Edgar Rice Burroughs." In *Under the Moons of Mars: A History and Anthology of "The Scientific Romance" in the Munsey Magazines, 1912–1920*, edited by Sam Moskowitz. Holt, Rinehart and Winston.
Porges, Irwin. 1975. *Edgar Rice Burroughs: The Man Who Created Tarzan*. Ballantine Books.
Reid, Connor. 2018. *The Science and Fiction of Edgar Rice Burroughs*. Glyphi Limited.
Roy, John Flint. 2012. *A Guide to Barsoom*. ReAnimus Press.
Verne, Jules. 2018 (1876). "Journey to the Center of the Earth." Dover Publications.
Weller, Sam. 2010. *Listen to the Echoes: The Ray Bradbury Interviews*. Melville House.
Zeuschner, Robert B. 2016. *Edgar Rice Burroughs: The Bibliography*. Edgar Rice Burroughs, Inc.

At the Earth's Core (1914), Chapter 1: "Toward the Eternal Fires"

EDGAR RICE BURROUGHS

I was born in Connecticut about thirty years ago. My name is David Innes. My father was a wealthy mine owner. When I was nineteen he died. All his property was to be mine when I had attained my majority—provided that I had devoted the two years intervening in close application to the great business I was to inherit.

I did my best to fulfill the last wishes of my parent—not because of the inheritance, but because I loved and honored my father. For six months I toiled in the mines and in the counting-rooms, for I wished to know every minute detail of the business.

Then Perry interested me in his invention. He was an old fellow who had devoted the better part of a long life to the perfection of a mechanical subterranean prospector. As relaxation he studied paleontology. I looked over his plans, listened to his arguments, inspected his working model—and then, convinced, I advanced the funds necessary to construct a full-sized, practical prospector.

I shall not go into the details of its construction—it lies out there in the desert now—about two miles from here. Tomorrow you may care to ride out and see it. Roughly, it is a steel cylinder a hundred feet long, and jointed so that it may turn and twist through solid rock if need be. At one end is a mighty revolving drill operated by an engine which Perry said generated more power to the cubic inch than any other engine did to the cubic foot. I remember that he used to claim that that invention alone would make us fabulously wealthy—we were going to make the whole thing public after the successful issue of our first secret trial—but Perry never returned from that trial trip, and I only after ten years.

I recall as it were but yesterday the night of that momentous occasion upon which we were to test the practicality of that wondrous invention. It was near midnight when we repaired to the lofty tower in which Perry had constructed his "iron mole" as he was wont to call the thing. The great nose rested upon the bare earth of the floor. We passed through the doors into the outer jacket, secured them, and then passing on into the cabin, which contained the controlling mechanism within the inner tube, switched on the electric lights.

Perry looked to his generator; to the great tanks that held the life-giving chemicals with which he was to manufacture fresh air to replace that which we consumed in breathing; to his instruments for recording temperatures, speed, distance, and for examining the materials through which we were to pass.

He tested the steering device, and overlooked the mighty cogs which transmitted its marvelous velocity to the giant drill at the nose of his strange craft.

Our seats, into which we strapped ourselves, were so arranged upon transverse bars that we would be upright whether the craft were plowing her way downward into the bowels of the earth, or running horizontally along some great seam of coal, or rising vertically toward the surface again.

At length all was ready. Perry bowed his head in prayer. For a moment we were silent, and then the old man's hand grasped the starting lever. There was a frightful roaring beneath us—the giant frame trembled and vibrated—there was a rush of sound as the loose earth passed up through the hollow space between the inner and outer jackets to be deposited in our wake. We were off!

The noise was deafening. The sensation was frightful. For a full minute neither of us could do aught but cling with the proverbial desperation of the drowning man to the handrails of our swinging seats. Then Perry glanced at the thermometer.

"Gad!" he cried, "it cannot be possible—quick! What does the distance meter read?"

That and the speedometer were both on my side of the cabin, and as I turned to take a reading from the former I could see Perry muttering.

"Ten degrees rise—it cannot be possible!" and then I saw him tug frantically upon the steering wheel.

As I finally found the tiny needle in the dim light I translated Perry's evident excitement, and my heart sank within me. But when I spoke I hid the fear which haunted me. "It will be seven hundred feet, Perry," I said, "by the time you can turn her into the horizontal."

"You'd better lend me a hand then, my boy," he replied, "for I cannot budge her out of the vertical alone. God give that our combined strength may be equal to the task, for else we are lost."

I wormed my way to the old man's side with never a doubt but that the great wheel would yield on the instant to the power of my young and vigorous muscles. Nor was my belief mere vanity, for always had my physique been the envy and despair of my fellows. And for that very reason it had waxed even greater than nature had intended, since my natural pride in my great strength had led me to care for and develop my body and my muscles by every means within my power. What with boxing, football, and baseball, I had been in training since childhood.

And so it was with the utmost confidence that I laid hold of the huge iron rim; but though I threw every ounce of my strength into it, my best effort was as unavailing as Perry's had been—the thing would not budge—the grim, insensate, horrible thing that was holding us upon the straight road to death!

At length I gave up the useless struggle, and without a word returned to my seat. There was no need for words—at least none that I could imagine, unless Perry desired to pray. And I was quite sure that he would, for he never left an opportunity neglected where he might sandwich in a prayer. He prayed when he arose in the morning, he prayed before he ate, he prayed when he had finished eating, and before he went to bed at night he prayed again. In between he often found excuses to pray even when the provocation seemed far-fetched to my worldly eyes—now that he was about to die I felt positive that I should witness a perfect orgy of prayer—if one may allude with such a simile to so solemn an act.

But to my astonishment I discovered that with death staring him in the face Abner Perry was transformed into a new being. From his lips there flowed—not prayer—but a clear and limpid stream of undiluted profanity, and it was all directed at that quietly stubborn piece of unyielding mechanism.

"I should think, Perry," I chided, "that a man of your professed religious-ness would rather be at his prayers than cursing in the presence of imminent death."

"Death!" he cried. "Death is it that appalls you? That is nothing by com-parison with the loss the world must suffer. Why, David within this iron cylinder we have demonstrated possibilities that science has scarce dreamed. We have harnessed a new principle, and with it animated a piece of steel with the power of ten thousand men. That two lives will be snuffed out is nothing to the world calamity that entombs in the bowels of the earth the discoveries that I have made and proved in the successful construction of the thing that is now carrying us farther and farther toward the eternal central fires."

I am frank to admit that for myself I was much more concerned with our own immediate future than with any problematic loss which the world might be about to suffer. The world was at least ignorant of its bereavement, while to me it was a real and terrible actuality.

"What can we do?" I asked, hiding my perturbation beneath the mask of a low and level voice.

"We may stop here, and die of asphyxiation when our atmosphere tanks are empty," replied Perry, "or we may continue on with the slight hope that we may later sufficiently deflect the prospector from the vertical to carry us along the arc of a great circle which must eventually return us to the surface. If we succeed in so doing before we reach the higher internal temperature we may even yet survive. There would seem to me to be about one chance in several million that we shall succeed—otherwise we shall die more quickly but no more surely than as though we sat supinely waiting for the torture of a slow and horrible death."

I glanced at the thermometer. It registered 110 degrees. While we were talking the mighty iron mole had bored its way over a mile into the rock of the earth's crust.

"Let us continue on, then," I replied. "It should soon be over at this rate. You never intimated that the speed of this thing would be so high, Perry. Didn't you know it?"

"No," he answered. "I could not figure the speed exactly, for I had no instrument for measuring the mighty power of my generator. I reasoned, however, that we should make about five hundred yards an hour."

"And we are making seven miles an hour," I concluded for him, as I sat with my eyes upon the distance meter. "How thick is the Earth's crust, Perry?" I asked.

"There are almost as many conjectures as to that as there are geologists," was his answer. "One estimates it thirty miles, because the internal heat, increasing at the rate of about one degree to each sixty to seventy feet depth, would be sufficient to fuse the most refractory substances at that distance beneath the surface. Another finds that the phenomena of precession and nutation require that the earth, if not entirely solid, must at least have a shell not less than eight hundred to a thousand miles in thickness. So there you are. You may take your choice."

"And if it should prove solid?" I asked.

"It will be all the same to us in the end, David," replied Perry. "At the best our fuel will suffice to carry us but three or four days, while our atmosphere cannot last to exceed three. Neither, then, is sufficient to bear us in safety through eight thousand miles of rock to the antipodes."

"If the crust is of sufficient thickness we shall come to a final stop between six and seven hundred miles beneath the earth's surface; but during the last hundred and fifty miles of our journey we shall be corpses. Am I correct?" I asked.

"Quite correct, David. Are you frightened?"

"I do not know. It all has come so suddenly that I scarce believe that either of us realizes the real terrors of our position. I feel that I should be reduced to panic; but yet I am not. I imagine that the shock has been so great as to partially stun our sensibilities."

Again I turned to the thermometer. The mercury was rising with less rapidity. It was now but 140 degrees, although we had penetrated to a depth of nearly four miles. I told Perry, and he smiled.

"We have shattered one theory at least," was his only comment, and then he returned to his self-assumed occupation of fluently cursing the steering wheel. I once heard a pirate swear, but his best efforts would have seemed like those of a tyro alongside of Perry's masterful and scientific imprecations.

Once more I tried my hand at the wheel, but I might as well have essayed to swing the earth itself. At my suggestion Perry stopped the generator, and as we came to rest I again threw all my strength into a supreme effort to move the thing even a hair's breadth—but the results were as barren as when we had been traveling at top speed.

I shook my head sadly, and motioned to the starting lever. Perry pulled it toward him, and once again we were plunging downward toward eternity at the rate of seven miles an hour. I sat with my eyes glued to the thermometer and the distance meter. The mercury was rising very slowly now, though even at 145 degrees it was almost unbearable within the narrow confines of our metal prison.

About noon, or twelve hours after our start upon this unfortunate journey, we had bored to a depth of eighty-four miles, at which point the mercury registered 153 degrees F.

Perry was becoming more hopeful, although upon what meager food he sustained his optimism I could not conjecture. From cursing he had turned to singing—I felt that the strain had at last affected his mind. For several hours we had not spoken except as he asked me for the readings of the instruments from time to time, and I announced them. My thoughts were filled with vain regrets. I recalled numerous acts of my past life which I should have been glad to have had a few more years to live down. There was the affair in the Latin Commons at Andover when Calhoun and I had put gunpowder in the stove—and nearly killed one of the masters. And then—but what was the use, I was about to die and atone for all these things and several more. Already the heat was sufficient to give me a foretaste of the hereafter. A few more degrees and I felt that I should lose consciousness.

"What are the readings now, David?" Perry's voice broke in upon my somber reflections.

"Ninety miles and 153 degrees," I replied.

"Gad, but we've knocked that thirty-mile-crust theory into a cocked hat!" he cried gleefully.

"Precious lot of good it will do us," I growled back.

"But my boy," he continued, "doesn't that temperature reading mean anything to you? Why it hasn't gone up in six miles. Think of it, son!"

"Yes, I'm thinking of it," I answered; "but what difference will it make when our air supply is exhausted whether the temperature is 153 degrees or 153,000? We'll be just as dead, and no one will know the difference, anyhow." But I must admit that for some unaccountable reason the stationary temperature did renew my waning hope. What I hoped for I could not have explained, nor did I try. The very fact, as Perry took pains to explain, of the blasting of several very exact and learned scientific hypotheses made it apparent that we could not know what lay before us within the bowels of the earth, and so we might continue to hope for the best, at least until we were dead—when hope would no longer be essential to our happiness. It was very good, and logical reasoning, and so I embraced it.

At one hundred miles the temperature had DROPPED TO 152½ DEGREES! When I announced it Perry reached over and hugged me.

From then on until noon of the second day, it continued to drop until it became as uncomfortably cold as it had been unbearably hot before. At the depth of two hundred and forty miles our nostrils were assailed by almost overpowering ammonia fumes, and the temperature had dropped to TEN BELOW ZERO! We suffered nearly two hours of this intense and bitter cold, until at about two hundred and forty-five miles from the surface of the earth we entered a stratum of solid ice, when the mercury quickly rose to 32 degrees. During the next three hours we passed through ten miles of ice, eventually emerging into another series of ammonia-impregnated strata, where the mercury again fell to ten degrees below zero.

Slowly it rose once more until we were convinced that at last we were nearing the molten interior of the earth. At four hundred miles the temperature had reached 153 degrees. Feverishly I watched the thermometer. Slowly it rose. Perry had ceased singing and was at last praying.

Our hopes had received such a deathblow that the gradually increasing heat seemed to our distorted imaginations much greater than it really was. For another hour I saw that pitiless column of mercury rise and rise until at four hundred and ten miles it stood at 153 degrees. Now it was that we began to hang upon those readings in almost breathless anxiety.

One hundred and fifty-three degrees had been the maximum temperature above the ice stratum. Would it stop at this point again, or would it continue its merciless climb? We knew that there was no hope, and yet with the persistence of life itself we continued to hope against practical certainty.

Already the air tanks were at low ebb—there was barely enough of the precious gases to sustain us for another twelve hours. But would we be alive to know or care? It seemed incredible.

At four hundred and twenty miles I took another reading.

"Perry!" I shouted. "Perry, man! She's going down! She's going down! She's 152 degrees again."

"Gad!" he cried. "What can it mean? Can the earth be cold at the center?"

"I do not know, Perry," I answered; "but thank God, if I am to die it shall not be by fire—that is all that I have feared. I can face the thought of any death but that."

Down, down went the mercury until it stood as low as it had seven miles from the surface of the earth, and then of a sudden the realization broke upon us that death was very near. Perry was the first to discover it. I saw him fussing with the valves that regulate the air supply. And at the same time I experienced difficulty in breathing. My head felt dizzy—my limbs heavy.

I saw Perry crumple in his seat. He gave himself a shake and sat erect again. Then he turned toward me.

"Good-bye, David," he said. "I guess this is the end," and then he smiled and closed his eyes.

"Good-bye, Perry, and good luck to you," I answered, smiling back at him. But I fought off that awful lethargy. I was very young—I did not want to die.

For an hour I battled against the cruelly enveloping death that surrounded me upon all sides. At first I found that by climbing high into the framework above me I could find more of the precious life-giving elements, and for a while these sustained me. It must have been an hour after Perry had succumbed that I at last came to the realization that I could no longer carry on this unequal struggle against the inevitable.

With my last flickering ray of consciousness I turned mechanically toward the distance meter. It stood at exactly five hundred miles from the earth's surface—and then of a sudden the huge thing that bore us came to a stop. The rattle of hurtling rock through the hollow jacket ceased. The wild racing of the giant drill betokened that it was running loose in AIR—and then another truth flashed upon me. The point of the prospector was ABOVE us. Slowly it dawned on me that since passing through the ice strata it had been above. We had turned in the ice and sped upward toward the earth's crust. Thank God! We were safe!

I put my nose to the intake pipe through which samples were to have been taken during the passage of the prospector through the earth, and my fondest hopes were realized—a flood of fresh air was pouring into the iron cabin. The reaction left me in a state of collapse, and I lost consciousness.

"The Glittering Lady"

Riccardo Gramantieri

In a 2012 article published in *Nature*, author and publisher Joshua Glenn coined the term "Radium Age" to define science fiction written between 1904 and 1933: "It emerged when the speed of change in science and technology was inducing vertigo on both sides of the Atlantic. More cynical than its Victorian precursor yet less hard-boiled than the generation that followed, this is sci-fi offering a dizzying, visionary blend of acerbic social commentary and shock tactics. It yields telling insights into its context, the early twentieth century" (Glenn, 204). The first three decades of the 20th century were marked by great scientific and technological progress. During that historical period, a veritable revolution took place in chemistry and physics. This was possible, in part, thanks to the discovery of radium by Marie and Pierre Curie. As a result of the Curies' work, the physics and technology of radioactivity underwent considerable growth. For example, radium made it possible to conduct a series of tests that led to the discovery of the atomic structure (Geiger and Marsden). In addition, radium was believed to be a substance capable of improving all health conditions. Besides the alleged beneficial and healthy properties, radium is characterized by radioluminescence. This feature gave it an almost divine halo effect.

To the readers who discovered all the allegedly wonderful properties of radium, both beneficial and aesthetic, it appeared as if scientists had discovered the fountain of eternal youth long sought after in classical and Medieval mythology. It is no surprise that an author of popular novels like Henry Rider Haggard (like many others), at the end of the 1910s, included this element in *When the World Shook*, one of his most famous lost race stories.

The Discovery and Marketing of Radium

Pierre and Marie Curie discovered the element radium in 1898. In particular, it was Marie who specialized in experimenting with radium. She won the Nobel Prize twice for her work with radium: in 1903 for contributions to physics and in 1911 for contributions to chemistry.

Marie Sklodowska Curie was born in Warsaw in 1867. She studied in Paris and initially worked with her husband Pierre and Antoine Henri Becquerel. She had just started her Ph.D. in 1898 when she coined the term "radioactivity" to describe the fact that thorium and uranium emitted what at that time were called "Becquerel rays" (Pasachof, 37). In the following years, the scientist dedicated her time to conducting additional experiments on radioactive materials. It was during this long work that Marie Curie discovered radium. In the biography written by her daughter Eve (1938), it is told that the initial result of this work was just one gram of radium obtained from eight tons of pitchblende. In light of such a huge amount of work, her husband Pierre jokingly said he hoped that after so much effort, radium would at least have "a very beautiful colour" (Curie, 168). Radium had something that was much more beautiful than a nice color; it was naturally luminous. In the laboratory, the few extracted fragments of material were phosphorescent like small fireflies in the night: "She was to remember for ever this evening of glow-worms, this magic" (Curie, 173).

Radium immediately appeared to be extraordinary, much more than the other radioactive elements such as uranium or polonium (the latter were also discovered by Curie in 1902), and its properties were soon put to use. As a source of emission of small particles, it made it possible for Ernest Rutherford (1911) to discover the atomic structure. Moreover, it turned out that it was much more radioactive than uranium, it generated heat spontaneously, it imprinted photographic plates, it made the atmosphere electrically-conductive, and it made other bodies able to emit phosphorescent light.

Radium soon became one of the first therapeutic means to fight cancer and lupus (the actual therapy was known as *curietherapy*). In just a few years, a veritable industry was created for the radium products which, at first, seemed to be almost a miracle. Luminescence was widely used in the watch industry, until a few decades later when the toxicity of these paints was discovered (Clark). In the world of medicine, radium made it possible to see the bones inside a human body; a radiograph could be obtained after some hour's exposure using a few milligrams of radium (Mould, 25). Its presumed therapeutic properties were used in the field of medicine; in addition to cancer treatment, doctors believed it could also be used to treat other conditions such as hypertension, diabetes, arthritis, rheumatism, gout, and tuberculosis.

The most common commercial applications included mineral water, spas, toothpaste, and cosmetics. The idea of drinkable radium spread very quickly, and newspapers began to promote the radium cocktail story. Water containing radium was said to improve one's physical and mental performance. Radium-infused water was considered to be a "healthful tonic" (Herbert, 297). The most famous of these waters was the Revigator, invented by R.W. Thomas and patented in 1912. It was described as a "radioactive water crock...—it was a large jar made of radium containing uranium ore with an attached spigot. Consumers were instructed to fill the jar every night and 'drink freely,' averaging between six and seven glasses each day" (Kang and Pedersen, 48). Tourist organizations took the opportunity in the spa-like business. It was believed that one hour and a half in the Sunshine Radon Health Mine three times a day for ten or eleven days would cure arthritis, sinusitis, migraine, eczema, and asthma (Caufield, 28). The cosmetics industry also took advantage of the miraculous properties of radium with products like radioactive toothpaste and beauty creams: "'Radiate Youth and Beauty,' 'Radium is Restoring Health to Thousands,' and 'Remarkable NEW Radium Cream Liniment Drives Our Pam from Aching Joints and Muscles *Instantly!*'" (Malley, 152; Kang and Pedersen, 47). That is not to mention the paraphernalia:

> By 1904, "radiomania" had escaped from the printed page and taken hold in America's living rooms. Lectures on radium were the latest thing at afternoon teas. Devices called spinthariscopes, magnified viewing tubes containing a miniscule speck of radium, became such popular Christmas gift that store shelves were emptied. Also popular were radium roulette, an expensive party game played at night with luminous parts, and home-made imitations of "liquid sunshine," called radium punch (usually done with back-lit glasses) [de la Pena, 189].

To the readers of popular magazines in which these wondrous ads appeared, radium came to look like a substance with endless beneficial properties. According to water- and cosmetics-producers, its ability to affect the atomic structure translated into the ability to promptly act on human cells in order to prevent their ageing. Radium was a miracle.

H.R. Haggard and the Model of Immortal Woman

Amid such excitement, even the adventurous and fantastic fiction of that time used radioactivity as a marvelous and technologically innovative element, sometimes in lieu of the usual metaphysical and spiritual elements. Before the discovery of radioactivity, immortality in adventure novels was only granted through reincarnation or via the transfer of the soul or consciousness;

"Radium and Beauty" (ad for Radior). *New York Tribune*, November 10, 1918.

later, a millennia-long life was granted due to the invention of extraordinary devices that exploited radioactive vapors (as in *When the World Shook* by Haggard, precisely). This shift from spiritualism to the imaginative use of chemistry discovery bears similarity to the Victorian popularization of mathematics (Valente).

Works of adventure and fantasy that use radium and radioactivity as a plot element become science fiction. Therefore, the science fiction genre adopts tropes from other popular radium age genres, such as adventure, fantasy, mystery, and horror. Were it not for Henry Rider Haggard's inclusion of scientific details and plot elements, *When the World Shook* (1919) would certainly fall into the genre of adventure. At its core, *When the World Shook* is a "lost world" story. Haggard set the standards for the "lost races" story with *King Solomon's Mines* (1885), but it was with the novel *She* (1886) that he defined a new type of story: the matriarchal lost world story. In this novel, and in his sequel *The Return of Ayesha*, (1905), the woman-goddess achieved immortality through mysterious natural phenomena such as the Flame in the great cavern and reincarnation.

At the end of the 19th century, the practices of theosophy and the occult were rising in popularity across Europe and in America. Modern theosophy adopted the ideas of Helena Blavatsky (1831–1891), a Russian occultist who, first in New York and then throughout the world, gained popularity for the philosophical and religious ideas she propagandized. Blavatsky's theosophy drew on Hindu and Buddhist traditions, to which she added the beliefs that reincarnation was real and that there were multiples planes of existence. The East retained a sense of isolation, pastoral beauty, and ancient wisdom: "The East was symbolic of the past, the morning of the world, the pre-evolutionary era" (Dijkstra, 335). The East is the place of choice for Spiritualists: western languages find it hard to convey the meaning of certain concepts that, on the contrary, are better expressed in eastern idioms, which are endowed with a special nicety, "pre-eminently the Sanskrit" (Blavatsky, 39).

Followers of the occult, on the other hand, claimed that the dead could communicate with and affect the real world. The beginnings of modern following of the Occult can be traced back to two sisters: Kate and Maggie Fox. They "were naughty little girls who amused themselves by making strange noises which superstitious persons interpreted as communications from the dead. This proving profitable to the sisters Fox, the business of producing 'spirit knocking' spread from town to town, and forthwith modern spiritism [*sic*] was born" (Bruce, 87). In Europe, the work and practices of Sir William Crookes, an English scientist devoted to the study of electrical conduction in gases and of spectroscopy, took an interest in the spiritualistic phenomena of the Fox sisters and other mediums such as Florence Cook. He brought to Europe, mainly to London, these new beliefs and, though involved in several allegations of fraud (Oppenheim, 346), helped to spread support for Occult beliefs thanks to the studies conducted by who believed in the truthfulness of the medium's work. Theosophy and the occult often overlapped. The souls with which the mediums claimed to come in contact often told of having travelled on astral planes that resembled Oriental landscapes such as the planet Mars described by Flournoy in his thorough study on the medium Hélène Smith; the souls themselves often had an oriental identity, such as Princess Simandini, or an eastern look as in the case of wise Martian Astanè with whom Hélène Smith was in contact (Flournoy). Souls presented themselves as ancient sages and conveyed messages with theosophical contents. The mediums expressed an image of the East that had filtered through the familiar theosophical writings (Fournoy; Jung).

These occult and theosophical beliefs, including metempsychosis (transfer of the soul between bodies), telepathy, and communication with the dead were readily used by authors of popular novels set in exotic places. Between the end of the 19th century and the beginning of the 20th, in pulp fiction magazines such as *Argosy, Popular Magazine*, and *Weird Tales*, exoticism and reincarnation were common topics.

Haggard drew upon popular Occult and theosophical beliefs in his novels as well. His queens were often ancient priestesses incarnate who, at the moment of their death, had freed their spirits in order to travel to other bodies. Haggard's queens resemble European mediums in many ways. With the introduction of a radiotechnology, Haggard transforms theosophical and spiritist fantasies into scientific romance.

In fact, the scientific romance had very little to do with science. Brian Stableford writes that the term initially identified the genre of the first novels by H.G. Wells, which combined fiction with speculative nonfiction: "A scientific romance is a story which is built around something glimpsed through a window of possibility from which scientific discovery has drawn back the curtain" (Stableford, 8). Later, the term was left to designate a type of science fiction that has much in common with the traditional British novel. With the introduction of the scientific element, Haggard continued this Wellsian tradition of biologic, evolutionary and masculine romance (Luckhurst, 31). Other examples are Arthur Conan Doyle's novels featuring Professor Challenger (Brantlinger, 376).

Haggard's novels all follow a similar narrative structure. A hero travels to exotic or unexplored lands (*She* is set in Africa, *The Return of Ayesha* in Tibet, and *When the World Shook* in the South Pacific), where he finds the ideal woman who lives in a place outside of time. They feel connected by very ancient and mysterious ties. Their love, however, usually does not have a happy ending, and the beloved cannot follow the man on his journey home. These beautiful and desolate locations are the chosen place for ancestral women (Gramantieri). The timeless settings reflect the heroine's mysterious and polarized figure: killer and lover, goddess and witch, and almost always immortal.

When the World Shook follows the same generic adventure plot found in *She* and its sequels. However, *When the World Shook* reaches into the realm of science fiction with its incorporation of details related to the popularization of radium and radioactivity. The discovery of radium and the fascination it had acquired in popular culture inspired Haggard to take a new approach. What better way to explain the fall of a lost civilization and the survival of its royalty?

In his survey of Haggard's work, R.D. Mullen describes *When the World Shook* as "The most science-fictional of Haggard's novels, for along with such psychic phenomena as metempsychosis we have suspended animation with survivors from a technologically advanced civilization 250,000 years in the past, a chart comparing the star patterns of that time with those of today, and a monstrous machine—one capable of changing the tilt of the earth" (291). *She* and *The Return of Ayesha*, where eternal youth and immortality were achieved through reincarnation, were fantasy novels. Haggard's reliance on radium and radioactivity and the description of devices capable of modifying the planet situates *When the World Shook* in the field of science fiction.

The novel follows protagonist Humphrey Arbuthnot on his journey to the South Pacific. Humphrey is the Vicar's son from Devonshire. He is a beautiful, athletic, and successful man who lives comfortably thanks to an inheritance. After his wife, Natalie, dies during childbirth, Humphrey goes on a trip to the Pacific islands with his friends. His two university friends play supporting roles. Bastin and Bickley are polar opposites. Bastin is a church-going man with a simple mind; Bickley, on the other hand, is a doctor and a firm atheist who is fully convinced that man is a casual descendant of monkeys.

An early episode demonstrates Haggard's inventive combination of generic elements characteristic of radium age science fiction. Haggard integrates details about science and technology through the theme of reincarnation. Before Natalie dies, she says to her husband: "Go where you seem called to go, far away. Oh! the wonderful place in which you will find me, not knowing that you have found me. Good-bye for a little while; only for a little while, my own, my own!" (Haggard, 41).

During a hurricane, their yacht shipwrecks on an uncharted island. Humphrey, Bastin, and Bickley are the only survivors. The trio encounter a tribe of cannibal natives who come to fear the white men because of Bickley's surgical skills. In one scene, Bickley removes a tumor from the body of Chief Marama. Bickley saves the life of Chief Marama, which causes the tribe to view the doctor as something of a magician.

Humphrey, Bastin, and Bickley explore the island. They discover a lake, which Chief Marama warned them was sacred and prohibited. Out of sheer curiosity, the men decide to explore further. In a cave, the men discover some mysterious machinery and two crystal sarcophagi. In one lies "a most wonderful old man, clad in a gleaming, embroidered robe" (Haggard, 137). In the other sarcophagus there is a young woman: "In truth, she was a splendid creature, and yet, I know not how, her beauty suggested more of the spirit than of the flesh" (138–9). The woman is enveloped by a sort of radioluminescence, which is the reason she is called the glittering lady.

The old man, Oro, was the King and scientist of an ancient civilization; she is Lady Yva, his daughter. They reigned over a continent, which sank 250,000 years ago as the result of Oro's mad science experiments. This island is all that is left of their civilization.

The narrative commences along the lines of *She* and *The Return of Ayesha*, with a romance between Humphrey and Yva. The meeting with the woman fulfills Natalie's premonition. It is as if the souls of the two women were connected to each other, as if Natalie's death had made Yva's resurrection possible. This combination of science and esoterism is one of the characteristic aspects of this Radium-Age science fiction, destined to soon disappear in the Golden Age of science fiction.

At the end, Yva offers Humphrey immortality and a place beside her on the throne. Humphrey, however, does not accept. Yva sacrifices her own life in order to prevent Oro's machine from destroying the planet.

Radium and Resurrection

As noted above, *When the World Shook* adapts the plot structure of *She* and *The Return of Ayesha*. Haggard updates the lost races trope by integrating techniques from the emerging genre of science fiction. In *She* and in its sequels *The Return of Ayesha* and *Wisdom's Daughter*, Haggard's female protagonists live on through the centuries by means of reincarnation. In *When the World Shook,* he resorts to radioactivity to explain Lady Yva's vitality. Haggard describes radium-infused water as her source of life.

When the World Shook was not the first or the last novel to draw upon the popularity of radium for the intrigue of adventure. For example, shortly before Haggard, Abraham Merritt in *The Moon Pool* (1918) told of the discovery of a civilization residing in a hidden world under the Pacific Ocean powered by a well of glowing radioactive water. A decade later, Ed Earl Repp's *The Radium Pool* (1929) describes a community of aliens who live in a desert cave lit by a green phosphorescence generated by radioactive water. In the underwater world described by Jack Williamson in *The Green Girl* (1930), radium is a source of energy that provides power.

The influence of the discovery of radium and the popularity of radioactive materials in the American market is clearly represented in chapter eleven of *When the World Shook*, which chronicles the resurrection of Oro and Yva. In the previous pages, Humphrey and friends go inside the cave and find the bodies of an old man and his daughter inside glass sarcophagi. Haggard narrates: "Indeed, in a way, it was unearthly. My senses were smitten, it pulled at my heart-strings, and yet its unutterable strangeness seemed to awake memories within me, though of what I could not tell. A wild fancy came to me that I must have known this heavenly creature in some past life" (139). Both bodies are enveloped in a phosphorescent halo. It is this property of radium that gives the girl her beauty and youth.

Humphrey and friends must try to bring them back to life. They try with the old man first. They approach the sarcophagus and watch as the crystals emit a warm, phosphorescent light:

—Great heavens!—I exclaimed,—here's magic.

—There's no such thing,—answered Bickley in his usual formula. Then an explanation seemed to strike him and he added,—Not magic but radium or something of the sort. That's how the temperature was kept up. In sufficient quantity it is practically indestructible, you see. My word! this old gentleman knew a thing or two [145–146].

When they try to bring the girl back to life, they once again find the same radioactive source of youth: "Then we lifted her from that narrow bed in which she had slept for—ah! how long? and perceived that beneath her also were crystal boxes of the radiant, heat-giving substance" (153). The men interpret this discovery ambiguously. Humphrey, an adventure writer, thinks it could be magic. Bickley, the scientist, embodies the point of view of Haggard, the science fiction writer; he concludes that the glow must be radioactive. The substance contained in the crystal boxes has allowed the girl and the old man to stay alive for 250,000 years.

The miraculous effects of radium are again described later on in the novel. In chapter XIV there is a description of a fountain in the shape of a woman, whose hands hold two cups made of black and white marble from which "a thin stream of sparkling water" (204) gushes out. It is the water of life. Here Haggard, through Yva's words, reiterates the properties of the glowing water "is very health-giving," she answered, "and if drunk continually, not less than once each thirty days, it wards off sickness, lessens hunger and postpones death for many, many years" (206). But youth is not the only effect radium has: when Humphry drank it, he "felt extremely strong and well, happier, too, than I had been for years" (205). In addition to feeling strong and happy, radioactive water is even capable of enhancing cognitive skill. Indeed, when Humphrey drinks the water of life, he acquires knowledge:

> I began to understand several problems that had puzzled me, and then lost their explanations in the midst of light, inner light, I mean. Moreover, of a sudden it seemed to me as though a window had been opened in the heart of that Glittering Lady who stood beside me. At least I knew that it was full of wonderful knowledge, wonderful memories and wonderful hopes, and that in the latter two of these I had some part; what part I could not tell. Also, I knew that my heart was open to her and that she saw in it something which caused her to marvel and to sigh [208–209].

Through its representation in science fiction, radium becomes a sort of modern philosopher's stone.

BIBLIOGRAPHY

Ashley, Mike. 2000. *The Time Machines: The Story of the Science-Fiction Pulp Magazines from the Beginning to 1950*. Liverpool UP.

Blavatsky Helena P. 1939. *Practical Occultism*. Theosophical Publishing House.

Brantlinger, Patrick. 2002. "Victorian Science Fiction." *A Companion to the Victorian Novel*. Edited by Patrick Brantlinger. Blackwell.

Bruce, H. Addington. 2013 [1914]. *Adventurings in the Psychical*. The Floating Press.

Caufield, Catherine. 1989. *Multiple Exposure. Chronicles of the Radiation Age.* U of Chicago P.

Clark, Claudia. 1997. *Radium Girls, Women and Industrial Health Reform: 1910–1935.* U of North Carolina P.

Curie, Eva. 1938. *Madame Curie.* William Heinemann.

De la Peña, Carolyn Thomas. 2005. *The Body Electric: How Strange Machines Built the Modern American.* New York UP.

Dijkstra, Bram. 1986. *Idols of Perversity: Fantasies of Feminine Evil in Fin-de-siècle Culture.* Oxford UP.

Flournoy, Theodore. 2015. *From India to the Planet Mars: A Case of Multiple Personality with Imaginary Languages.* Princeton UP.

Geiger, Hans, and Marsden Ernest. 1909. "On a Diffuse Reflection of the α-Particles." *Proceedings of the Royal Society of London* 82: 495–500.

Glenn, Joshua. 2012. "Science Fiction: The Radium Age." *Nature* 489, no. 7415: 204–205.

Gramantieri, Riccardo. 2018. "Il Deserto Dell'Anima" [The Desert of Jungian Anima]. *Il Minotauro-problemi E Ricerche Di Psicologia Del Profondo* XLV, no. 2: 49–61.

Gunn, James E. 2002. *The Road to Science Fiction: Volume I: From Gilgamesh to Wells.* Scarecrow.

Haggard, Henry Rider. 1919. *When the World Shook.* Longmans, Green and Co.

Herbert Paul N. 2011. *God Knows All Your Names: Stories in American History.* Author House.

Jung, Carl Gustav. 1983. *Collected Works of C.G. Jung, Volume 1: Psychiatric Studies: Psychiatric Studies.* Princeton UP.

Kang, Lydia, and Pedersen, Nate. 2017. *Quackery: A Brief History of the Worst Ways to Cure Everything.* Workman Publishing.

Luckhurst, Patrick. 2005. *Science Fiction.* Polity Press.

Malley, Marjorie C. 2011. *Radioactivity. a History of a Mysterious Science.* Oxford UP.

Mould, Richard F. 1993. *A Century of X-rays and Radioactivity in Medicine.* Institute of Physics Publishing.

Mullen, Richard Dale. 1978. "The Books of H. Rider Haggard: A Chronological Survey." *Science Fiction Studies* 5, no. 3: 287–291.

Oppenheim, Janet. 1985. *The Other World: Spiritualism and Psychical Research in England, 1850–1914.* Cambridge UP.

Pasachof, Naomi. 1996. *Marie Curie and the Science of Radioactivity.* Oxford UP.

Rutherford Ernest. 1911. "The Scattering of α and β Particles by Matter and the Structure of the Atom." *Philosophical Magazine* 21: 669–688.

Stableford, Brian. 1985. *Scientific Romance in Britain 1890–1950.* St. Martin's.

Valente, Ken. G. 2008. "'Who Will Explain the Explanation?': The Ambivalent Reception of Higher Dimensional Space in the British Spiritualist Press, 1875–1900." *Victorian Periodicals Review* 41, No. 2: 124–149.

Wilt, Judith. 1981. "The Imperial Mouth: Imperialism, the Gothic and Science Fiction." *Journal of Popular Culture* 14: 618–628.

When the World Shook (1919)
Chapter 11: Resurrection

H. Rider Haggard

We reached the sepulcher without stopping to look at the parked machines or even the marvelous statue that stood above it, for what did we care about machines or statues now? As we approached we were astonished to hear low and cavernous growlings.

"There is some wild beast in there," said Bickley, halting. "No, by George! it's Tommy. What can the dog be after?"

We peeped in, and there sure enough was Tommy lying on the top of the Glittering Lady's coffin and growling his very best with the hair standing up upon his back. When he saw who it was, however, he jumped off and frisked round, licking my hand.

"That's very strange," I exclaimed.

"Not stranger than everything else," said Bickley.

"What are you going to do?" I asked.

"Open these coffins," he answered, "beginning with that of the old god, since I would rather experiment on him. I expect he will crumble into dust. But if by chance he doesn't I'll jam a little strychnine, mixed with some other drugs, of which you don't know the names, into one of his veins and see if anything happens. If it doesn't, it won't hurt him, and if it does—well, who knows? Now give me a hand."

We went to the left-hand coffin and by inserting the hook on the back of my knife, of which the real use is to pick stones out of horses' hoofs, into one of the little air-holes I have described, managed to raise the heavy crystal lid sufficiently to enable us to force a piece of wood between it and the top. The rest was easy, for the hinges being of crystal had not corroded. In two minutes it was open.

From the chest came an overpowering spicy odor, and with it a veritable breath of warm air before which we recoiled a little. Bickley took a pocket thermometer which he had at hand and glanced at it. It marked a temperature of 82 degrees in the sepulcher. Having noted this, he thrust it into the coffin between the crystal wall and its occupant. Then we went out and waited a little while to give the odors time to dissipate, for they made the head reel.

After five minutes or so we returned and examined the thermometer. It had risen to 98 degrees, the natural temperature of the human body.

"What do you make of that if the man is dead?" he whispered.

I shook my head, and as we had agreed, set to helping him to lift the body from the coffin. It was a good weight, quite eleven stone I should say; moreover, it was not stiff, for the hip joints bent. We got it out and laid it on a blanket we had spread on the floor of the sepulcher. Whilst I was thus engaged I saw something that nearly caused me to loose my hold from astonishment. Beneath the head, the center of the back and the feet were crystal boxes about eight inches square, or rather crystal blocks, for in them I could see no opening, and these boxes emitted a faint phosphorescent light. I touched one of them and found that it was quite warm.

"Great heavens!" I exclaimed, "here's magic."

"There's no such thing," answered Bickley in his usual formula. Then an explanation seemed to strike him and he added, "Not magic but radium or something of the sort. That's how the temperature was kept up. In sufficient quantity it is practically indestructible, you see. My word! this old gentleman knew a thing or two."

Again we waited a little while to see if the body begun to crumble on exposure to the air, I taking the opportunity to make a rough sketch of it in my pocket-book in anticipation of that event. But it did not; it remained quite sound.

"Here goes," said Bickley. "If he should be alive, he will catch cold in his lungs after lying for ages in that baby incubator, as I suppose he has done. So it is now or never."

Then bidding me hold the man's right arm, he took the sterilized syringe which he had prepared, and thrusting the needle into a vein he selected just above the wrist, injected the contents.

"It would have been better over the heart," he whispered, "but I thought I would try the arm first. I don't like risking chills by uncovering him."

I made no answer and again we waited and watched.

"Great heavens, he's stirring!" I gasped presently.

Stirring he was, for his fingers began to move.

Bickley bent down and placed his ear to the heart—I forgot to say that he had tested this before with a stethoscope, but had been unable to detect any movement.

"I believe it is beginning to beat," he said in an awed voice.

Then he applied the stethoscope, and added, "It is, it is!"

Next he took a filament of cotton wool and laid it on the man's lips. Presently it moved; he was breathing, though very faintly. Bickley took more cotton wool and having poured something from his medicine-chest on to it, placed it over the mouth beneath the man's nostrils—I believe it was sal volatile.

Nothing further happened for a little while, and to relieve the strain on my mind I stared absently into the empty coffin. Here I saw what had escaped our notice, two small plates of white metal and cut upon them what I took to be star maps. Beyond these and the glowing boxes which I have mentioned, there was nothing else in the coffin. I had no time to examine them, for at that moment the old man opened his mouth and began to breathe, evidently with some discomfort and effort, as his empty lungs filled themselves with air. Then his eyelids lifted, revealing a wonderful pair of dark glowing eyes beneath. Next he tried to sit up but would have fallen, had not Bickley supported him with his arm.

I do not think he saw Bickley, indeed he shut his eyes again as though the light hurt them, and went into a kind of faint. Then it was that Tommy, who all this while had been watching the proceedings with grave interest, came forward, wagging his tail, and licked the man's face. At the touch of the dog's red tongue, he opened his eyes for the second time. Now he saw—not us but Tommy, for after contemplating him for a few seconds, something like a smile appeared upon his fierce but noble face. More, he lifted his hand and laid it on the dog's head, as though to pat it kindly. Half a minute or so later his awakening senses appreciated our presence. The incipient smile vanished and was replaced by a somewhat terrible frown.

Meanwhile Bickley had poured out some of the hot coffee laced with brandy into the cup that was screwed on the top of the thermos flask. Advancing to the man whom I supported, he put it to his lips. He tasted and made a wry face, but presently he began to sip, and ultimately swallowed it all. The effect of the stimulant was wonderful, for in a few minutes he came to life completely and was even able to sit up without support.

For quite a long while he gazed at us gravely, talking us in and everything connected with us. For instance, Bickley's medicine-case which lay open showing the little vulcanite tubes, a few instruments and other outfit, engaged his particular attention, and I saw at once that he understood what it was. Thus his arm still smarted where the needle had been driven in and on the blanket lay the syringe. He looked at his arm, then looked at the syringe, and nodded. The paraffin hurricane lamps also seemed to interest and win his approval. We two men, as I thought, attracted him least of all; he just summed us up and our garments, more especially the garments, with a few shrewd glances, and then seemed to turn his thoughts to Tommy, who had seated himself quite contentedly at his side, evidently accepting him as a new addition to our party.

I confess that this behavior on Tommy's part reassured me not a little. I am a great believer in the instincts of animals, especially of dogs, and I felt certain that if this man had not been in all essentials human like ourselves, Tommy would not have tolerated him. In the same way the sleeper's clear liking for Tommy, at whom he looked much oftener and with greater kindness than he did at us, suggested that there was goodness in him somewhere, since although a dog in its wonderful tolerance may love a bad person in whom it smells out hidden virtue, no really bad person ever loved a dog, or, I may add, a child or a flower.

As a matter of fact, the "old god," as we had christened him while he was in his coffin, during all our association with him, cared infinitely more for Tommy than he did for any of us, a circumstance that ultimately was not without its influence upon our fortunes. But for this there was a reason as we learned afterwards, also he was not really so amiable as I hoped.

When we had looked at each other for a long while the sleeper began to arrange his beard, of which the length seemed to surprise him, especially as Tommy was seated on one end of it. Finding this out and apparently not wishing to disturb Tommy, he gave up the occupation, and after one or two attempts, for his tongue and lips still seemed to be stiff, addressed us in some sonorous and musical language, unlike any that we had ever heard. We shook our heads. Then by an afterthought I said "Good day" to him in the language of the Orofenans. He puzzled over the word as though it were more or less familiar to him, and when I repeated it, gave it back to me with a difference indeed, but in a way which convinced us that he quite understood what I meant. The conversation went no further at the moment because just then some memory seemed to strike him.

He was sitting with his back against the coffin of the Glittering Lady, whom therefore he had not seen. Now he began to turn round, and being too weak to do so, motioned me to help him. I obeyed, while Bickley, guessing his purpose, held up one of the hurricane lamps that he might see better. With a kind of fierce eagerness he surveyed her who lay within the coffin, and after he had done so, uttered a sigh as of intense relief.

Next he pointed to the metal cup out of which he had drunk. Bickley filled it again from the thermos flask, which I observed excited his keen interest, for, having touched the flask with his hand and found that it was cool, he appeared to marvel that the fluid coming from it should be hot and steaming. Presently he smiled as though he had got the clue to the mystery, and swallowed his second drink of coffee and spirit. This done, he motioned to us to lift the lid of the lady's coffin, pointing out a certain catch in the bolts which at first we could not master, for it will be remembered that on this coffin these were shot.

In the end, by pursuing the same methods that we had used in the instance of his own, we raised the coffin lid and once more were driven to retreat from the sepulcher for a while by the overpowering odor like to that of a whole greenhouse full of tuberoses, that flowed out of it, inducing a kind of stupefaction from which even Tommy fled.

When we returned it was to find the man kneeling by the side of the coffin, for as yet he could not stand, with his glowing eyes fixed upon the face of her who slept therein and waving his long arms above her.

"Hypnotic business! Wonder if it will work," whispered Bickley. Then he lifted the syringe and looked inquiringly at the man, who shook his head, and went on with his mesmeric passes.

I crept round him and took my stand by the sleeper's head, that I might watch her face, which was well worth watching, while Bickley, with his medicine at hand, remained near her feet, I think engaged in disinfecting the syringe in some spirit or acid. I believe he was about to make an attempt to use it when suddenly, as though beneath the influence of the hypnotic passes, a change appeared on the Glittering Lady's face. Hitherto, beautiful as it was, it had been a dead face though one of a person who had suddenly been cut off while in full health and vigor a few hours, or at the most a day or so before. Now it began to live again; it was as though the spirit were returning from afar, and not without toil and tribulation.

Expression after expression flitted across the features; indeed these seemed to change so much from moment to moment that they might have belonged to several different individuals, though each was beautiful. The fact of these remarkable changes with the suggestion of multiform personalities which they conveyed impressed both Bickley and myself very much indeed. Then the breast heaved tumultuously; it even appeared to struggle. Next the eyes opened. They were full of wonder, even of fear, but oh! what marvelous eyes. I do not know how to describe them, I cannot even state their exact color, except that it was dark, something like the blue of sapphires of the deepest tint, and yet not black; large, too, and soft as a deer's. They shut again as though the light hurt them, then once more opened and wandered about, apparently without seeing.

At length they found my face, for I was still bending over her, and, resting there, appeared to take it in by degrees. More, it seemed to touch and stir some human spring in the still-sleeping heart. At least the fear passed from her features and was replaced by a faint smile, such as a patient sometimes gives to one known and well loved, as the effects of chloroform pass away. For a while she looked at me with an earnest, searching gaze, then suddenly, for the first time moving her arms, lifted them and threw them round my neck.

The old man stared, bending his imperial brows into a little frown, but did nothing. Bickley stared also through his glasses and sniffed as though in disapproval, while I remained quite still, fighting with a wild impulse to kiss her on the lips as one would an awakening and beloved child. I doubt if I could have done so, however, for really I was immovable; my heart seemed to stop and all my muscles to be paralyzed.

I do not know for how long this endured, but I do know how it ended. Presently in the intense silence I heard Bastin's heavy voice and looking round, saw his big head projecting into the sepulcher.

"Well, I never!" he said, "you seem to have woke them up with a vengeance. If you begin like that with the lady, there will be complications before you have done, Arbuthnot."

Talk of being brought back to earth with a rush! I could have killed Bastin, and Bickley, turning on him like a tiger, told him to be off, find wood and light a large fire in front of the statue. I think he was about to argue when the Ancient gave him a glance of his fierce eyes, which alarmed him, and he departed, bewildered, to return presently with the wood.

But the sound of his voice had broken the spell. The Lady let her arms fall with a start, and shut her eyes again, seeming to faint. Bickley sprang forward with his sal volatile and applied it to her nostrils, the Ancient not interfering, for he seemed to recognize that he had to deal with a man of skill and one who meant well by them.

In the end we brought her round again and, to omit details, Bickley gave her, not coffee and brandy, but a mixture he compounded of hot water, preserved milk and meat essence. The effect of it on her was wonderful, since a few minutes after swallowing it she sat up in the coffin. Then we lifted her from that narrow bed in which she had slept for—ah! how long? and perceived that beneath her also were crystal boxes of the radiant, heat-giving substance. We sat her on the floor of the sepulcher, wrapping her also in a blanket.

Now it was that Tommy, after frisking round her as though in welcome of an old friend, calmly established himself beside her and laid his black head upon her knee. She noted it and smiled for the first time, a marvelously sweet and gentle smile. More, she placed her slender hand upon the dog and stroked him feebly.

Bickley tried to make her drink some more of his mixture, but she refused, motioning him to give it to Tommy. This, however, he would not do because there was but one cup. Presently both of the sleepers began to shiver, which caused Bickley anxiety. Abusing Bastin beneath his breath for being so long with the fire, he drew the blankets closer about them.

Then an idea came to him and he examined the glowing boxes in the coffin. They were loose, being merely set in prepared cavities in the crystal. Wrapping our handkerchiefs about his hand, he took them out and placed them around the wakened patients, a proceeding of which the Ancient nodded approval. Just then, too, Bastin returned with his first load of firewood, and soon we had a merry blaze going just outside the sepulcher. I saw that they observed the lighting of this fire by means of a match with much interest.

Now they grew warm again, as indeed we did also—too warm. Then in my turn I had an idea. I knew that by now the sun would be beating hotly against the rock of the mount, and suggested to Bickley, that, if possible, the best thing we could do would be to get them into its life-giving rays. He agreed, if we could make them understand and they were able to walk. So I tried. First I directed the Ancient's attention to the mouth of the cave which at this distance showed as a white circle of light. He looked at it and then at me with grave inquiry. I made motions to suggest that he should proceed there, repeating the word "Sun" in the Orofenan tongue. He understood at once, though whether he read my mind rather than what I said I am not sure. Apparently the Glittering Lady understood also and seemed to be most anxious to go. Only she looked rather pitifully at her feet and shook her head. This decided me.

I do not know if I have mentioned anywhere that I am a tall man and very muscular. She was tall, also, but as I judged not so very heavy after her long fast. At any rate I felt quite certain that I could carry her for that distance. Stooping down, I lifted her up, signing to her to put her arms round my neck, which she did. Then calling to Bickley and Bastin to bring along the Ancient between them, with some difficulty I struggled out of the sepulcher, and started down the cave. She was more heavy than I thought, and yet I could have wished the journey longer. To begin with she seemed quite trustful and happy in my arms, where she lay with her head against my shoulder, smiling a little as a child might do, especially when I had to stop and throw her long hair round my neck like a muffler, to prevent it from trailing in the dust.

A bundle of lavender, or a truss of new-mown hay, could not have been more sweet to carry and there was something electric about the touch of her, which went through and through me. Very soon it was over, and we were out of the cave into the full glory of the tropical sun. At first, that her eyes might become accustomed to its light and her awakened body to its heat, I set her down where shadow fell from the overhanging rock, in a canvas deck chair that had been brought by Marama with the other things, throwing the rug about her to protect her from such wind as there was. She nestled gratefully into the soft seat and shut her eyes, for the motion had tired her. I noted, however, that she drew in the sweet air with long breaths.

Then I turned to observe the arrival of the Ancient, who was being borne between Bickley and Bastin in what children know as a dandy-chair, which is formed by two people crossing their hands in a peculiar fashion. It says much for the tremendous dignity of his presence that even thus, with one arm round the neck of Bickley and the other round that of Bastin, and his long white beard falling almost to the ground, he still looked most impos-ing.

Unfortunately, however, just as they were emerging from the cave, Bastin, always the most awkward of creatures, managed to leave hold with one hand, so that his passenger nearly came to the ground. Never shall I forget the look that he gave him. Indeed, I think that from this moment he hated Bastin. Bickley he respected as a man of intelligence and learning, although in comparison with his own, the latter was infantile and crude; me he tolerated and even liked; but Bastin he detested. The only one of our party for whom he felt anything approaching real affection was the spaniel Tommy.

We set him down, fortunately uninjured, on some rugs, and also in the shadow. Then, after a little while, we moved both of them into the sun. It was quite curious to see them expand there. As Bickley said, what happened to them might well be compared to the development of a butterfly which has just broken from the living grave of its chrysalis and crept into the full, hot radiance of the light. Its crinkled wings unfold, their brilliant tints develop; in an hour or two it is perfect, glorious, prepared for life and flight, a new creature.

So it was with this pair, from moment to moment they gathered strength and vigor. Near-by to them, as it happened, stood a large basket of the luscious native fruits brought that morning by the Orofenans, and at these the Lady looked with longing. With Bickley's permission, I offered them to her and to the Ancient, first peeling them with my fingers. They ate of them greedily, a full meal, and would have gone on had not the stern Bickley, fearing untoward consequences, removed the basket. Again the results were wonderful, for half an hour afterwards they seemed to be quite strong. With my assistance the Glittering Lady, as I still call her, for at that time I did not know her name, rose from the chair, and, leaning on me, tottered a few steps forward. Then she stood looking at the sky and all the lovely panorama of nature beneath, and stretching out her arms as though in worship. Oh! how beautiful she seemed with the sunlight shining on her heavenly face!

Now for the first time I heard her voice. It was soft and deep, yet in it was a curious bell-like tone that seemed to vibrate like the sound of chimes heard from far away. Never have I listened to such another voice. She pointed to the sun whereof the light turned her radiant hair and garments to a kind of golden glory, and called it by some name that I could not understand. I shook my head, whereon she gave it a different name taken, I suppose, from another language. Again I shook my head and she tried a third time. To my delight this word was practically the same that the Orofenans used for "sun."

"Yes," I said, speaking very slowly, "so it is called by the people of this land."

She understood, for she answered in much the same language:

"What, then, do you call it?"

"Sun in the English tongue," I replied.

"Sun. English," she repeated after me, then added, "How are you named, Wanderer?"

"Humphrey," I answered.

"Hum-fe-ry!" she said as though she were learning the word, "and those?"

"Bastin and Bickley," I replied.

Over these patronymics she shook her head; as yet they were too much for her.

"How are you named, Sleeper?" I asked.

"Yva," she answered.

"A beautiful name for one who is beautiful," I declared with enthusiasm, of course always in the rich Orofenan dialect which by now I could talk well enough.

She repeated the words once or twice, then of a sudden caught their meaning, for she smiled and even colored, saying hastily with a wave of her hand towards the Ancient who stood at a distance between Bastin and Bickley, "My father, Oro; great man; great king; great god!"

At this information I started, for it was startling to learn that here was the original Oro, who was still worshipped by the Orofenans, although of his actual existence they had known nothing for uncounted time. Also I was glad to learn that he was her father and not her old husband, for to me that would have been horrible, a desecration too deep for words.

"How long did you sleep, Yva?" I asked, pointing towards the sepulcher in the cave.

After a little thought she understood and shook her head hopelessly, then by an afterthought, she said,

"Stars tell Oro to-night."

So Oro was an astronomer as well as a king and a god. I had guessed as much from those plates in the coffin which seemed to have stars engraved on them.

At this point our conversation came to an end, for the Ancient himself approached, leaning on the arm of Bickley who was engaged in an animated argument with Bastin.

"For Heaven's sake!" said Bickley, "keep your theology to yourself at present. If you upset the old fellow and put him in a temper he may die."

"If a man tells me that he is a god it is my duty to tell him that he is a liar," replied Bastin obstinately.

"Which you did, Bastin, only fortunately he did not understand you. But for your own sake I advise you not to take liberties. He is not one, I think, with whom it is wise to trifle. I think he seems thirsty. Go and get some water from the rain pool, not from the lake."

Bastin departed and presently returned with an aluminum jug full of pure water and a glass. Bickley poured some of it into a glass and handed it to Yva who bent her head in thanks. Then she did a curious thing. Having first lifted the glass with both hands to the sky and held it so for a few seconds, she turned and with an obeisance poured a little of it on the ground before her father's feet.

A libation, thought I to myself, and evidently Bastin agreed with me, for I heard him mutter,

"I believe she is making a heathen offering."

Doubtless we were right, for Oro accepted the homage by a little motion of the head. After this, at a sign from him she drank the water. Then the glass was refilled and handed to Oro who also held it towards the sky. He, however, made no libation but drank at once, two tumblers of it in rapid succession.

By now the direct sunlight was passing from the mouth of the cave, and though it was hot enough, both of them shivered a little. They spoke together in some language of which we could not understand a word, as though they were debating what their course of action should be. The dispute was long and earnest. Had we known what was passing, which I learned afterwards, it would have made us sufficiently anxious, for the point at issue was nothing less than whether we should or should not be forthwith destroyed—an end, it appears, that Oro was quite capable of bringing about if he so pleased. Yva, however, had very clear views of her own on the matter and, as I gather, even dared to threaten that she would protect us by the use of certain powers at her command, though what these were I do not know.

While the event hung doubtful Tommy, who was growing bored with these long proceedings, picked up a bough still covered with flowers which, after their pretty fashion, the Orofenans had placed on the top of one of the baskets of food. This small bough he brought and laid at the feet of Oro, no doubt in the hope that he would throw it for him to fetch, a game in which the dog delighted. For some reason Oro saw an omen in this simple canine performance, or he may have thought that the dog was making an offering to him, for he put his thin hand to his brow and thought a while, then motioned to Bastin to pick up the bough and give it to him.

Next he spoke to his daughter as though assenting to something, for I saw her sigh in relief. No wonder, for he was conveying his decision to spare our lives and admit us to their fellowship.

After this again they talked, but in quite a different tone and manner. Then the Glittering Lady said to me in her slow and archaic Orofenan:

"We go to rest. You must not follow. We come back perhaps tonight, perhaps next night. We are quite safe. You are quite safe under the beard of Oro. Spirit of Oro watch you. You understand?"

I said I understood, whereon she answered:

"Good-bye, O Humfe-ry."

"Good-bye, O Yva," I replied, bowing.

Thereon they turned and refusing all assistance from us, vanished into the darkness of the cave leaning upon each other and walking slowly.

Future Predictions
of Past Technologies

"In 1999" and the History of the Future

Ivy Roberts

The radical scientific discoveries of the first two decades of the 20th century fuel the imagination of Radium Age science fiction. In questioning the substance of the natural world, scientists were reevaluating the very nature of matter and energy, and therefore of reality as well. The observation of seemingly impossible phenomena led to the discovery of the electron (Thompson 1897), the radioactivity of radium, and to the nonexistence of the luminiferous aether. Research into the radioactivity of elements revealed inconsistencies in the fundamental laws of Thermodynamics. The vast leaps ahead in scientific knowledge confounded the mind and the imagination.

Writing in the late 1910s, future chemist and engineer Burrell Franklin Ruth (1901–1954) let his imagination run wild. Like other Radium Age writers of speculative fiction, Ruth led a double life. He aspired to be a scientist while also being an avid reader of popular science and science fiction pulps. "In 1999" (1921) chronicles achievements of pivotal scientists throughout the 20th century, several of whom have real-world counterparts. Ruth mentions Marie and Pierre Curie, and Ernest Rutherford and Frederick Soddy. Both pairs made significant advances in the field of radioactivity in the first decades of the 20th century. Ruth also drew inspiration from H.G. Wells' *The World Set Free* (1914). Ruth's short speculative fiction also shows the marks of an avid reader of Gernsback's science and technology magazines.

B.F. Ruth was just 20 years old when "In 1999" was published in *Science and Invention* ("Necrology" 1954; *Burrell Franklin Ruth Papers*). In 1921, Ruth was an undergraduate studying chemical engineering at Michigan State College. For all intents and purposes, he was still an amateur scientist. Ruth would go on to become a professor and chemist specializing in filtration. "In 1999" is the only work of fiction that Ruth would ever publish.

Ruth grew up in Detroit during a period of great change and transformation in the fields of science, technology, and engineering.[1] The tone of his story reflects a burgeoning culture of science still driven by the belief in technological determinism and progress. "In 1999" does not read like a work of fiction; Ruth frames his story as a public address. Its matter-of-fact tone invites the reader to negotiate between future speculation and historical fact. The story fits clearly into the science-fictional form of *future history*. As Csicsery-Ronay (2008) observes, "Unlike real prophecies, sf's are narrated in the past tense. They don't pretend to predict a future, but to explain a *future past*" (76). By writing in the past tense, future history makes Ruth's 1999 feel inevitable.

Ruth's optimistic tone reflects that of Radium Age science culture, which entertained the possibility that radical new inventions could solve issues stemming from overpopulation, particularly hunger and energy. Ruth's 20th century witnesses the birth of renewable energy and social equality. "In 1999" rehashes a handful of speculative inventions that had been proposed in the first decades of the 20th century on the pages of Gernsback pulps. *Electrical Experimenter* and *Science and Invention* hosted annual competitions for perpetual motion machines.[2] Scientific speculations in the form of academic lectures explored the possibility of drawing heat from the Earth's core.[3]

During the Radium Age, the most commonly discussed source of energy was the atom. The possibility of generating energy from atomic forces and radioactive substances was, at the time, referred to by as the theory of atomic disintegration. Ruth draws on the work of Rutherford and Soddy to explain how their theory of atomic disintegration could be utilized to create a source of pure, clean, and everlasting energy: nuclear fusion.

"In 1999" … in 1921: Reading Future History in Context

Ruth's future history takes the form of a lecture delivered by the president of the American Academy of Science. The story assumes an authoritative tone lacking in plot. If there are characters, they take the form of real world scientists and fictional ones. "In 1999" touches upon advances in fields of science and technology, including energy (perpetual motion, atomic energy), space travel and interplanetary communication, transportation, and resource management. This hypothetical president, our narrator, highlights a series of scientific discoveries and subsequent inventions that were instrumental in bringing about a "Utopian Age of Science."

Ruth focuses on two particular industries: energy and transportation. In the first case, Ruth describes the role nuclear energy played in creating sustainability and enabling interplanetary travel. In the second case, Ruth describes inventions, including dirigibles and jets, that make travel safe and fast. An elaborate intra-planetary transportation system brings about the end of hunger by facilitating the mass transit of food.

The address begins with a series of hyperbolic congratulations. In summarizing achievements in science and technology, the address identifies the 20th century as "an era that surpasses the greatest expectations": "the Golden Age of Science." Ruth's explanation of the developments in science, technology, and industry, and their impact on the shape of society is indicative of a way of thinking about progress as determined by technology.

Ruth speculates on the state of war and peace in the 20th century. Writing several years after the end of the Great War (World War I), Ruth envisions the peace that will soon come as the result of scientific discoveries and technological achievements. As a result of the devastation brought on by the Great War, Ruth anticipates a time of global harmony. An American president sits at the head of a world government, and that union brought about a century of peace. Speaking from the context of a culture infused with the promise of new technology, Ruth expects progress to turn out for the better. He describes how weapons of war will be converted into peace-making machines. The discussion of atomic disintegration applied to solving the problem of the global population crisis differs dramatically from the image that nuclear energy would later adopt: hazardous radioactive fallout from atomic bombs and reactor meltdowns. Ruth also looks forward to the ways that nuclear energy will be applied as a solution to social issues. At his time of writing, popular science was ablaze with the potential in applying the power of the atom to energy production.

In addition to atomic disintegration, Ruth incorporates two other Radium Age hot topics in science and technology: interplanetary communication, and the hunger crisis. Ruth credits a fictional scientist named Thomas Soddy for the 1938 invention of space travel. Ruth likely models this figure after Frederick Soddy, who would win a 1921 Nobel Prize in chemistry for his achievements in the study of radioactive elements. Thomas Soddy's achievement comes from the application of nuclear energy to space craft propulsion engines.

There may be more to Ruth's naming of Thomas Soddy than is at first immediately apparent. Ruth was an aspiring chemist, and "In 1999" demonstrates his familiarity with popular science and the theory of atomic disintegration. Ruth writes:

> After the occurrences of several successive manifestations, the latter were immediately identified as radioactive in origin. It was admitted that atomic disintegration had at last been accomplisht, and that the fate of the world was in the hands of its unknown discoverer, who might destroy the planet at his whim. With deep secrecy,

science kept its knowledge, and waited for the discoverer to make himself known either as a benefactor or destroyer of mankind.

But Ruth does not associate his Thomas Soddy with research on radioactivity or the theory of atomic disintegration. Rather, Soddy's contribution comes later, in 1938, with his invention of an atomic engine:

> One of the most spectacular inventions resulting from Signa Beth's discovery was that of Thomas Soddy's space navigating apparatus in 1938. By utilization of the terrific recoil developed in a certain method of disintegration, this instrument was able to leave the earth's surface like a sky rocket and travel beyond its gravitational orbit in any direction, at a tremendous rate of speed.

Ruth's youthful and optimistic attitude is evident in his identification with the works of chemist Frederick Soddy, and his fascination with the overlap of science fact and speculative fiction in the contemporary literature of his time. In his contributions to popular science, Frederick Soddy integrates scientific experimentation and science fact with imaginative speculation on the outcomes of scientific progress into the distant future.

Chapter 11 of Soddy's *Interpretation of Radium* (1909) reads like a combination of popular science and science fiction (Brossmann and Sovacool, 208). For example, Soddy writes:

> Our outlook on the physical universe has been permanently altered. We are no longer the inhabitants of a universe slowly dying from the physical exhaustion of its energy, but of a universe which has in the internal energy of its material components the means to rejuvenate itself perennially over immense periods of time, intermittently and catastrophically, which is the first possibility that presents itself, or continuously and in orderly fashion, if there exist compensating phenomena still outside the ken of science [181].

In "Radioactivity and the Evolution of the World," Soddy entertains wild speculations about the promise of atomic energy, equating the discovery of radioactivity, disintegration theory, and the potential to harness the energy in radioactive material to the discovery of fire. STS scholar Richard Sclove describes Soddy's chapter 11: "imagination is let loose to weave a stunning cosmological tapestry from which emerges, in turn, the single fullest expression of Soddy's Utopian hopes" (172). Soddy was uniquely concerned with the impact of discovery and invention on society (Kauffman, xx). He understood better than most how scientific discovery can lead to technological applications that can be applied both for the betterment or destruction of the world.

Ruth and Gernsback's Universe

Judging by the popular culture references littered throughout his short story, Ruth was likely an avid reader of the Hugo Gernsback pulp magazines

Can You

write a snappy, short story, having some scientific fact as its theme? If you can

Write

such fiction we would like to print it. The story which is appearing in the ELECTRICAL EXPERIMENTER at present has aroused so much enthusiasm among our readers that we have decided to publish more

Stories

from time to time. If you have the knack, try your hand at it. It is worth while. However, please bear in mind that only scientific literature is acceptable, altho not necessarily dealing with electrical subjects. "Baron Münchhausen" is a good example. Suppose you try. We pay well for such original stories.

"Can You Write Stories," *Science and Invention*. June 1915.

during the 1910s: *Electrical Experimenter* and *Science and Invention*. Ruth's response to Gernsback's open call for scientifiction further indicates that he was an regular reader of popular science who was already familiar with the trends in its discourse. Gernsback solicited contributions from readers beginning with the inaugural issue of *Electrical Experimenter* in May of 1913: "We invite our readers to contribute articles to this journal and we will pay well for all excepted matter. New experiments, new designs of electrical apparatus, new electrical tricks, etc., will be welcomed; good photographs are especially desirable" (2). Op-eds, scientific lectures, how-to articles, and scientifiction mingled casually on the pages of Gernsback's magazines, blending any recognizable distinction between science fact and science fiction. In his op-eds, Gernsback wrote actively on the possibilities of interplanetary travel and communication, and speculated widely about the application of radio telegraphy.[4] Gernsback's magazines also promoted speculative inventions that could be applied to solving social problems related to energy production, transportation, overpopulation, and hunger. Ruth reflects on these trends in presenting an intraplanetary subway, which drew power from the earth's core in order to transport food from third world agricultural centers to population centers in the northern hemisphere.[5]

The confluence of popular science and science fiction would not become apparent until the launching of Gernsback's magazine devoted entirely to short fiction: *Amazing Stories* (1926): "*Amazing stories* gave a name to fiction treating the speculative and otherworldly through the lens of systematic real-

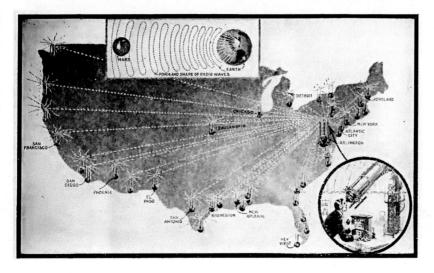

C.S. Brainin, "Interplanetary Communication," *Electrical Experimenter*. November 1919: 641.

ism: scientifiction" (Wythoff, 2). However, Gernsback had been soliciting works of short fiction from his reading audience since 1911, in the pages of *Electrical Experimenter* (Ashley 2000, 1). Ashley adds:

> By mid–1915, The *Electrical Experimenter* was broadening its coverage beyond the confines of radio, and an increasing emphasis was being given to the wider aspects of scientific experimentation. With this expansion Gernsback reintroduced the scientific story [after *Ralph 124C41+*], starting with another series of his own: "Baron Munchausen's New Scientific Adventures," which began in the May 1915 issue [Ashley 2004, 34–5].

Gernsback's raison d'etre was "to stimulate the imagination and inspire the inventor" (Ashley 2004, 37).

In his "Evolution of Science Fiction" (1952), Gernsback historicizes the role of short stories in his magazines. With *Ralph 124C41+* (1911–12), Gernsback inaugurated a tradition of popular science that encouraged outrageous speculation. It was in these pages of *Electrical Experimenter* and *Science and Invention* that Ruth would have read Gernsback's "The Scientific Adventures of Munchausen" and Jacque Morgan's "Mr. Fosdick," two early scientifiction serials that paved the way for what the genre would become. Editions of these magazines from the teens and twenties usually opened with a speculative article penned by Gernsback and/or his coeditor, H.W. Secor. Editorials like "Radium and Evolution" (*Electrical Experimenter*, November 1916, 467) and "Imagination Versus Facts" (*Electrical Experimenter*, November 1917, 435) blurred boundaries between science fact and speculative fiction.

Ruth, Wells and Soddy

In addition to its connection to the tone and style of Hugo Gernsback's popular science, Ruth also borrows heavily from H.G. Wells' 1914 novel *The*

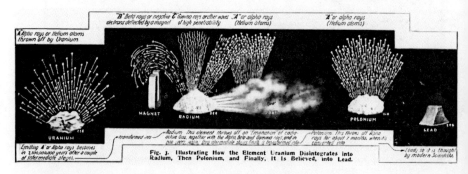

"The Wonders of Radium," *The Electrical Experimenter*. September 1915: 179–183; 236–237.

World Set Free. For instance, Ruth's characterization of Signa Beth, the Indian physicist who would discover nuclear fission in 1925, bears remarkable similarity to a creation of Wells. Ruth writes: "Early in 1925, the great Indian physicist, Signa Beth, announced his discovery of a method of releasing the immense energy stored in the atom, and his intentions of benefiting mankind. Thus the most monumental discovery ever made by science was disclosed." In *The World Set Free*, Wells writes of the 1953 invention of an atomic generator: "the Dass-Tata engine—the invention of two among the brilliant galaxy of Bengali inventors the modernization of Indian thought was producing at this time—which was used chiefly for automobiles, aeroplanes, waterplanes, and such-like, mobile purposes" (50). Ruth's Signa Beth and Wells' "Bengali inventors" have no apparent real world counterparts.

Both Ruth and Wells write at length of the role that Frederick Soddy played in advancing the possibility of applying radioactivity to energy production. Scholars have noted how several of Wells' fictional scientists in *The World Set Free* resemble Soddy in both character and scientific achievement (Haynes 212; Morrison 152–3; Campos 38–39; Sclove 177; Brossmann and Sovacool 208; Seed 2003; Guston 2012). Professor Rufus delivers an academic lecture that copies many of the main ideas in Soddy's text. Wells also writes about a chemist named Holsten who applies the theory of atomic disintegration to the process of "transmutation," the scientific approximation of alchemy (Morrison 153; Jenkin 129; Kauffman 11). Additionally, Wells dedicated his novel to Soddy's *The Interpretation of Radium* (1909). Chapter 11 of Soddy's work of popular science, "Radioactivity and the Evolution of the World," incorporates the seeds of Well's introductory chapter as well as the inspiration for a work of science fiction that speculates on the destructive power of atomic weapons in a post-war era.

Mirroring Wells' dedication to Soddy, Ruth also transparently pays homage to the great chemist. "In 1999" takes the lead from Wells in fictionalizing Soddy's contribution to the study of radioactivity. Frederick Soddy's achievements in the study of radioactivity extend far beyond the realms of hard science. Both Wells and Ruth honored Soddy because his popular science was composed with great imagination. A comparative analysis of Soddy's writing on chemistry and the speculative fiction of the first two decades of the 20th century shows how the genre of science fiction developed into its modern form.

At Ruth's time of writing, Frederick Soddy, in partnership with physicist Ernest Rutherford, claimed fame for their experiments with radium and radioactivity.[6] They proposed a groundbreaking theory of atomic disintegration that would change the way that people thought of the fundamental substance of the universe: the atom. Atomic disintegration theory supposes that elements organically and naturally degrade while emitting energy in the form of radioactivity. Rutherford and Soddy speculated that atoms contained within themselves an infinite amount of energy. If that energy could be controlled, atomic generators could power the world. Atomic disintegration provides the theoretical foundation for modern processes of atomic fusion.

Rutherford and Soddy observed radioactive decay, which appeared to defy the foundation of modern physics. The first law of thermodynamics states that energy cannot be created or destroyed. As historian of science T.J Trenn (1977) explains it:

> The difficulty now in recovering the conceptual state involving atomic disintegration as chemical genesis without a priori specifying a particulate residue is a further indication of the grave difficulties encountered in their pioneering research. Although perhaps "inconvenient" from a modern perspective, this half-way theoretical structure formed a distinct and important stage in the formulation of a full theory [3].

Rutherford and Soddy's atomic disintegration theory was radical because it challenged the laws of thermodynamics. The discovery of radioactivity prompted physicists and chemists to reassess the nature of matter. To entertain the theory of atomic disintegration meant to reevaluate the structure of the atom.

Read as a work of fiction, Ruth's characterization and narration fall short. As a history of the future, Ruth excels in reflecting upon science theory and speculating future progress from within the frame of Radium Age culture. Ruth projects contemporary scientific theory into the technological possibilities of the future. Ruth's associations with Gernsback, Wells, and Soddy reveal the way that popular science and the yet-to-be named science fiction percolated into Radium Age culture. In Gernsback's pulps, scientifiction masqueraded as op-eds, and vice versa.

Ruth envisions a 20th century global empire ruled by American leadership and made possible by scientific knowledge and technological force. Ruth's rhetoric privileges the American perspective. While he acknowledges global contributions, he censors the voices and perspectives of others. Still, Ruth makes an effort in nodding to the achievements of non–Western scientists (Signa Beth) and incorporating a global perspective ("farming countries"). "In 1999" presents a promising vision of how science and technology can solve global issues in hunger, wealth inequality, population distribution, and energy consumption. But it fails to interrogate its own privileged perspective from that of a white American man. Ruth's 1999 is optimistic but naïve. Readers should want to ask: what would Signa Beth have to say on the matter?

The history of the future requires us to consider reflexive frames of reference. "In 1999" cannot be read and fully understood from the perspective of a 21st century reader. The irony with this type of science fiction comes down to imaginative speculation and the role that tense plays in a reader's understanding of possibility. Popular science can speculate on possibility; science fiction can make it seem so real that it has already become a reality.

NOTES

1. Obituary states that Ruth was born in Traverse City. College directory states that lived in Detroit before entering college. Michigan State University college catalog, 1921: 223.

2. See for example John Adams, "Will These Perpetual Motion Schemes Work?" *Electrical Experimenter,* Nov. 1919: 649; "Perpetual Motion Contest Awards," *Electrical Experimenter,* Feb 1920: 1013. "Prizes," *Science and Invention,* August 1925: 364.

3. See for example Gernsback, "Tapping the Earth's Heat," *Electical Experimetner,* March 1917; Gernsback, "The Earth's Interior Molten?" *Electrical Experimenter,* April 1920: 1226; T. O'Connor Sloane, "Tapping the Earth's Heat," *Science and Invention,* Nov 1920: 724–5.

4. See for example Hugo Gernsback, "The Moon Rocket," *Electrical Experimenter,* March 1920, 1098; Gernsback, "Interplanetary Messages," *Electrical Experimenter,* April 1919; Gernsback, "The Elusive Martian Canals," *Electrical Experimenter,* Oct 1919, 490; C. S. Brainin, "Interplanetary Communication," *Electrical Experimenter,* Nov 1919, 641.

5. See for example Hugo Gernsback, "Speeds," *Electrical Experimenter,* Aug 1919; "Future Rapid Transit," *Electrical Experimenter,* May 1919, 7, 66–67; Clement Fizandie (Author of "Doctor Hackenshaw's Secrets"), "A Tunnel Through the Center of the Earth!" *Science and Invention,* July 1922; Gernsback, "Tapping the Earth's Heat," *Electical Experimenter,* March 1917; Gernsback, "The Earth's Interior Molten?" *Electrical Experimenter,* April 1920, 1226; T. O'Connor Sloane, "Tapping the Earth's Heat," *Science and Invention,* Nov 1920, 724–5.

6. See also Nelson, Craig. *The Age of Radiance: The Epic Rise and Dramatic Fall of the Atomic Era.* New York: Scribner, 2014; Trenn, T.J. *The Self-Splitting Atom: The History of the Rutherford-Soddy Collaboration.* London, UK: Taylor and Francis, 1977; Claudio Tuniz, *Radioactivity: A Very Short Introduction.* Cambridge, UK: Oxford University Press, 2012.

BIBLIOGRAPHY

Ashley, Mike. 2000. *The Time Machines: The Story of the Science-fiction Pulp Magazines from the Beginning to 1950.* Liverpool: Liverpool UP.
Ashley, Mike, and Robert A.W. Lowndes. 2004. *The Gernsback Days: A Study of the Evolution of Modern Science Fiction from 1911 to 1936.* Wildside Press.
Brossmann, Brent, and Benjamin K. Sovacool. 2013. "Fantastic Futures and Three American Energy Transitions," *Science as Culture* 22, no. 2: 204–212.
Burrell Franklin Ruth Papers, RS 11/4/52, Special Collections Department, Iowa State University Library.
Campos, Luis A. 2015. *Radium and the Secret of Life.* U of Chicago P.
Csicsery-Ronay, Istvan. 2008. *The Seven Beauties of Science Fiction.* Wesleyan UP.
Gernsback, Hugo. 1952. "The Evolution of Modern Science Fiction." Gernsback.
Guston, David H. 2012. "The Pumpkin or the Tiger? Michael Polanyi, Frederick Soddy, and Anticipating Emerging Technologies." *Minerva* 50, no. 3: 363–379.
Haynes, Roslynn D. 1980. *H.G. Wells: Discoverer of the Future: The Influence of Science on His Thought.* Macmillan.
Jenkin, John G. 2011. "Atomic Energy Is 'Moonshine': What Did Rutherford Really Mean?" *Physics in Perspective* 13, no. 2: 128–145.
Kauffman, George B., ed. 2012. *Frederick Soddy (1877–1956): Early Pioneer in Radiochemistry.* Springer Science & Business Media.
Morrisson, Mark. 2007. *Modern Alchemy: Occultism and the Emergence of Atomic Theory.* Oxford UP on Demand.
"Necrology." 1954. *Chemical and Engineering News,* Jan. 25.
Nelson, Craig. 2014. *The Age of Radiance: The Epic Rise and Dramatic Fall of the Atomic Era.* Scribner's.

Ruth, Franklin. 1921. "In 1999," *Science and Invention,* April, 1302, 1361–3.

Sclove, Richard E. 1989. "From Alchemy to Atomic War: Frederick Soddy's 'Technology Assessment' of Atomic Energy, 1900–1915." *Science, Technology, & Human Values* 14, no. 2: 163–194.

Seed, David. 2003 "H.G. Wells and the Liberating Atom," *Science Fiction Studies*: 33–48.

Soddy, Frederick. 1922 [1909]. *The Interpretation of Radium and the Structure of the Atom,* 4th ed. G.P. Putnam's Sons.

Trenn, T.J. 1977. *The Self-Splitting Atom: The History of the Rutherford-Soddy Collaboration.* Taylor and Francis.

Tuniz, Claudio. 2012. *Radioactivity: A Very Short Introduction.* Oxford UP.

Wells, H.G. 1914. *The World Set Free: A Story of Mankind.* Bernhard Tauchnitz.

Westfahl, Gary. 2007. *Hugo Gernsback and the Century of Science Fiction.* McFarland.

Wythoff, Grant. 2016. *The Perversity of Things: Hugo Gernsback on Media, Tinkering, and Scientifiction.* U of Minnesota P.

"In 1999: Scientific Progress in the Last Century" (1921)

B. Franklin Ruth

"Thirty Foot Tubes..." from "In 1999," *Science and Invention.* July 1921. "...Thirty-Foot Tubes were erected thru the Earth's diameter, Reaching from a large industrial center on one side to some extensive agricultural area upon the other. Africa, China, Australia, and Parts of South America were touched. As these tubes were sunk, they were lined with Browning's Electro-Heat Converting apparatus, which turned the intense heat of the bowels of the earth into an immense voltage. Giving an electric current but left the interiors of the tubes relatively cool and insulated from the fiery medium through which they passed and the elevator-like carriers were dropt thru the center of the earth. The momentum gained in the 4000-mile drop carried the cars past the center of the earth and up to within a few feet of the opposite surface. At this point they were caught by automatic Catches and Giant Electric hoists hauled them to the surface...."

Presidential Address Before the American Academy of Science, September 1999.

Gentlemen of the Academy:

At the close of this 20th century we look back upon a more brilliant array of scientific achievements than man has ever been privileged to see, or imagine. Within the last few decades our earth has entered upon an era that surpasses the greatest expectations of the 19th century philosophers. Civilization has advanced at a rate comparable to a geometric progression, and today we are living in the Golden Age of Science. In looking back upon this century, we should review some of the most significant achievements of the past, and to note their bearing upon progress and their relevance to the science of today.

The dawn of modern science occurred in 1898, when the discovery of radium and its radioactive properties was made by the Curie's. The importance of this discovery can never be too greatly emphasized, for it marks the actual conception and birth of the principles upon which today's science is founded. The untiring investigations of those great pioneers of modern science, Rutherford and Soddy, in the field of radioactivity, soon caused them to announce the hypotheses of atomic disintegration and evolution of the elements.[1] Although these theories were at first discredited and regarded in the same light as Perpetual Motion, the undeniable existence of enormous reservoirs of energy in the minute atom, as evidenced by radium, soon attracted the attention not only of scientific circles, but of the whole world.[2] Research became busy with the momentous question whether artificial means could accelerate of retard the processes of spontaneous disintegration. Civilized nations became excited and expectant. Vivid fiction, exploiting the imaginary results of the discovery of atomic disintegration, was widely read, and increased the credulity of the people.[3]

It was at about this period that the Great War occurred. Altho [sic] this world disaster took a great toll of like, it proved to be an impetus to scientific advancement. At the close of the War the United States found itself the creditor of almost the entire European continent, whose nations were on the verge of bankruptcy and revolution. Unrest was widespread.[4] Crises between labor and capital were imminent. Numerous strikes occurred, and Bolshevik uprising in Russia threatened to undermine all governmental control and order. The air seemed charged with something that stifled all thoughts of resuming prewar existence. Over all hung unconscious, vague dread, grasped in its entirety by only a few minds of scientific prominence. Prophets and religious fanatics preached the end of the world and the arrival of the Millennium. The world was ripe for some cataclysm that would overwhelm civilization and possibly sweep all life from the planet.

Suddenly, in 1924, occurred the first phenomenon of a series, which created physical disturbances sufficiently powerful to attract general attention. Scientific investigators, however, with the aid of their delicate instruments, had detected weaker but similar disturbances at pervious periodic intervals. The world waited anxiously for words that might come from scientific men, identifying the cause of the mysterious phenomena. Scientists knew that the peculiar nature of the disturbances could only be explained as the result of some human agency capable of exercising extraordinary powers over the physical universe. After the occurrences of several successive manifestations, the latter were immediately identified as radioactive in origin. It was admitted that atomic disintegration had at last been accomplisht [*sic*], and that the fate of the world was in the hands of its unknown discoverer, who might destroy the planet at his whim. With deep secrecy, science kept its knowledge, and waited for the discoverer to make himself known either as a benefactor or destroyer of mankind.

Early in 1925, the great Indian physicist, Signa Beth, announced his discovery of a method of releasing the immense energy stored in the atom, and his intentions of benefiting mankind.[5] Thus the most monumental discovery ever made by science was disclosed.

From that date, science bounded forward. The commercialization of Signa Beth's discovery and its direct application to the immense stores of energy contained in the atoms of the common heavy elements brought unprecedented benefits to mankind. With almost unlimited power waiting to be unleashed by the pressure of a finger, men laid aside their work and took a holiday. It was like the discovery that water could be turned into steam and made to work for us,—multiplied a million times.

Close upon the discovery of atomic disintegration came that of the transmutability of matter. This was the natural sequence of the analysis of the properties of by-products formed during the successive steps of disintegration. The result of this discovery, as we all know today, was the immediate de-monetization of gold and all precious metals. In a day the world was threatened with its greatest financial panic.

Fortunately, there was at the head of our government a man of great foresight and ability who saw the threatened disaster and took immediate steps to avert it. At a joint meeting of the representatives of various governments, measures were taken to meet the crises, and thru [*sic*] pressure brought to bear from certain sources a coalition of nations was formed under a single government. This we know today as the United States of the World.[6] It was in effect a League of Nations similar to the plan advanced by the great Wilson in 1919. It arranged for a semi-annual world congress at Washington, and enforced its decrees by means of an International Police. Paper notes on the World Government were issued as legal currency, and substituted for all outstanding metal currency. Threatened Bolshevik outbreaks in Russia, and labor crises in Europe and America were immediately quelled by the efficient iron hand of the international government. Thus was civilization again saved from destruction.

One of the most apparent effects of the world coalition was the abolishment of war. The United States as principal creditor of the bankrupt nations, held a unique position in the league, both as its sponsor and guardian. The former president of the United States was elected president of the World Congress. But he also represented the United States.

The reason for the disappearance of war, we are led to believe, was the potential power held by the United States. When the Great War came to an end in 1918, many new and terrible inventions were perfected too late to be used in actual warfare. The possession of these secrets by the United States constituted an effectual curb to the aggressive instincts of any nation inclined to war.

One of the most spectacular inventions resulting from Signa Beth's discovery was that of Thomas Soddy's space navigating apparatus in 1938.[7] By utilization of the terrific recoil developed in a certain method of disintegration, this instrument was able to leave the earth's surface like a sky rocket and travel beyond its gravitational orbit in any direction, at a tremendous rate of speed.

The effect of this invention upon the lay mind at that time can hardly be imagined. Nineteen years before, powerful waves of mysterious but undoubtedly ethereal origin had been received by some of the larger radio stations. The scientific explanations and press exploitations of these unidentified waves created such widespread excitement at the time that when Soddy returned from his epoch-making explorations of Mars and Venus in 1938, and confirmed these attempted Martian communications of 1919, and testified as to the residence on Mars and Venus of highly civilized beings, the people of the earth became wildly excited.[8] Results followed speedily. Intercourse between the inhabited planets of our solar system was quickly established. Interplanetary laws governing spatial navigation were quickly formulated and ratified, so that today we witness our great interplanetary merchant marine, touching all planets in the solar system, and many of the nearer stars. Trips of exploration are bringing in reports of new discoveries every day. Excursion ships dash thru [sic] space at regular hours, bound for other planets.

Soddy's invention truly marks the beginning of the Utopian era of Science. Mankind began to live a life of ease and indulgence, yet governed by sobriety and health.

Due to the congestion of our cities, some of which had a population of fifty-five millions, and to existing agricultural conditions, it was increasingly difficult, during the early sixties, to furnish enough food. The great Browning's discovery of a method permitting the direct conversion of heat into electricity enabled engineers of the period to solve this problem adequately. Thirty-foot tubes were excavated thru [*sic*] the earth's diameter, reaching from a large industrial center on one side to some extensive agricultural area upon the other.[9] Africa, China, Australia, and parts of South America were touched. As these tubes were sunk, they were lined with Browning's electro-heat converting apparatus, which turned the intense heat of the bowels of the earth into an immense voltage, giving an electric current, but left the interiors of the tube relatively cool and insulated from the fiery medium thru [*sic*] which they passed.

Food, produced easily and in large quantities in the farming countries, was quickly hauled over extensive railroad systems to the mouths of the tubes, and regular consignments dropped through in specially designed cars. The momentum gained in the four thousand mile drop easily carried the cars past the center of the earth, where gravity began to exert its counterpull, up to within several feet of the opposite surface. The moment they started to fall back, they were caught and held by automatic catches. Giant electric hoists completed their journey to the surface.

It is to these great engineering feats that credit must be given for the comfort of our modern city life. They may easily be regarded as among the most beneficial gifts to mankind that science has produced in the last four decades, for they make possible our present-day existence. Today we are so dependent for food upon these earth-piercing tubes, that if they all should be damaged simultaneously, there would be much suffering and hardship before repairs could be effected. Possibly many deaths might result from starvation. These tubes are indeed the arteries of our daily existence.

Some of the most widely known of Science's improvements have been those of transportation and travel. Speed, as demanded by the ease and luxury-loving internationalite of today, has been furnished by the prolific genius of science. Huge liners of the air, several thousand feet in length, inflated with helium gas (which is a plentiful end-product of the disintegration process), driven by powerful atomic engine at several hundred miles per hour, and luxuriously fitted with accommodations for at least a thousand passengers, ply the great Atlantic and Pacific between breakfast time and dinner. Our skies today are filled with wings swiftly propelled by noiseless thorio-actinic motors. Since the helium-filled ship came into general use, more than forty-five years ago, not a life has been lost in aerial transportation. Certainly this is a magnificent record, and a worthy tribute to the science that made it possible. Progress in Education has been no less rapid. Today we have our great university cities, endowed by a benevolent government, for the free use of all mankind. Free higher-education to any who desire it as much a right of the world citizen of today as liberty was of the American of a century ago. Thousands of investigators in pure science now finish their education in the immense national universities of Mars and Venus, as all learning went to Europe to receive its degree in 1900.

In biology, geology, bacteriology, zoology, engineering, chemistry, and all branches of science there has been rapid achievement. In biology, I understand, the synthetic production of living organisms has been lately accomplished, and promises wonderful achievements. It is no great flight of fancy to say that if we were able one billion years from now to look upon those warm, steamy, cooling, and sill lifeless planets, where our intrepid spacefliers have recently placed cultures of synthetic Amoeba, we might hope to see a creature occupying a place in that planetary existence comparable to that now filled by earth's human race.

In medical science there has been such progress that death by sickness and disease are rare, whereas continued pain is hardly known, and certainly avoidable. By observing scientific methods of right living and obeying natural laws, one may expect to live for more than one hundred years. That is a period of existence nearly twice that of the average man fifty years ago. Gentlemen, I ask you, can the coming century be filled with such an array of achievements? Possibly. Who can tell? Biology holds hopes which some of use may live to see realized.

NOTES

1. Ernest Rutherford and Frederick Soddy proposed the theory of atomic disintegration in the first decade of the twentieth century, as the result of work put forth by the Curies. Ruth draws heavily on the figure of chemist Frederick Soddy based on the popularity of his monograph, *The Interpretation of Radium* (1909). The theory of atomic disintegration was an early indicator for the application of radioactive materials for use in generation of atomic energy and nuclear fusion.

2. Ruth's reference to perpetual motion is important as an indicator of speculative inventions for solutions to the energy crisis. Perpetual motion had gradually been accepted as an impossibility, a thing of *fantasy*. H.W. Secor, "Perpetual Motion: The Folly of the Ages" *Electrical Experimenter*, Jan 1916, 478–480; 514. Clement Fezandie, "Dr. Hackensaw's Secrets of Perpetual Motion," *Science and Invention*, Nov 1924, 660–1. John Adams, "Will These Perpetual Motion Schemes Work?, *Electrical Experimenter*, Nov 1919, 649. "Perpetual Motion Context Awards," *Electrical Experimenter*, Feb 1920. "Perpetual Motion," *Electrical Experimenter*, August 1917, 249; 280.

3. Here, Ruth is likely referencing Radium Age science fiction including Wells' *The World Set Free* (1914). Both *The World Set Free* and "In 1999" deal with themes of war and peace, machines and energy, and a future social utopia. Wells dedicates his novel to Soddy, in particular the inspiration he drew from chapter 11 of *Interpretation of Radium* (1909).

4. Here, Ruth acknowledges the potential danger of war machines and the crises that devistated the world during and immediately after "the Great War" (World War I).

5. "Signa Beth" resembles H.G. Wells' fictional Bengali inventors of the "Dass-Tata" machine in *The World Set Free* (1914).

6. H.G. Wells also speculated on the formation of a world government in *The World Set Free*, chapter 3.

7. For a contemporary perspective on the potential for space travel, see Hugo Gerns-back, "The Moon Rocket," *Electrical Experimenter*, March 1920, 1098.

8. For contemporary examples of the possibility of interplanetary communication, see Hugo Gernsback, "Interplanetary Messages," *Electrical Experimenter*, April 1919; Hugo Gernsback, "The Elusive Martian Canals," *Electrical Experimenter*, Oct 1919, 490; C. S. Brainin, "Interplanetary Communication," *Electrical Experimenter*, Nov 1919, 641.

9. For further speculation on how heat from the earth's core could be utilized as an energy source, see Hugo Gernsback, "Tapping the Earth's Heat," *Electical Experimenter*, March 1917; Hugo Gernsback, "The Earth's Interior Molten?" *Electrical Experimenter*, April 1920, 1226; T. O'Connor Sloane, "Tapping the Earth's Heat," *Science and Invention*, Nov 1920, 724–5.

Scientifiction, Relativism and the Multiverse

Introduction to "The Man from the Atom"

Riccardo Gramantieri

At the end of his career as editor, Hugo Gernsback wrote that science fiction is the "truly, scientific, prophetic Science-Fiction with the full accent on SCIENCE" (1953, 22). Almost thirty years before he had written, "science fiction in other words furnished a tremendous amount of scientific education and fires the reader's imagination more perhaps than anything else of which we know" (1926, 195).

Origin of science fiction can be traced back to the early 1910s, in the technical magazines published by Hugo Gernsback.[1] At the start of the 20th century, this editor, inventor, and author solidified an idea of science fiction that held steadfast for decades. Unlike the fantasy or adventure novel, Gernsback's science fiction had to have a current scientific theory as a starting point or as the resolving argument of the plot. Hugo Gernsback used the term "scientifiction" in the 1910s and the 1920s to label the type of stories he published in his magazines. In the first issue of *Amazing Stories* in April 1926, Gernsback was still using the term. Later on, the spelling was modified to the "science fiction," a term coined by Gernsback in the leading article in the first issue of *Science Wonder Stories* published in 1929. Therefore, we can definitely say, with Gary Westfahl, that:

> Gernsback had effectively created the genre of science fiction and had imprinted his image upon all of its text; that he had an impact on all works of science fiction published since 1926, regardless of whether he played any direct role in their publication; that he had influenced perceptions of the works published before 1926 now acknowledge as science fiction; and that the overall effects of his work were overwhelmingly positive, as demonstrated by the vibrant, fascinating genre that he had fashioned [2007, 3].

Returning to Gernsback's idea that science fiction had to have a current scientific or technical underpinning, in those early 1910s, the world of theoretical and experimental physics was undergoing a revolution. The tale "The Man from the Atom" (1923) by G. Peyton Wertenbaker draws on both the theory of the atomic planetary model and the theory of relativity. Wertenbaker's story is an example of the type of "proto" science fiction that Gernsback published in his magazines, and thus an example of the suggestions that early 20th century physics instilled in contemporary authors (Evans, 51).

The Atom as a Solar System

The hypothesis that matter consists of extremely small particles can be traced back to ancient times. The Greek philosopher Democritus was the first, between the fifth and the fourth century BCE, to talk about atoms: *a-temno*, or indivisible elementary structures of matter. For centuries, the concept was a mere philosophical speculation, and it was not until 1738 that the Swiss physician Daniel Bernoulli grasped the corpuscular structure of gases. However, it was with John Dalton in *New System in Chemical Philosophy* (1808) that the assumption that matter was formed by indivisible atoms became a fundamental starting point for science. It was at that moment that it was established that matter is formed by atoms considered to be homogenous and compact particles. However, the discovery of cathodic rays by Johann Wilhelm Hittorf in 1869 brought about a breakthrough in physics. Rays were formed by negatively-charged sub-atomic particles. Hittford's discovery revolutionized knowledge about the atom, thought to be indivisible.

In 1904, physicist Sir Joseph John Thomson discovered the existence of negatively-charged electrons within the atom. Subsequently, the atom planetary model was developed by Ernest Rutherford. As the result of experiments conducted between 1908 and 1912, Rutherford, along with Hans Wilhelm Geiger and Ernest Marsden, reimagined the atom as having a very small positive nucleus and an external negative electron to equalize the charge. Their model resembled a planetary system: the nucleus in place of the sun, and the electrons which rotated around the small nucleus just like the planets. The following year, the physicist Gordon S. Fulcher observed that "certainly the Rutherford atom seems much too simple to explain these spectral phenomena, though perhaps these and other objections may be overcome" (274). Changes to the model were not made until some twenty years later, when James Chadwick discovered neutrally-charged particles called neutrons.

In 1905, Albert Einstein published his theory of special relativity ("Zur Elektrodynamik bewegter Körper"). In addition to proposing that the speed of light is constant, Einstein introduced the principle of relativity: that all physical laws are the same in all inertial systems. Space and time contract and dilate respectively, depending on the speed of the reference system. The theory of relativity then disproves the existence of "absolute time." The famous twin paradox can be used to explain Einstein's counterintuitive theory:

> Known as the twin paradox, it had two twin brothers, A and B, say, of which B stays at rest in his inertial frame while A takes off in a spacecraft attaining high speed. A goes far and returns after a considerable time as measured by B. But, since A was moving relative to B with high speed, A would be younger than B ... because A's watch would run slower than B's. Also, since A and B ... meet at the same place at the beginning and the end of the experiments, the effect must be real [Narlikar, 27].

Hence, time "dilates," or changes in speed depending on the experience of an observer, as the result of dramatic changes in speed. The theory of relativity is expressed in mathematical terms with the famous equation $E = mc^2$, which presents a relationship between mass and time.

In addition to making radical progress in the field of physics in the first decades of the 20th century, Einstein's theories fascinated science fiction writers. During this period, science fiction matured alongside physics as stories drew upon the progress of real science. Hard science, and science fiction in turn, opened up possibilities of dimensions, time sequences, microcosmic or macrocosmic universes, and galaxies (Rogers, 90).

Technique, Science, Science Fiction

The term "pulp" derives from the plant-based substance used to make paper and is used to refer to the tabloid-sized magazines that published popular fiction in the early 20th century. The first pulp magazine was *Argosy*, published by the editorial group Munsey beginning in 1896 (Gunn, 105). Many of the stories published in *Argosy* might be characterized as "proto" science fiction, which suggests that science fiction emerged as the result of genre mash-ups and the cultivation of a mass audience.

Pulp science fiction is synonymous with the name Hugo Gernsback because of his magazine empire, including but not limited to *Modern Electrics*, *Electrical Experimenter*, *Radio News*, *Radio-Electronics*, *Science and Invention*, *Television News*, *Amazing Stories* and *Wonder Stories*. Hugo Gernsback was born in Luxembourg on August 16, 1884. An inventor in the field of batteries and radiophony, he emigrated to the United States in 1904. In 1905, he immediately set up his first company, Telimco (The Electro Importing Company), for the assembly and distribution of radio and electrical components. In 1908, he began publicizing Telimco through the publication of a catalog. In 1913, he founded *Electrical Experimenter*, at first an electro-technics magazine consisting of only a few pages. *Electrical Experimenter* gradually began to incorporate advertising, technical and how-to articles, and short fiction. Gernsback intended his magazine for an audience of amateur scientists and engineers. The fiction he wrote and edited was intentionally written for such an audience; it was an adventurous re-writing of scientific theory. In 1920, the magazine changed its name to *Science and Invention*.

"The Man from the Atom"

G. Peyton Wertenbaker's "The Man from the Atom" not only discloses innovative scientific theories of the time; it also represents the Gernsbackian

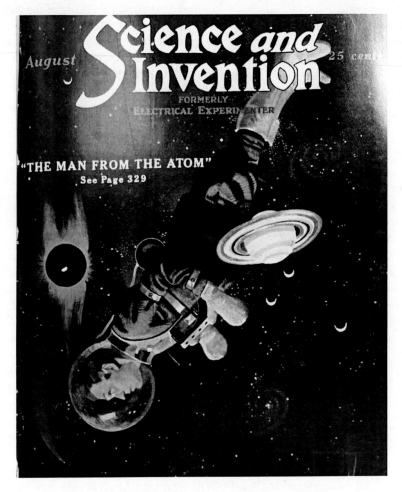

Science and Invention **cover design, August 1923.**

vision of science fiction. In his July 1926 *Amazing Stories* op-ed, Gernsback adds: "[Science fiction] is designed to reach those qualities of the mind which are aroused only by things vast, things cataclysmic, and things unfathomably strange. It is designed to reach that portion of the imagination which grasps with its eager, feeble talons after the unknown" (291). Wertenbaker shared this vision.

"The Man from the Atom" was published in *Science and Invention* in August 1923. Wertenbaker also penned a sequel, which was published in the May 1926 issue of *Amazing Stories*. The author was only 16 years old at the time of his story's original publication. He later abandoned the genre to become an editor and journalist. Though young, Wertenbaker's stories demonstrate many of the themes that would eventually become hallmarks of the science fiction genre. Ashley writes: "His story is emotionally strong and considers the fate of an explorer who travels through into the macrocosm only to discover he cannot return to Earth because, with time relative to mass, the Earth had grown old and died within minutes of his own subjective time. Wertenbaker was Gernsback's first important writing discovery" (47).

"The Man from the Atom" tells the story of Professor Martyn, a brilliant but isolated inventor. His latest invention is a wearable machine able to transform its user's size (like Marvel's Ant-Man). Professor Martyn asks one of his students, Kirby, to test the device. First, Kirby grows large. The boy gradually turns into a giant and sees the Earth become smaller and smaller under his feet. He grows so large, the planet's rotation causes him to slip off the Earth. To him, the planets and the sun are as big as marbles. The most distant stars seem to come closer and closer and revolve around him. He manages to swim through the ether.[2]

First the stars and then the nebulae surround him. Then the rotating nebulae transform into the electrons, which form the matter in a macroscopic universe. Kirby finds himself inside a molecule, the atoms of which are formed by our galaxies. Finally, he emerges from the sea on an unknown planet. The atoms he saw were our galaxies, none other than the electrons forming the water molecules of this alien ocean. Kirby wakes on the beach and decides to try reversing the process. As Kirby becomes small again, he re-enters our galaxy to discover that the solar system has changed beyond recognition. Though Kirby has been gone only a few hours, billions of years have elapsed on Earth.

Planets Like Atoms, Atoms Like Planets

"The Man from the Atom" was not original in imagining a world contained in infinitesimal matter. In "The Diamond Lens" (1858), Fitz-James O'Brien describes the invention of a very powerful microscope and the discovery of a world inside a drop of water. *The Adventures of a Micro-Man* (1902) by Edwin Pallander concerns a scientist who invents microgen gas, which makes things smaller. In *The Girl in the Golden Atom*, which appeared in the pulp magazine *All-Story* in 1919, Ray Cummings describes an indentation in a gold ring as a canyon in the subatomic universe. Authors who tackled the topic of miniaturization imagined that the protagonist would see a world similar to ours.

In the stories that preceded Wertenbaker's, the transition from the infinitely large to the infinitely small takes place continuously; narratives focus on the scientific conundrum while omitting the events that occur through corpuscular states. Wertenbaker's brilliant idea to describe the transition between universes makes it possible for the story to offer insight into the theory of relativity and the nature of subatomic particles. In "The Man from the Atom," Kirby observes the subatomic particles around him, and simultaneously the flowing of time. Along Kirby's relativistic journey, each world is an atom of a larger universe and Earth is a subatomic particle in a macroscopic universe. Unlike the stories that preceded it, by inserting the acceleration of the passage of time, Wertenbaker talks about miniaturization from a relativistic viewpoint.

Wertenbaker describes Rutherford's planetary atomic model when Kirby, by now of giant proportions with respect to the Earth, realizes that he has penetrated into another universe: "Was not this system of a great ball effect with a nucleus within similar to what the atom was said to be? Could the nucleus and its great shell be opposite poles of electrical energy, then? In other words, was this an electron—a huge electron composed of universes? The idea was terrible in its magnitude, something too huge for comprehension" (388). He understands that the galaxies of our universe are none other than electrons rotating in the matter of another universe.

The significance of Einstein's theory is indicated throughout the plot. To clarify the connection, Gernsback added an editorial comment on the first page of the initial publication appearing in *Science and Invention*, August 1923:

> If you are interested in Einstein's Theory of Relativity, you cannot afford to miss this story. It is one of the big scientific stories of the year and is worth reading and rereading many times. If the Theory of Relativity has been a puzzle to you, this story, written in plain English, cannot fail to hold your interest from start to finish. The thoughts expressed in this story are tremendous. It will give you a great insight, not only into the infinitely large, but also the infinitely small. Better yet, relativity is brought home to you in a most ingenious and easily understandable manner [Gernsback, 329].

The end of Wertenbaker's story illustrates the most disturbing suggestion in Einstein's theory. Upon returning to Earth, Kirby discovers that the universe he knew has aged irrevocably: "Seconds it took them to cover what I knew to be billions of trillions of light-years.... Perhaps all mankind had died away from a world stripped of air and water. In ten minutes of my life..." (Wertenbaker 1923, 389–390).

It is also worth noting that Wertenbaker suggests the existence of a multiverse. During his journey, Kirby penetrates in another universe and thinks "The stars, universes within universes! And those universes but nebulae in another great universe! Suddenly I began to wonder. Could there be nothing more in infinity than universe after universe, each a part of another greater one?" (Wertenbaker 1923, 388). Hence our galaxy is not simply the atom of matter that makes up another universe, but instead there are many universes connected to one another in a chain.

Like most stories from the Gernsback Age, "The Man from the Atom" was certainly naïve. The scientists described by Wertenbaker and other authors who wrote for Gernsback's magazines are super-hobbyists. The reason can be found in the type of authors Gernsback initially presented. Gernsback did not want science fiction by regular pulp writers. Instead he encouraged the man on the street, the everyday hobbyist, and the amateur experimenter to write scientific fiction (Drown, 92). "It was these people who could be the new Edisons, Bells, Teslas, and Marconis of the world. In their fiction they could envisage a future that they might in turn create" (Ashley and Lowndes, 43–44). Professor Martyn is a solitary genius, more of a bricoleur than a researcher: "one of those mysterious outcasts, geniuses whom Science would not recognize because they scorned the pettiness of the men who represented Science. Martyn was first of all a scientist, but almost as equally he was a man of intense imagination" (Wertenbaker 1923, 329). Yet Martyn represents the typical scientist of the stories that Gernsback published in *The Electrical Experimenter* and *Science and Invention*. Examples of these types of inventors, both ingenious and solitary, can be found in Gernsback's *Ralph 124C41+* (1911–12; 1925) and Jacques Morgan's "Mr. Fosdick" series (1912–1913). Professor Martyn described in "The Man in the Atom" is, like them, a brilliant, resourceful man able to always be far ahead of his time.

NOTES

1. In their critical works on this literary genre, some scholars consider *Amazing Stories* the starting point. Mike Ashley's *The History of the Science Fiction Magazine* (1974–78) starts right from 1926 with *Amazing*. Gary Westfahl states that the birth of science fiction resides in the publishing work of Gernsback (1998; 2007). Other scholars, though recognizing *Amazing* and other Gernsback's magazine as milestones, felt compelled to add introductory chapters to their science fiction stories that mentioned all those fantasy tales that, from ancient times to the 20th century, could be seen as forerunners of the genre (Gunn 1975; Pohl 1974; Ashley & Tymn 1985). Critic Brian W. Aldiss, on the other hand, expressly maintains that science fiction originated in 1818 with the publication of *Frankenstein* by Mary Shelley, considered to be a spin-off of the Gothic genre, and clearly indicated how the Gothic topoi have transformed into those of science fiction (Aldiss 1973).

2. Wertenbaker's reference to the "ether" hails back to the pre–Einsteinian belief that empty space consisted of a substance. Popular understanding of wave theory and the transmission of light did not percolate into popular culture until well into the 20th century, assisted by evidence provided by the failed Michelson-Morley experiments. See Michelson, Albert and Edward Morley, "On the Relative Motion of the Earth and the Luminiferous Ether," *American Journal of Science* (1887).

BIBLIOGRAPHY

Aldiss, Brian W. 1973. *Billion Year Spree: The History of Science Fiction*. Weidenfeld & Nicolson.

Ashley, Mike. 2000. *The Time Machines: The Story of the Science-Fiction Pulp Magazines from the Beginning to 1950*. Liverpool UP.

Ashley, Mike, and Lowndes, Robert A. 2004. *The Gernsback Days. a Study of the Evolution of Modern Science Fiction from 1911 to 1936*. Wildside Press.

Ashley, Mike, and Tymn, Marshall B. 1985. *Science Fiction, Fantasy and Weird Fiction Magazines*. Greenwood.

Butler, Octavia. 1986. "Black Scholar Interview with Octavia Butler: Black Women and the Science Fiction Genre." *The Black Scholar* 17, no. 2: 14–18,

De Camp, L. Sprague, Catherine Crook De Camp, and Jane Whittington Griffin. 1983. *Dark Valley Destiny: The Life of Robert E. Howard*. Bluejay Books Inc.

Drown, Eric. 2006. "'A Finer and Fairer Future': Commodifying Wage Earners in American Pulp Science Fiction." *Endeavour* 30, no. 3: 92–97.

Evans, Arthur B. 2014. "Histories." In *The Oxford Handbook of Science Fiction*, edited by Rob Latham, 47–58. Oxford UP.

Fulcher, Gordon S. 1913. "The Rutherford Atom." *Science* XXVIII, no. 973: 274–276.

Gernsback, Hugo. 1923. "Introduction to 'The Man from the Atom.'" *Science and Invention* XI, no. 4: 329.

Gernsback, Hugo. 1926. "A New Sort of Magazine." *Amazing Stories* 1, no. 1: 3.

Gernsback, Hugo. 1926. "The Lure of Scientifiction." *Amazing Stories* 1, no. 3: 195.

Gernsback, Hugo. 1926. "Fiction Versus Fact." *Amazing Stories* 1, no. 4: 291.

Gernsback, Hugo. 1929. "Science Wonder Stories." *Science Wonder Stories* 1, no. 1: 5.

Gernsback, Hugo. 1953. "The Impact of Science-Fiction on World Progress." *The Journal of Science Fiction* 4: 22–26.

Gunn, James. 1975. *Alternate Worlds: The Illustrated History of Science Fiction*. Prentice-Hall,.

James Edward. 2014. "Yellow, Black, Metal, and Tentacled." In *Black and Brown Planets: The Politics of Race in Science Fiction*, edited by Isiah Lavender, 195–222. UP of Mississippi.

Moskowitz, Sam. 1963. *Explorers of the Infinite: Shapers of Science Fiction*. World Publishing Co.

Narlikar, Jayant V. 2010. *An Introduction to Relativity*. Cambridge UP.

Nelson, Emmanuel Sampath. 2005. *The Greenwood Encyclopedia of Multiethnic American Literature: A–C*. Greenwood Press.

Perry, Tom. 1978. "An Amazing Story: Experimenter in Bankruptcy." *Amazing Stories*, May, 101–119.

Pohl, Frederik. 1975. "The Publishing of Science Fiction." In *Science Fiction: Today and Tomorrow*, edited by Reginald Bretnor. 17–44. Penguin.

Rogers, Ivor A. 1976. "The Gernsback Era, 1926–1937." In *Anatomy of Wonder*, edited by Neil Barron, 79–116. R.R. Bowker.

Sadoul, Jacques. 1973. *Histoire de la Science-Fiction Moderne*. Albin Michel.

Wertenbaker, G. Peyton. 1923. "The Man from the Atom." *Science and Invention* XI, no. 4: 329, 386–390. [Reprinted in *Amazing Stories* 1, no. 1: 62–66].

Westfahl, Gary. 1998. *The Mechanics of Wonder: The Creation of the Idea of Science Fiction*. Liverpool UP.

Westfahl, Gary. 2007. *Hugo Gernsback and the Century of Science Fiction*. McFarland.

"The Man from the Atom" (1923)

G. Peyton Wertenbaker

If you are interested in Einstein's Theory of Relativity, you cannot afford to miss this story. It is one of the big scientific stories of the year and it is worth reading and rereading many times. If the Theory of Relativity has been a puzzle to you, this story, written in plain English, cannot fail to hold your interest from start to finish. The thoughts expressed in this story are tremendous. It will give you a great insight, not only into the infinitely large, but also the infinitely small. Better yet, relativity is brought home to you in a most ingenious and easily understandable manner.

—EDITOR [Hugo Gernsback].

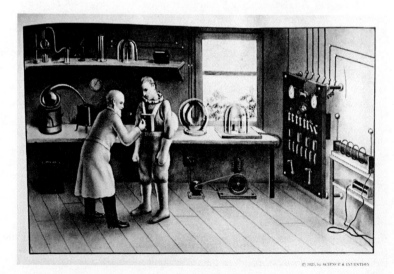

© 1923, by SCIENCE & INVENTION

I

I am a lost soul, and I am homesick. Yes, homesick. Yet how vain is homesickness when one is without a home! I can but be sick for a home that has gone. For my home departed millions of years ago, and there is now not even a trace of its former existence. Millions of years ago, I say, in all truth and earnestness. But I must tell the tale—though there is no man left to understand it.

I well remember that morning when my friend, Professor Martyn, called me to him on a matter of the greatest importance. I may explain that the Professor was one of those mysterious outcasts, geniuses whom Science would not recognize because they scorned the pettiness of the men who represented Science. Martyn was first of all a scientist, but almost as equally he was a man of intense imagination, and where the ordinary man crept along from detail to detail and required a complete model before being able to visualize the results of his work, Professor Martyn first grasped the great results of his contemplated work, the vast, far-reaching effects, and then built with the end in view.

The Professor had few friends. Ordinary men avoided him because they were unable to understand the greatness of his vision. Where he plainly saw pictures of worlds and universes, they vainly groped among pictures of his words on printed pages. That was their impression of a word. A group of letters. His was of the picture it presented in his mind. I, however, though I had not the slightest claim to scientific knowledge, was romantic to a high degree, and always willing to carry out his strange experiments for the sake of the adventure and the strangeness of it all, And so the advantages were equal. I had a mysterious personage ready to furnish me with the unusual. He had a willing subject to try out his inventions, for he reasoned quite naturally that should he himself perform the experiments, the world would be in danger of losing a mentality it might eventually have need of.

And so it was that I hurried to him without the slightest hesitation upon that, to me, momentous day of days in my life. I little realized the great change that soon would come over my existence, yet I knew that I was in for an adventure, certainly startling, possibly fatal. I had no delusions concerning my luck.

I found Professor Martyn in his laboratory bending, with the eyes of a miser counting his gold, over a tiny machine that might easily have fitted in my pocket. He did not see me for a moment, but when he finally looked up with a sigh of regret that he must tear his eyes away from his new and wonderful brain-child, whatever it might be, he waved me a little unsteadily into

Opposite: Science and Invention, **"Fitting on the Apparatus." August 1923.**

a chair, and sank down in one himself, with the machine in his lap. I waited, placing myself in what I considered a receptive mood.

"Kirby," he began abruptly at last, "have you ever read your Alice in Wonderland?" I gasped, perhaps, in my surprise.

"Alice in—! are you joking, Professor?"

"Certainly not," he assured me. "I speak in all seriousness."

"Why, yes, I have read it many times. In fact, it has always struck me as a book to appeal more to an adult than to a child. But what—I can't see just how that is important." He smiled.

"Perhaps I am playing with you unduly," he said, "but do you remember the episode of the two pieces of cheese, if my own recollection is correct, one of which made one grow, the other shrink?"

I assented. "But," I said incredulously, "certainly you cannot tell me you have spent your time in preparing magical cheeses?" He laughed aloud this time, and then, seeing my discomfort, unburdened himself of his latest triumph.

"No Kirby, not just that, but I have indeed constructed a machine that you will be incapable of believing until you try it. With this little object in my lap, you could grow forever, until there was nothing left in the universe to surpass. Or you could shrink so as to observe the minutest of atoms, standing upon it as you now stand upon the earth. It is an invention that will make scientific knowledge perfect!" He halted with flushed face and gleaming eyes. I could find nothing to say, for the thing was colossal, magnificent in its possibilities. If it worked. But I could not resist a suspicion of so tiny a machine.

"Professor, are you in absolute earnest?" I cried.

"Have I ever jested about so wonderful a thing?" he retorted quietly. I knew he had not.

"But surely that is merely a model?"

"It is the machine itself!"

II

I was too astounded to speak at first. But finally, "Tell me about it," I gasped. "This is certainly the most fantastic invention you have made yet! How does it work?"

"I am afraid," suggested Professor Martyn, "that you could not understand all the technical details. It is horribly complicated. And besides, I am anxious to try it out. But I will give you an idea of it.

"Of course, you know that an object may be divided in half forever, as you have learned in high school, without being entirely exhausted. It is this principle that is used in shrinking. I hardly understand the thing's mechanism myself—it was the result of an accident—but I know that the machine not only divides every atom, every molecule, every electron of the body into two exactly equal parts, but it accomplishes the same feat in itself, thus keeping pace with its manipulator. The matter it removes from the body is reduced to a gaseous form, and left in the air. There are six wires that you do not see, which connect with the body, while the machine itself is placed on the chest, held by a small belt that carries wires to the front of the body where the two controlling buttons are placed.

"When the user wishes to grow, he presses the upper button, and the machine then extracts atoms from the air which it converts, by a reverse method from the first, into atoms identical to certain others in the body, the two atoms thus formed joining into one large particle of twice the original size.

"As I said, I have little idea of my invention except that it works by means of atomic energy. I was intending to make an atomic energy motor, when I observed certain parts to increase and diminish strangely in size. It was practically by blind instinct that I have worked the thing up. And now I fear I shall not be able to discover the source of my atomic energy until I can put together, with great care, another such machine, for I am afraid to risk taking this apart for analysis."

"And I," I said suddenly, with the awe I felt for such a discovery quite perceptible, I fear, in my tone, "I am to try out this machine?"

"If you are willing," he said simply. "You must realize, of course, that there are a multitude of unknown dangers. I know nothing of the complete effects of the machine. But my experiments on inanimate objects have seemed satisfactory."

"I am willing to take any risks," I said enthusiastically, "If you are willing to risk your great machine. Why, don't you realize, Professor, that this will revolutionize Science? There is nothing, hardly, that will be unknown. Astronomy will be complete, for there will be nothing to do but to increase in size enough to observe beyond our atmosphere, or one could stand upon worlds like rocks to examine others."

"Exactly. I have calculated that the effect of a huge foot covering whole countries would be slight, so equally distributed would the weights be. Probably it would rest upon tall buildings and trees with ease. But in space, of course, no support should be necessary.

"And then, as you said, one could shrink until the mysteries of electrons would be revealed. Of course, there would be danger in descending into apparent nothingness, not knowing where a new world-atom could be found upon which to stand. But dangers must be risked."

"But now, Kirby," remarked the Professor officially, "time passes, and I should like you to make your little journey soon that I may quickly know its results. Have you any affairs you would like to put in order, in case—"

"None," I said. I was always ready for these experiments. And though this promised to be magnificently momentous, I was all ready. "No, if I return in a few hours, I shall find everything all right. If not, I am still prepared." He beamed in approval.

"Fine. Of course you understand that our experiment must take place at some secluded spot. If you are ready, we can proceed at once to a country laboratory of mine that will, I think, be safe."

I assented, and we hastily donned our overcoats, the Professor spending a moment or two collecting some necessary apparatus. Then we packed the machine in a safe box, and left his home.

"Are you all ready, Kirby?" The Professor's voice was firm, but my practiced ear could detect the slightest vibrations that indicated to me his intense inner feelings. I hesitated a moment. I was not afraid of going. Never that. But there seemed something partaking almost of finality about this departure. It was different from anything I had ever felt before.

"All ready, Professor," I said cheerfully after a brief moment.

"Are you going to magnify or minimize yourself?"

"It shall be growth," I answered, without a moment's hesitation there. The stars, and what lay beyond…. It was that I cared for. The Professor looked at me earnestly, deeply engrossed in thought. Finally he said, "Kirby, if you are to make an excursion into interstellar space, you realize that not only would you freeze to death, but also die from lack of air."

Walking to a cabinet in the rear of the room, he opened it and withdrew from it some strange looking paraphernalia. "This," he said, holding up a queer looking suit, "is made of a great quantity of interlocking metal cells, hermetically sealed, from which the air has been completely exhausted so as to give the cells a high vacuum. These separate cells are then woven into the fabric. When you wear this suit, you will, in fact, be enclosed in a sort of thermos bottle. No heat can leave this suit, and the most intensive cold cannot penetrate through it."

I quickly got into the suit, which was not as heavy as one might imagine. It covered not only the entire body, but the feet and hands as well, the hand part being a sort of mitten.

After I had gotten into the suit, the Professor placed over my head a sort of transparent dome which he explained was made of strong unbreakable Bakelite. The globe itself really was made of several globes, one within the other. The globes only touched at the lower rim. The interstices where the globes did not touch formed a vacuum, the air having been drawn from the spaces. Consequently heat could not escape from the transparent head piece nor could the cold come in. From the back of this head gear, a flexible tube led into the interior; this tube being connected to a small compressed oxygen tank, which the Professor strapped to my back.

He then placed the wonder machine with its row of buttons on my chest, and connected the six wires to the arms and other parts of my body.

Professor Martyn grasped my hand then, and said in his firm, quiet voice:

"Then goodbye, Kirby, for awhile. Press the first button when you are ready to go. May the Fates be with you!"

The Professor next placed the transparent head gear over my head and secured it with attachments to my vacuum suit. A strange feeling of quietness and solitude came over me. While I could still see the Professor, I could hear him talk no longer as sounds cannot pierce a vacuum. Once more the Professor shook my hand warmly.

Then, somehow, I found myself pressing down the uppermost of three buttons. Instantly there was a tingling, electric flash all through my body. Martyn, trees, distant buildings, all seemed to shoot away into nothingness. Almost in panic, I pushed the middle button. I stopped. I could not help it, for this disappearing of all my world acted upon my consciousness. I had a strange feeling that I was leaving forever.

I looked down; and Professor Martyn, a tiny speck in an automobile far below, waved up to me cheerfully as he started his car and began to speed away. He was fleeing the immediate danger of my growth, when my feet would begin to cover an immense area, until I could be almost entirely in space. I gathered my courage quickly, fiercely, and pressed the top button again. Once more the earth began to get smaller, little by little, but faster. A tingling sensation was all over me, exhilarating if almost painful where the wires were connected upon my forearms, my legs, about the forehead, and upon my chest.

It did never seem as though I was changing, but rather that the world was

"The Man from the Atom." *Amazing Stories.* **April 1926.**

shrinking away, faster and faster. The clouds were falling upon me with threatening swiftness, until my head broke suddenly through them, and my body was obscured, and the earth below, save tiny glimpses, as though of a distant landscape through a fog. Far away I could see a few tall crags that broke through even as had I, scorning from their majestic height the world below. Now indeed, if never before, was my head "among the clouds!"

But even the clouds were going. I began to get an idea of the earth as a great ball of thick cloud. There was a pricking sensation beneath my feet, as though I stood upon pine needles. It gave me a feeling of power to know that these were trees and hills.

I began to feel insecure, as though my support were doing something stealthy beneath me. Have you ever seen an elephant perform upon a little rolling ball? Well that is how I felt. The earth was rotating, while I no longer could move upon it. While I pondered, watching in some alarm as it became more and more like a little ball a few feet thick, it took matters in its own hand. My feet slipped off, suddenly, and I was lying absolutely motionless, powerless to move, in space!

I watched the earth awhile as it shrank, and even observed it now as it moved about the sun. I could see other planets that had grown at first a trifle larger and were now getting smaller again, about the same size as the earth, tiny balls of no more than a couple of inches in diameter....

It was getting much darker. The sun no longer gave much light, for there was no atmosphere to diffuse it. It was a great blinding ball of fire near my feet now, and the planets were traveling about it swiftly. I could see the light reflected on one side, dark on the other, on each planet. The sun could be seen to move perceptibly too, though very slightly. As my feet grew larger, threatening to touch it, I hastily drew them up with ease and hung suspended in the sky in a half-sitting position as I grew.

Turning my head away all at once, I observed in some surprise that some of the stars were growing larger, coming nearer and nearer. For a time I watched their swift approach, but they gradually seemed to be getting smaller rather than larger. I looked again at my own system. To my amazement, it had moved what seemed about a yard from its former position, and was much smaller. The planets I saw no longer, but there were faint streaks of light in circles about the sun, and I understood that these were the tracks of the worlds that now moved about their parent too swiftly to be followed with the eye.

I could see all the stars moving hither and yon now, although they still continued to appear closer and closer together. I found a number lying practically on the plane of my chest, but above that they seemed to cease. I could now see no planets, only the tiny sun moving farther and farther, faster and faster along its path. I could discern, it seemed to me, a trend in its and its companions' path. For on one side they seemed to be going one way, and the opposite way on the other. In front, they seemed to move across my vision. Gradually I came to understand that this was a great circle swinging vastly about me, faster and faster.

I had grown until the stars were circling now about my legs. I seemed to be the center of a huge vortex. And they were coming closer and closer together, as though to hem me about. Yet I could not move all of me away. I could only move my limbs and head in relation to my stationary body. The nearest star, a tiny bright speck, was a few yards away. My own sun was like a bright period upon a blackboard. But the stars were coming nearer and nearer. It seemed necessary for me to move somehow, so I drew my legs up and shot them out with all my force. I began to move slowly away, having acted upon what little material substance there was in the ether.

The stars were soon only a few feet apart below me, then a few inches, and suddenly, looking out beyond them, I was struck with the fact that they seemed to be a great group, isolated from a number of far distant blotches that were apart from these. The stars were moving with incredible swiftness now about a center near which was what I imagined to be the sun, though I had lost track of it somehow. They merged closer and closer together, the vast group shrunk more and more, until finally they had become indistinguishable as entities. They were all part of a huge cloud now, that seemed somehow familiar. What did it suggest? It was pale, diffused at the ends, but thick and white in the center, like a nebul—a nebula! That was it! A great light broke over me. All these stars were part of a great system that formed a nebula. It explained the mystery of the nebulae.

And there were now other nebulae approaching, as this grew smaller. They took on the resemblance of stars, and they began to repeat the process of closing in as the stars had done. The stars, universes within universes! And those universes but nebulae in another great universe! Suddenly I began to wonder. Could there be nothing more in infinity than universe after universe, each a part of another greater one? So it would seem. Yet the spell was upon me and I was not ready to admit such simplicity yet. I must go on. And my earth! It could not even be found, this sphere that had itself seemed almost the universe.

But my growth was terribly fast now. The other nebulae were merging, it would seem at first, upon me. But my slow progress through space became faster as I grew larger, and even as they came upon me, like flying arrows now, I shot above them. Then they, too, merged. The result was a vast nucleus of glowing material.

A great light began to grow all about me. Above I suddenly observed, far away, a huge brightness that seemed to extend all over the universe. But it began definitely. It was as though one were in a great ball, and the nebulae, a sunlike body now, were in the center. But as I became larger with every instant, the roof-like thing diffused, even as before things had converged, and formed into separate bodies, like stars. I passed through them finally, and they came together again behind me as I shot away, another great body.

A coincidence suddenly struck me. Was not this system of a great ball effect with a nucleus within similar to what the atom was said to be? Could the nucleus and its great shell be opposite poles of electrical energy, then? In other words, was this an electron—a huge electron composed of universes? The idea was terrible in its magnitude, something too huge for comprehension.

And so I grew on. Many more of these electrons, if such they were, gathered together, but my luck held and I passed beyond this new body thus formed—a molecule? I wondered. Suddenly I tired of the endless procession of stars coming together, forming ever into new stars that came together too. I was getting homesick. I wanted to see human faces about me again, to be rid of this fantastic nightmare. It was unreal. It was impossible. It must stop.

A sudden impulse of fear took hold upon me. This should not go on forever. I had to see my earth again. All at once, I reached down, and pressed the central button to stop.

But just as a swiftly moving vehicle may not stop at once, so could not I. The terrific momentum of my growth carried me on, and the machine moved still, though slower. The stars seemed shooting upon me, closing about me. I could see no end of them before me. I must stop or they would be about me.

Closer in they came, but smaller and smaller. They became a thousand pinpoints shooting about me. They merged into a thick, tenuous cloud about me, thicker and thicker. I was shooting up now, but my growth had stopped. The cloud became a cold, clammy thing that yielded to the touch, and—and it was water! Yes, pure water! And I was floating in it....

Years....

Suddenly I shot up, out of the water, and fell back. Strength returned to me, and warmth, and love of life. It was water, something I knew, something familiar, a friend. And so I swam, swam on and on, until my feet touched bottom, and I was leaping forth out of the water, on to the sand....

IV[1]

There is no need to drag the tale out. I awoke finally from an exhausted sleep, and found myself in a world that was strange, yet familiar. It might have been a lonely part of the earth, except for an atmosphere of strangeness that told me subconsciously it was another world. There was a sun, but it was far distant, no larger than my moon. And vast clouds of steam hung over the jungles beyond the sand, obscuring them in a shimmering fog, obscuring the sun so that it danced and glimmered hazily through the curtain. And a perpetual twilight thus reigned.

I tried to tell myself I was in some strange manner home. But I knew I was not. At last, breaking beneath the weight of homesickness and regret, I surrendered to a fit of weeping that shamed my manhood even as I wept. Then a mood of terrible, unreasoning anger against Fate enveloped me, and I stormed here and there about the beach.

And so, all through the night, I alternately wept and raged, and when the dawn came I sank again in peaceful slumber....

When I awoke, I was calm. Obviously, in stopping I told myself I had been left in a cloud of atoms that proved to be part of another group of matter, another earth or atom, as you will. The particular atoms I was in were part of the ocean.

The only thing to do was to return. I was ashamed of my madness now, for I had the means of return. In the third button ... the bottom button. I saw no reason for delay. I splashed back into the water, and swam hastily out to the point where it seemed I had risen. I pushed the lowest button. Slowly I felt myself grow smaller and smaller, the sense of suffocation returned, only to pass away as the pinpoints shot about me again, but away this time. The whole nightmare was repeated now, reversed, for everything seemed to be opening up before me. I thrilled with joy as I thought of my return to my home, and the Professor again. All the world was friend to me now, in my thoughts, a friend I could not bear to lose.

And then all my hopes were dashed. How, I thought, could I strike my own earth again? For even if I had come to the right spot in the water to a certainty, how could I be sure I would pass between just the right cloud of molecules? And what would lead me to the very electron I had left? And, after the nucleus, why should I not enter the wrong nebula? And even if I should hit the right nebula, how should I find my own star, my own earth? It was hopeless, impossible! ... And yet, so constituted is human nature that I could hope nevertheless!

My God! Impossible as it is, I did it! I am certain that it was my own nebula I entered, and I was in the center, where the sun should be. It sounds fantastic, it *is* fantastic. The luck of a lifetime, an infinity, for me. Or so it should have been. But I looked where the sun ought to be found, in the central cluster. I halted early and watched long with a sinking heart. But the sun—was gone!

I lay motionless in the depths of space and I watched idly the stars that roamed here and there. Black despair was in my heart, but it was a despair so terrible that one could not comprehend its awfulness. It was beyond human emotion. And I was dazed, perhaps even a little mad.

The stars were tiny pinpoints of light, and they shot back and forth and all around like purposeless nothings. And ever would they collide, and a greater pinpoint would be born, or a thousand pieces of fragments would result. Or the two might start off on new tracks, only to collide again. Seconds it took them to cover what I knew to be billions of trillions of light-years.

And gradually the truth dawned upon me, the awful truth. These stars were suns, even as mine had been, and they grew and died and were reborn, it seemed now, in a second, all in a second. Yet fair races bloomed and died, and worlds lived and died, races of intelligent beings strove, only to die. All in a second. But it was not a second to them. My immense size was to blame on my part.

For time is relative, and depends upon size. The smaller a creature, the shorter its life. And yet, to itself, the fly that lives but a day has passed a lifetime of years. So it was here. Because I bad grown large, centuries had become but moments to me. And the faster, the larger I grew, the swifter the years, the millions of years had rolled away. I remembered how I had seen the streaks that meant the planets going about the sun. So fast had they revolved that I could not see the circuit that meant but a second to me. And yet each incredibly swift revolution had been a year! A year on earth, a second to me! And so, on an immensely greater scale, had it been as I grew. The few minutes that meant to me the sun's movement through the ether of what seemed a yard had been centuries to the earth. Before I had lived ten minutes of my strange existence, Professor Martyn had vainly hoped away a lifetime, and died in bitter despair. Men had come and died, races had flourished and fallen. Perhaps all mankind had died away from a world stripped of air and water. In ten minutes of my life...

And so I sit here now, pining hopelessly for my Mother Earth. This strange planet of a strange star is all beyond my ken. The men are strange and their customs, curious. Their language is beyond my every effort to comprehend, yet mine they know like a book. I find myself a savage, a creature to be treated with pity and contempt in a world too advanced even for his comprehension. Nothing here means anything to me.

I live here on sufferance, as an ignorant African might have lived in an incomprehensible, to him, London.[2] A strange creature, to play with and to be played with by children. A clown ... a savage...! And yearn as I will for my earth, I know I may never know it again, for it was gone, forgotten, nonexistent a trillion centuries ago!

Notes

1. The omission of a part III seems to be a typographical error in *Science and Invention*. That error was reproduced when the story was reprinted in *Amazing Stories*. Some reproductions begin part III at: "The Professor next placed the transparent head gear over my head and secured it with attachments to my vacuum suit."

2. One cannot help but highlight the racist remark written by Wertenbaker at the end of the tale. The writer describes the main character, lost on an unknown planet "as an ignorant African might have lived… a strange creature… a savage…!" This attitude towards African people was almost widespread at that time. Edward James writes: "we might expect science fiction writers, as authors of a genre of popular literature, to reflect the racial prejudice in their own society to some extent" (195). Almost all of the writers of traditional science fiction where Caucasian, and they were almost all Anglo Saxon Protestants, and this would explain Wertenbaker's remark. Unfortunately, it must be said that in the so-called early and Golden Age science fiction, there was a form of racism that was almost unconscious, but at times plainly avowed. The heroes and the beautiful women described in the tales and shown on the magazine cover pages were Caucasian, and the creatures they faced in lands lost in time were often black or yellow-skinned. For a pulp author like Robert E. Howard there has been talk of "aryanism" (De Camp 150).

In the early decades of the spread of science fiction, African American authors were very few. The few works written by non-white authors that appeared were written by professional journalists and not by pulp authors. The first African American science fiction novel is considered *Blake, or the Huts of America* (1857) by Martin Delany (Nelson 90). Another example is *Black No More* (1931) by George S. Schuyler. Since the 1960s, African American authors began to assert themselves. Samuel Delany was the first widely known African American writer to have grown up within the science fiction publishing market (no relation with Martin Delany). To explain the small number of African American authors at the birth of science fiction, Octavia Butler said "that science fiction began as a boy's genre. So, it was white, it was adolescent and it involved a particular kind of adolescent best described as a nerd. So, this did not make it popular with blacks or adults or women for quite a long time" (16).

About the Contributors

Beth **Atkins** is a graduate of the English program at the University of Texas of the Permian Basin (MA 2019). She received a BA in biology with a minor in English from the University of Texas San Antonio in 2014. Her research interests fall at the intersections of science and the imagination in literature. Her MA thesis focuses on Sylvia Plath, *The Stepford Wives*, ecofeminism, science history, and Donna Haraway's cyborg theory.

Bodhisattva **Chattopadhyay** is a senior researcher at the Department of Culture Studies and Oriental Languages, University of Oslo. He is also a fellow of the Imaginary College, Center for Science and the Imagination, Arizona State University. He is the founding editor of the book series *Studies in Global Genre Fiction* (Routledge), and coeditor-in-chief of *Fafnir: Nordic Journal of Science Fiction and Fantasy Research*.

Riccardo **Gramantieri** holds a master's degree in engineering and psychology. He has published books on A.E. van Vogt (2011) and William S. Burroughs (2012). His interdisciplinary work includes books linking American literature, paranoia and mental disorders (with G. Panella, 2012) and post–9/11 society, literature and trauma (2016). His articles have appeared in the *MOSF Journal of Science Fiction* and *Il Minotauro*.

Joanna **Harker Shaw** is a writer and researcher from Scotland with an interest in collaborative literature and especially the relationship between Percy Bysshe and Mary Wollstonecraft Shelley. She holds an MA in Russian literature from University College London and is completing a novel on the Shelleys as part of her English literature and creative writing Ph.D. at St Mary's University, Twickenham.

Christin **Hoene** is the Leverhulme Early Career Fellow in the School of English at the University of Kent and a researcher in residence at the British Library. Her work focuses on depictions of sound and sound technology in colonial literature and on the history of the radio in the context of the British Empire. She is the author of *Music and Identity in Postcolonial British South-Asian Literature* (Routledge, 2015).

Ivy **Roberts** is an interdisciplinary scholar specializing in film studies, science, technology, and society and cultural history. She teaches film studies at Virginia

Commonwealth University and is a professor of digital media at the University of Maryland University College. Her research investigates early media history from cultural contexts. She holds a Ph.D. from Virginia Commonwealth University's interdisciplinary program in media, art and text.

Jessie F. **Terrell**, Jr., is an administrator of the Facebook discussion group "For the Love of All Things Edgar Rice Burroughs." In addition, he is a consultant to the University of Louisville for their Edgar Rice Burroughs Memorial Collection and a regular contributor to Burroughs-themed fan publications including *ERB-APA*, the *Chicago Muckers* magazine, and the *National Capital Panthans*.

Rob Welch holds a Ph.D. in literature and criticism from Indiana University of Pennsylvania. He is a specialist in transatlantic literature of the late 19th century and lectures at St. Vincent College while also teaching graduate classes in literary theory. He has published on the work of Stephen Crane, George du Maurier, and Ambrose Bierce.

Index